"The unlikely search for a buried Spanish galleon in the Yuma desert propels the action in Steven Law's *Yuma Gold*. The possibility of buried treasure brings forth plot twists, action, and a cast of characters you won't soon forget."

—Thomas Cobb, author of *Crazy Heart* and *Shavetail*

"Start reading at your own risk. You won't want to put it down. Memorable characters, a captivating setting, and exciting plot twists will keep you turning the pages."

—Cotton Smith, author of *Ride for Rule Cordell*

A Second Chance

In less than an hour the crew had moved the entire camp to a spot fifty feet from the flag. Ben calculated that if the flag was anywhere close to the mainmast, which was in the center of the ship, then fifty feet away was a safe distance to place their tent. After everything was set up, they built a campfire and cooked some beans and bacon out of Francis's provisions, then brewed some coffee and thought about the dig. Ben took his coffee and walked out to the flag, where he stood and looked down at the ground trying to imaging what lay beneath. The excitement within him made him realize that this was the first time in his life that he felt a real purpose for his existence. All of his years had been spent learning and paying a hard price just to breathe the air. It was possible now, he thought, that his time had come. Time to forgive all those who had caused him pain. Time to truly live.

D0204643

YUMA GOLD

STEVEN LAW

BERKLEY BOOKS, NEW YORK

THE BERKLEY PUBLISHING GROUP
Published by the Penguin Group
Penguin Group (USA) Inc.
375 Hudson Street, New York, New York 10014, USA
Penguin Group (Canada), 90 Eglinton Avenue East, Suite 700, Toronto, Ontario M4P 2Y3, Canada
(a division of Pearson Penguin Canada Inc.)
Penguin Books Ltd., 80 Strand, London WC2R 0RL, England
Penguin Group Ireland, 25 St. Stephen's Green, Dublin 2, Ireland (a division of Penguin Books Ltd.)
Penguin Group (Australia), 250 Camberwell Road, Camberwell, Victoria 3124, Australia
(a division of Pearson Australia Group Pty. Ltd.)
Penguin Books India Pvt. Ltd., 11 Community Centre, Panchsheel Park, New Delhi—110 017, India
Penguin Group (NZ), 67 Apollo Drive, Rosedale, Auckland 0632, New Zealand
(a division of Pearson New Zealand Ltd.)
Penguin Books (South Africa) (Pty.) Ltd., 24 Sturdee Avenue, Rosebank, Johannesburg 2196,
South Africa

Penguin Books Ltd., Registered Offices: 80 Strand, London WC2R 0RL, England

This is a work of fiction. Names, characters, places, and incidents either are the product of the author's
imagination or are used fictitiously, and any resemblance to actual persons, living or dead, business
establishments, events, or locales is entirely coincidental. The publisher does not have any control
over and does not assume any responsibility for author or third-party websites or their content.

YUMA GOLD

A Berkley Book / published by arrangement with the author

PRINTING HISTORY
Berkley edition / November 2011

Copyright © 2011 by Steven A. Anderson.
Cover illustration by Dennis Lyall.
Cover design by Diana Kolsky.
Interior text design by Kristin del Rosario.

All rights reserved.
No part of this book may be reproduced, scanned, or distributed in any printed or electronic form
without permission. Please do not participate in or encourage piracy of copyrighted materials in
violation of the author's rights. Purchase only authorized editions.
For information, address: The Berkley Publishing Group,
a division of Penguin Group (USA) Inc.,
375 Hudson Street, New York, New York 10014.

ISBN: 978-0-425-24450-0

BERKLEY®
Berkley Books are published by The Berkley Publishing Group,
a division of Penguin Group (USA) Inc.,
375 Hudson Street, New York, New York 10014.
BERKLEY® is a registered trademark of Penguin Group (USA) Inc.
The "B" design is a trademark of Penguin Group (USA) Inc.

PRINTED IN THE UNITED STATES OF AMERICA

10 9 8 7 6 5 4 3 2 1

If you purchased this book without a cover, you should be aware that this book is stolen property. It
was reported as "unsold and destroyed" to the publisher, and neither the author nor the publisher has
received any payment for this "stripped book."

For Andy and Marsha:
For giving me life and love

EDMOND DANTES: God is no more real than your treasure, Priest.

ABBE FARIA: Perhaps . . .

—Alexandre Dumas père, *The Count of Monte Cristo*
from Jay Wolpert's screenplay

Acknowledgments

Foremost I want to thank best-selling author, former Green Beret, Vietnam veteran, expert tracker, and cowboy Don Bendell, for his friendship, belief in me, and hearty endorsement. Secondly I want to thank my good friend L. D. Clark, novelist and literary scholar, for his undivided attention and advice, in English and in Spanish.

To my kindred spirit and Ozarks treasure, Dan R. Manning, not only for taking the time to read this work and offer his input, but mostly for always understanding and nurturing my artistic commitments.

A special thanks to Rachel Stirewalt, who sacrificed a beautiful spring day and time with her children to come to my aid for some last-minute reading.

Lastly to my longtime mentor and friend Jory Sherman, who over a decade ago steered me down a path of apprenticeship that has led to many publications, including this one. I barely write a word without thinking of his literary and spiritual teachings.

Chapter One

Holiday of the Gods:
Imperial Valley, California, 1904

THE winds from the sand hills had calmed during the night, leaving a haze at sunrise. By midday the sky was brilliant and cloudless, and out on the flats the scorching heat quickly transformed the new layer of damp sand into a thin, porous crust. The People prepared all day, gathering nuts and mesquite beans, painting their faces with earth pigment and gypsum, donning their nicest cottons, to meet at their primitive shelter.

It was a perfect day for stories.

Under the shade of a straw sombrero Raul stepped into the shelter and knelt on a palm-leaf mat in front of his grandfather, Indigo. The old Indian sat in a battered wooden rocking chair abandoned years ago by a traveler going west. He wore a cotton shirt and dungarees once worn by the farmhands. Short pieces of hemp rope kept the cuffs of the dungarees tied tight around his ankles to keep out the draft. Even in the hottest place in America, he constantly complained of being cold. He smoked a clay pipe, stuffed with secondhand tobacco, a wad he'd fished out of the proprietor's spittoon, separated, and dried on a fence rail in the sun. He was a self-proclaimed simple man, but frugal all the same and wise even beyond his ninety years. "Vulgar" and "disgusting" were the words often used by the proprietor's wife when describing him. She scowled at the sight of his foraging through the waste of others. Nevertheless, it was a holiday, and he was now proving that manners were neither beneath him nor forgotten. This gray, ponytailed elder calmly removed the pipe from his lips and gestured to Raul to take off his hat for the ceremony. Raul looked sheepishly at the others as he pulled off the sombrero and set it next to him on the sand floor.

Due to the low height of the shelter, Raul's mother, Yudexy, had to stoop as she walked to her father to take his pipe. With her other hand she took his and pressed her lips above his wrinkled, sun-baked knuckles. He nodded his appreciation as she walked back and resumed her place kneeling on the floor. He raised both arms and proclaimed: *"¡Los dioses son felices!"*

During his eleven years of life Raul had heard many stories on this holiday, but never the same story. The older he became the more he anticipated this day of history: not so much for what he learned about the People as for the enlightenment that would enrich his coming manhood. In the past years he had heard stories of his great-grandfather, and his great-great grandfather, of how they survived famine or fought the Mojave, the Yavapai, the Navajo, and the Apache for the rights of the land. He learned about the arrival of the Spaniards, and the Anglos. He never knew what the new story would be, but he still tried to guess. He felt strongly that this year it would be about the arrival of the proprietor who now employed them, since his grandfather complained so much about him.

But it was not so. On this holiday his grandfather went back many summers, over three hundred of them, back to when the great sea from the south filled the flats where they now made their home. The hills above the shores had been the home of the People for thousands of summers, where they hunted and from which they went to the shores for fish. And there were many accounts of sightings of the great Spanish ships that sailed to these shores and set anchor to explore. The People traded with the Spanish and led them up trails into the desert and across to the Sierra, where legend told there were great caches of gold. But the Spanish were beginning to wear out their welcome, were rude and forceful to the Cahuilla, to the point of battle.

At this point of the story, the old Indian raised his hands to the air and shouted, *"¡Pero los dioses sonrieron en nosotros ese dia!"*

He went on to explain how the earth shook and the waters rolled, a mountain in the south broke in two and the waters drained from the valley. Many of the Spaniards drowned trying to save their ships in the whirling waters, and the rest died in a battle in which the People were victorious. The waters never returned to the valley, and the seabed became a graveyard for the ships, eventually buried by the sandstorms. For many moons, the elder said, the masts of the great ships could be seen above the dunes, until the gods brought windstorm after windstorm, burying them as deep as if they had never existed.

Raul could not help wondering what it all meant. His grandfather was so proud of the legends and always believed that the People would eventually prosper. Yet here they were living in hard times and hungry on the ranch of an Anglo. He put this question of hard luck to his grandfather, who, with pipe in hand again, grabbed a glowing ember to light it and looked confidently at his grandson, assuring him that only the gods could answer his question and that, in their time, they would.

Yuma Territorial Prison, 1904

Ben Ruby's walk out through the sally port was as nerve-racking as the walk in had been eight years ago. Most parolees jumped with joy and headed straight for the Bounty Saloon, but Ben did not feel that way, for he knew that real trouble lay in wait ahead of him. As Abel Winthrop had told him, it is one thing to be a rabbit in a cage, fed and taken care of, protected in a sense, but once let loose, the rabbit has to be leery of coyotes, wolves, and rattlesnakes. It has to watch every move, listen to every sound, and not for one moment forget that it is a rabbit. After eight years, Ben had forgotten nothing.

The guard shut the gate, and Ben stopped walking, turned, and looked back through the iron rails at Superintendent Morris T. Baker. Ben didn't want to look back, but Baker had treated him fairly over the years and deserved his respect for that. Baker stood there in the sun, a man of sixty, wearing a herringbone vest over a white cotton shirt, his full gray beard shaded by his black felt hat, and gazed out through the rails. The two men looked at each other for a moment. Ben's dusty, frayed, tattered clothing, bare feet, and scraggly beard clearly setting him apart from Baker. He was sure, too, that the rusty tin box he clutched under his arm added more contrast.

"Watch yourself, Ben," Baker said, and extended a hand through the gate toward him.

The two men shook hands.

"Gonna need a bath and a shave," Ben said.

"Try Rosa's place there on Main Street. Yuma Hotel don't allow parolees."

Ben nodded, then walked out into the road toward Yuma. He stopped for a moment and looked to his right, toward the Colorado River and its winding course into the desert. Freedom already felt different. Almost a decade in the isolated and sometimes cool shade, the hot Arizona sun now bore down on him like punishing fire. Reality had begun to set in. He would need a lot more than a bath and shave to make it where he was going.

He headed down Main Street looking for Rosa's, but

every so often he looked enough sideways, and sure enough there was a man following him. He didn't even have to get a good look at him to know who he was. Not his name, but Ben knew for certain who he was working for. Young men dressed in clean, expensive clothing out following someone around weren't likely self-made men. Young men around here worked on ranches, the copper mines, for the railroad, as freighters, or store clerks, and wore the clothes of working men. This man had a different kind of job, with a man Ben wanted to avoid, and was surely up to no good.

After another quick, sidelong glance, Ben shifted abruptly to his right and went up onto the plank walk. If not for the years of calluses that had built up on his feet, he might have worried about splinters, but his steps were steady and agile. After several lengthy strides on the walk, he slid off into an alley and backed up against the building. Nosy passersby gave him curious looks, but he paid them no mind. In just a few seconds he could hear boot steps on the walk. The young man was running, which was all Ben needed to know to prove he was being followed. When the man rounded the corner, Ben stuck out his foot and tripped him to a sprawling display on the dusty alley ground. His brown hat went tumbling away. He was only a kid. He tried to get up, but before he was steady on his feet, Ben had him lifted by the lapels and pushed against the building wall. He pressed a forearm against the kid's throat and held down his other arm with a firm grasp.

The kid hacked and choked, his freckled face red and grimacing. He was a bit taller than Ben, better than six foot and a good twenty pounds heavier. But experience gave Ben the edge.

"You tell Gorum I'll meet him at the Yuma Hotel," Ben said. "Six o'clock. Got it, kid?"

The kid nodded slowly.

"All right now. I'm gonna let you loose. But swallow your pride and don't try nothing stupid. That fancy Colt under your coat won't be enough to save you."

The kid nodded and Ben backed away slowly. There was a bit more hacking and coughing while Ben reached down and grabbed the kid's hat and handed it back to him.

"What's your name, kid?"

"Redman. Casey Redman."

"All right, Redman. Don't worry, you'll be chugging beers by nightfall. Now, go on."

Ben watched the kid dust off his hat and walk out of the alley. Ben thought he was lucky that L. J. Gorum had sent a young, inexperienced buck and not a couple of old Mexican badgers from the ranch—they would not have been so careless, and Ben would have been spitting blood instead of bathwater.

THOUGH THE BATH AND SHAVE WERE FOREMOST ON HIS mind, Ben stopped first at a mercantile. All parolees were given an appropriated fifty dollars to help them get settled again, plus any money they had when they went in. All Ben had had on him during his arrest was the money from his employer, which was confiscated and returned. Lucky for him, however, when someone dies in prison that money can go to the prisoner's family or an heir. Abel Winthrop didn't have any family to speak of, so on his deathbed he told Superintendent Baker to give the money to Ben. A hundred dollars was a tidy sum, and if used wisely, it could give a man a good head start on a new life. Most parolees blew it in the saloons in less than a week. Ben, however, would need every penny of those hundred dollars, and he needed to be sober.

He took twenty dollars out of the tin box and bought a new change of clothes: a set of long handles, brown dungarees, a white cotton shirt, a pair of boots, and a brown felt hat. It had been a long time since he'd worn clothes that had a new feel and smell. The clothes he wore now were the same ones he'd worn into the prison eight years ago. Many times soiled, many times mended, and only washed in the rain. They had to be a bit rank, but he'd grown so used to them that the only people they would bother were those who got close to him, like at the mercantile, or Consuela, the buxom *señorita* that poured his bathwater at Rosa's. In fact, at first he had a hard time getting any help from Consuela. After pouring hot water from the kettle, she made him throw his old clothes into the stove and added two sticks of wood to stoke up the fire.

Consuela came forward with another steaming kettle, holding the bottom with a folded towel while she tipped it forward. Ben was quite impressed with the new porcelain tub, a longer one that fit his body well, the water clean enough to see through. The last time he'd had a bath the tub was nothing more than a livestock trough, water warmed by the sun, gritty and gray, with a froth of horse saliva floating on the edges. Sure, he had used some lye soap, which did a fair job of cutting through the scum, but nothing like the concoction that Consuela had poured in this tub, which bubbled up with a sweet smell of lilac. Ben ducked his head under the water, held his breath for a moment, then came back up, pushed his long hair back, and wiped the water off his face.

"Now, that's more like it," Consuela said, settling in a wooden chair next to the tub. "You'd almost pass for a gentleman now."

The hostess crossed her legs, pulled her dress up, revealing a bit of thigh, and adjusted a garter. "What else can I get for you?"

"I believe I had a shave comin'."

The down look on her face showed that she hadn't expected such an answer. How different it must be for her, Ben thought, to have a man fresh out of prison, who hadn't had the touch of a woman in God knows how long, reject her advance. It's not that he didn't find her attractive. She was pretty enough. He just didn't find *whores* attractive. All he had to do was recall his first job as a cowhand, at age sixteen. Three cowboys came back late to the bunkhouse, bragging about the whore they'd poked in Kansas City. All night long he could hear them moan and scratch, and then before daylight they were nearly in tears, shedding their long handles and exposing the beet red and fiery results to the entire crew. It took almost a month for it to clear up. They couldn't even take a leak without grimacing. That was enough for Ben to know he wanted to stay clear of whores.

Consuela was quick to get back to her other business, grabbing a razor, a brush, and a cup. She poured a dab of water into the cup and stirred the brush around, making a sudsy paste. Ben tilted his head back and closed his eyes.

"Leave the mustache," he said.

Consuela gently painted the cream around his cheeks and chin. When finished, she reached down and grabbed the strap that hung on the side of the tub and ran the razor back and forth on it. She lifted the razor and then suddenly let out a gasp. Ben opened his eyes to find Gorum taking the razor from her hand. His old boss wore black gloves and a black suit, a gray tie and a shirt white as snow. His salt-and-pepper hair was slick and combed back, he had a black mustache waxed on the ends, and his whole face—not just his mouth—wore a broad grin. Above his narrow nose his green eyes glared out through a permanent squint.

"Vamoose," Gorum said, nudging Consuela off the chair.

She stood quickly and rushed out of the room, and Gorum took her place in the chair. He laid the razor on his lap and took off his coat, then his gloves, a finger at a time, all the while smirking at Ben.

Ben rose a little in the tub and saw two of Gorum's hired men standing near the door. One was Casey Redman, the freckle-faced kid he'd already met. The other one Ben recognized as Paulson Duff, a man he remembered well. Duff had worked for Gorum since the tycoon came to the valley in '78, and had quickly become Gorum's right-hand man. He was older and burly now, with curly black hair that rolled from under a gray felt cattleman's hat, and a bushy mustache under a red nose that looked more like a sore big toe. Ben knew Duff well enough to realize that if he'd been assigned to follow him from the prison, he would never have lured him into the alley, and Ben wouldn't have made it to the bathhouse. He'd have been tied up somewhere in a livery stall until Gorum got what he wanted. And Ben knew what that was.

He glanced quickly at the tin box on the washstand. The box seemed safe, but he was certainly trapped.

"It's been a long time," Gorum said. "How has your stay in Yuma been?"

Duff snorted.

"I got your invitation to the hotel—I appreciate that," Gorum continued. "But why wait any longer? It's been so long since we've had a pleasant conversation."

Gorum raised the razor and held it up to Ben's throat. Ben clutched the sides of the tub and leaned back as far away as he could. His quick movement caused waves of soapy water to splash over the edges.

"What are you worried about?" Gorum asked. "You paid for a shave—I want to make sure you get what's owed."

Gorum gently ran the razor up the side of Ben's neck, and the wet hair bunched up on the blade. He swished and cleaned the blade in the bathwater, then continued on.

Ben had never felt so helpless. Not even in prison. He might as well have been tied hand and foot to a fence post with a wet rope. He wasn't going anywhere.

Gorum made two more swipes down Ben's neck and one on each side of his face, each time washing off the blade before he returned. He put the blade up to his chin and looked directly into his eyes. "Pity we didn't have a chance to talk before they sent you away. I only got one side of the story. From the men who arrested you, and the tidbit in the paper."

"Who are you kidding?" Ben said. "You know the truth."

Gorum made a couple of light swipes off Ben's chin. "Nobody really knows the truth. We mostly have opinions, or assumptions, but rarely do we know the truth."

"Stolen dynamite—on a wagon I was teaming for you."

Gorum pressed a little harder with the razor. "So, what's your plan after prison?"

Ben thought about Gorum's question, and knew what he was after, but didn't want to take the lead.

"I lost eight years of my life," Ben said. "Isn't that payment enough?"

"Of course you would think that way. But I know you and you know me. You've already thought a lot about it. You've had eight years to think about it. I'm a businessman. I lost product. Product that you were responsible for. I paid five thousand dollars for that dynamite. That's a lot of money for a ranch hand."

Ben felt the pressure building and knew that Gorum would pile on more than he thought he could bear.

"I also lost a good team of horses and a Springfield wagon," Gorum said. "Sold at auction to the highest bidder."

Ben took a deep breath and exhaled slowly. "So that's the way it is. Non-negotiable."

"That's what I always liked about you, Ben. You see things so clearly."

Ben glanced at all of the men in the room. The kid shifted his eyes around, which clued Ben that he was oblivious to it all. Duff sneered in his habitual condescending manner.

Ben looked straight into Gorum's smiling eyes. "I need at least two months."

"Two months?" Gorum laughed.

"You know my word is good."

"Yes—yes it is." Gorum rinsed the razor and held it high over his shoulder, and Duff came and retrieved it. Gorum rubbed his hands together and put them in a praying position across his mouth. "But let's just be certain we are straight about the amount."

Ben was confused by Gorum's direction. "Five thousand . . . that—"

"That was the amount eight years ago. Money grows over time. A dollar doesn't buy as much as it did in '96, and of course there's interest."

"Just how much interest?"

"Get me a towel," Gorum said.

Duff returned with a towel and handed it to Gorum. Still facing Ben, Gorum grabbed each end of the towel, pulled it tight, and then, like a thick garrote, quickly pushed it around Ben's neck. Ben grimaced and reached for the towel with both hands, gripping it tightly as he kicked and splashed soapy water out onto the floor, but Gorum held him firmly. Ben could hardly breathe.

Gorum gritted his teeth. "Don't stroke me like some cat, Ruby! Two months, my ass. A ranch hand can't earn that amount in two years!"

Ben groaned and gasped for air.

Gorum pushed harder. "What did you learn in that prison? Where's the stash?"

Ben spit out his words slowly. "You want anything from me, you have to let me go."

"It's not that easy—"

"You kill me now, you get nothing."

"I'll get it anyway!"

"You know me . . . I won't let that happen."

"I disagree. I've waited eight years to get what's mine! I could wait a few more days. Major Duff here has ways of getting information."

Duff took off his coat, rolled up his sleeves, and stepped closer. His arms were as thick as corner posts and his clenched fists as big as sledgehammers.

"You can do it the hard way," Gorum said, "or the easy way."

Duff was convincing, but Ben wouldn't allow himself to be intimidated. He couldn't. What he had was worth too much to turn over to Gorum. He'd rather take it to his grave.

"You really think this method will work on me?" Ben asked.

"It's a proven method. Besides, what have I got to lose?"

"How about ten thousand in gold?"

Gorum held tight and looked at Ben a moment, as if studying his sincerity, and then let up with the towel. Ben rose from the water coughing and held his throat.

Gorum flipped the towel over his shoulder. He held up a hand to hold Duff back. "Where?"

"Give me two months and I'll bring it to you." His voice was hoarse, and he spoke with intermittent coughs. "Ten thousand in gold. I know that's more than you expected to get out of me. Is that not worth waiting for? We could spend the next twenty-four hours wasting a lot of time, trying to get information you'll never get, or you can let me go get started."

Gorum laughed out loud, as did the rest of them. Eventually the leader stood from the chair. "All right. Get him his clothes."

Duff lost his smug grin and gained a look of disappointment. The kid came forward with the package from the mercantile and dropped it onto the chair.

Gorum took the towel from his shoulder and tossed it to Ben. "My office. Two months. If you're not there we'll be coming to get you. And you know what that means."

Ben sat there in the tub, towel in his hand and draping over the side, and simply nodded at Gorum. Along with the kid, Gorum turned and walked out of the bathhouse. Duff gave Ben one final smirk before leaving the room. Ben exhaled a long breath, thankful that he was still alive and not bruised and bloody, but more so that the rusty box was still safe on the washstand.

WHEN GORUM REACHED THE FRONT WALK, HE STOPPED, turned, and looked back through the door. Ben was always a nose-to-the-grindstone man, he thought. Practical, not foolish. Dependable. Had he changed in prison?

Duff grunted. "Ten thousand in gold—my ass."

Gorum pinched his lips and shook his head. "No, he's on to something. Ben is no big thinker, but he knows he can't con me. Remember, we have a good source at the prison. I was told Ben spent a lot of time with that old thief, Abel Winthrop. He goes a long way back, to the army. Back in the old days the army would pay in gold. It makes sense. There's a stash somewhere, and Ben knows where it is."

"Yuma's lost gold?" Duff said. "The Aravaipa Mine?"

"Could be."

"What do we do then?"

"Take the kid, and better take Calhoun. Might need our best gun on this one."

"I can handle Ruby. We don't need Calhoun."

Gorum looked sternly at Duff. "You take Calhoun. And when Ben finds the money, you come back with it. And I'm saying all of it. You hear?"

"Yes sir."

"And Ben—well, you know what we do with deserters. Just leave him where you find him . . . and you know what I mean."

Chapter Two

❧❧

BEN needed a lot of supplies that were likely to be more abundant in Yuma, but he didn't want Gorum to know too much. The bastard owned the city, with snitches and informants all over town. The supplies he bought would tell a story, and stories were better, and in this case safer, when they unfolded a little at a time. With that in mind, he settled on a horse, a saddle, saddlebags, a pair of spurs, a canteen, a few camping items, and a skinning knife. That was no more than any man would procure to head out into the desert on a ride, so it wouldn't tell too much.

He was particularly proud of the horse he'd bought. For years he'd bought horses for himself or the ranchers he'd worked for, and never really cared what color they were or their markings. What mattered the most to him was intelligence. He could see it in their eyes and witness it in how they behaved around horse people. This particular horse was undoubtedly a seasoned mare; a ranch horse, seven years old, and keen to a good rider. She stood sixteen hands,

black with a white blaze and one white foreleg. The man he
bought her from said her name was Patty, and Ben wasn't
real fond of that name. It just didn't seem right calling a
horse "Patty." A mule maybe, but not a horse. He supposed
it didn't matter because she came right to him when he
whistled. In this case a whistle was as good as a name.

HE FOLLOWED THE BANK OF THE COLORADO, WHICH LED
directly to Cibola. It was a two-day ride, so he camped that
night a few miles across the river from the village of Picacho. The faint sound of piano music, laughing, and shouting
resonated in the night air. When Ben heard the saloon noise
of Picacho, there was comfort in knowing he was on the
right path and could camp for the night. He didn't want to
get too close, however, out of fear that tavern strays might
be a bit too interested in his presence.

Ben didn't mind so much the nights alone in the desert,
but being close to the village gave him some comfort. Being
close also told him he was halfway to Cibola. He'd ridden
the river trails before, but that was many years ago. It was
much quicker to follow some of the known passes outside
the river valley, and he appreciated the occasional diversion
to get away from the river's muddy smell and noisy rapids.

After a day of riding, he felt in his thighs and hips just
exactly how long it had been since he'd been in the saddle.
He was sore and stiff, and he did squats and stretching exer-
cises to limber himself. His knee joints popped, and he realized that age was also setting in on him. He was thirty-three
when he was sent to prison. It was hard to fathom that he
was in his forties, still not settled down with a place of his
own, a wife and children. Maybe he wasn't meant to have
that kind of life. Maybe it would be harder to get now, being
marked as a criminal. He tried not to think of such things.

He built a small enough fire to break the chill around
him, but not too big that it would attract attention. Desert

nights were not to be reckoned with. In the daytime the heat could kill any man without a wide-brimmed hat and a canteen of water, but at night he turned up the collar of his coat and appreciated a thick flannel blanket and the luxury of some mesquite and ironwood to kindle the fire.

After brewing some coffee and snacking on some jerky, Ben sat down in front of the fire with the tin box. He opened it to inspect the contents and recalled the day Abel Winthrop had given it to him. It had seemed no different than any other day with his elderly cell mate, but that all changed the moment Abel produced the box. The ailing man had pulled the box from under his cot, handed it to Ruby, then lay his head back down, pulled his blanket up to his chin, and coughed profusely. Ruby had grabbed a damp cloth from a bowl of water near the cot and dabbed it on Abel's forehead.

"I won't live to see this through," Abel said. "But you will."

"See what through?"

"Everything you need to find the treasure is in this box."

"You really expect me to believe that story?"

"It's more than just a belief, Ben. I know how you felt when you first got here, the lost feeling, the regrets. But some things happen for a reason. I believe this is your destiny."

"Come on, Abel. You know how many of those stories float around."

Abel coughed and drew a hand from under the blanket and grabbed Ruby's wrist firmly. "No, you listen to me! I know my life isn't worth much now, but in my best day I would have bet my life on it."

"Then why didn't you get if for yourself?"

Abel released Ruby's wrist, took a long breath, and relaxed on the cot. "I was like you, I wasn't sure of it. I was riding with a herd of stolen horses, and the gang I was working with was stupid and crazy. I thought there had to be more to life and started thinking about the story. The more I thought about it, the more I felt it had to be true.

Before I could reach Imperial Valley, a band of deputy marshals arrested us at our night camp. I haven't seen a day of freedom since."

Ruby had pondered the old man's words and opened the box. There were several items in the box. The one that stood out the most was a silver pendant on a chain. Ruby pulled it out and looked it over. It was hand-engraved, about the size of a silver dollar, and in the center was a round blue sapphire.

"That came from a man named Jeb Hostetter. We served in the Eighth Calvary together. We were on a peace mission and got into a scuffle with Apaches. I saved Jeb's life, and he gave that to me. Said it belonged to his mother."

"What does it have to do with the treasure?"

"Hostetter is in Cibola. He works under contract with the government, building canals to irrigate the valley. After leaving the army, he worked in the salt mines. He knows how to build desert mine shafts."

"Mine shafts?"

"The ship is under thirty to forty feet of sand and silt. Maybe more. You'll have to mine down to it. Hostetter will tell you how to do it."

"Why would he want to help me?"

"You show him the pendant. He'll help you."

"He might think I just stole it off you in prison."

"Not if you tell him the story of how I got it. No one else knows that. You're a good egg, Ruby. Any man who looks at you long enough will know that."

A coyote howled in the distance, and Ruby looked up and out into the desert darkness. He closed the lid of the box, then put it back in the saddlebag. The connection did make sense, and Ruby wanted to believe it all, but in some ways he still lacked the faith.

He kicked the fire to stoke it up and added two more pieces of driftwood and three dead stalks of cholla. He pulled the blanket over himself and lay on his side next to the fire. He stared into the dancing flames and thought about his faith, or maybe his doubt. He had an equal share of both, that was for sure.

HE ARRIVED IN CIBOLA LATE THE NEXT AFTERNOON. IT was a town not much bigger than Picacho, and similar, too, with many workers from the irrigation projects. He'd heard about the canal production while in prison. Many Yumans laughed at the idea of bringing water to a parched desert and claimed that if God had wanted water there it would already be there. The other side of the argument used examples of how the Indians had done it successfully, though on a much smaller scale. Scientists, engineers, and hopeful farmers flocked to the area, and did so first to Cibola through the stage line. When they got off the stage, they sought jobs constructing the canals, which was another promise by the government optimists. Those who succeeded pitched tents outside of town and went to work for a man named Jeb Hostetter.

Hostetter's office was next to the Cibola post office and across the dusty street from the stage stop. The office was the only modern wooden structure, compared to the many adobe buildings native to the town. Singing from rowdy patrons came from an adobe cantina not far from the stage stop. Ruby had thought about a taste of good whiskey, but cantinas produced trouble, and after eight years of lockup he decided to stay as far away from trouble as he could.

A sign near the door of Hostetter's office read DISTRICT DAM & CANAL AUTHORITY. Ben tied his horse to a rail, walked up the step to the door, and walked right in. It was a fairly large room, narrow in width but long in length, with a high ceiling, similar to railroad offices he remembered from Missouri and Kansas. The floor, however, had a rough finish with a few oval wool rugs scattered throughout the room in front of tables and desks. Near a corner was a long, tilted table with rolls of paper lying about and one engineering drawing tacked open on it. Toward the back of the room a gray-headed man sat at a desk, looking at a ledger through round eyeglasses.

Ruby walked toward the back of the room and halfway to the desk. Hostetter looked up and over his glasses.

"If you're looking for a job, I don't have any," Hostetter said.

Ruby kept walking until he reached the desk.

Hostetter took off his glasses. "Maybe you didn't hear me."

Ruby tossed the pendant onto the face of the open ledger. Hostetter looked down, put his glasses back on, and slowly picked up the memento of the past.

"I'm guessing Abel is dead," Hostetter said.

"About three months ago."

Hostetter gave Ruby a good look, then pointed to a chair next to him. "Have a seat. Can I offer you a drink?"

"You got any whiskey? Been a while since I had some of the good stuff."

Hostetter opened a drawer of his desk and produced a bottle and two shot glasses. "I hear what you're saying. It's all beer and tequila around here. That stuff will work in a pinch, but it's hard to beat good Kentucky bourbon." He pulled the cork and filled both glasses, then handed one to Ben.

"Thanks," Ben said, then extended a hand. "Name's Ben Ruby. I spent some time with Abel in Yuma."

Hostetter shook his hand. "Good to know you."

They both tipped back the drinks. Ruby smacked his lips, then set the glass down on the desk.

"Like another?" Hostetter asked.

"No, thanks. I'll savor that one for a bit."

Hostetter grinned and sat back down in his chair. He picked up the pendant again. Ruby commenced to telling the story, like Abel had told it to him.

Hostetter listened intently, then poured himself another drink. "Abel was a good man. Too bad he got mixed up with that rowdy bunch of horse thieves. But you know, those were desperate times. Could have happened to anyone."

"I met good and bad in that prison," Ruby said. "Some deserved to be there. Abel wasn't one of them."

"What about you?" Hostetter asked.

Ben thought about the question, thumbed his empty glass. "I'd rather you know me a little better first. I could tell you the story, but right now it would just be a story."

"So what brings you here? Besides delivering old memories."

"Abel said I could trust you."

"Trust me? With what?"

"What I'm about to tell you now has to stay between you and me."

Hostetter nodded. "All right, you have my word."

Ben shifted in his chair. "For the past five years I've listened to Abel tell a story. A story about an old Spanish ship, buried in the sands west of here."

Hostetter started laughing. "Yeah, I've heard that one, and many others. But I didn't believe them, and neither did Abel."

"There is one he believed. I'm not completely convinced, but at this point I have nothing better to do with my life."

"Than chasing an old tale? I beg to differ with you. There are many places you could go and find work."

"I have tried working for other people and that hasn't worked yet. And you just said you had no jobs. So I'm going to do something for myself."

Hostetter scratched inside his curly gray hair. "You've got a point there. But what does it have to do with me?"

"Abel said you worked in the salt mines. I need someone to instruct me on how to build a shaft in those dunes."

"I see. What is it about this story that makes you believe there's anything to it?"

"You might laugh again, but I believe it's a little bit spiritual."

"No, that's no laughing matter." Hostetter stood up from

his desk, reached behind him to a rack, and grabbed his gray
Stetson. "Why don't you take a walk with me?"

Ruby thought it was a little awkward to be leaving in the
middle of a request like the one he'd just made, but he
decided to oblige the man his time and reasoning. He followed Hostetter out the door and down the walk until it
stepped off into the street. They had to wait on a team and
buckboard passing before they could cross. Ruby paid particular attention to the cargo and noticed the buckboard was
loaded down with pickaxes, shovels, lanterns, and canvas
bundles.

"It's a bit of a boomtown now," Hostetter said. "Ever
since the government announced their funding of the dam
and canals. But I'm always a bit leery of a frenzy."

As they walked west out of town, the tent communities
became more visible, and before long they could see people
digging. Men and women, some older children, all digging.

"What is your fear?" Ben asked.

"Only one thing: the source of the water."

"The Colorado?"

"That's not the source, that's the result. The source is the
Rockies. The snowmelt, the rain. What I can see that many
can't, especially those pompous asses in Washington, is that
water levels are rising."

Ruby watched the many diggers work steadily and eagerly
on a trench that led directly east. He and Hostetter followed
the trail of the trench and stopped at a much wider, dry canal.

"The water level doesn't seem too high here," Ben said.

"That's because the gate at the river hasn't been opened. If
it were opened, the canal as it is couldn't handle the rush
of water that would come. We have gates and dams on both
sides of the river."

"When can you open them?"

"Not until the water levels go down at least three feet,"
Hostetter said. "And I don't see that happening for several
months."

"So these people—digging—may not see water anytime soon?"

"Exactly. They might as well play faro. They'd have better odds."

The two men kept walking down the bank of the canal until the rage of the Colorado could be heard, and that familiar muddy smell took over the air. They stopped close to a large wooden gate and several men with mules hauling soil in iron buckets.

Hostetter pointed at the workers. "Here are some of the men I employ. More are further downriver working on the dam project. Others are on the west side dams."

"What are they doing here?"

"Building a levee to try and control the rising water."

Ben and Hostetter walked up to the top of the levee and peered off into the rushing current. The water was less than five feet down.

Hostetter removed his hat and combed his fingers through his thick gray hair, then put his hat back on and placed his hands on his hips. He took a deep breath. "I pray to God it doesn't get much higher than this."

Ben studied the line of the riverbank. "What is too high?"

Hostetter pointed downriver. "See that canal gate?"

Ben acknowledged the wooden gate supported by large timbers. Men scurried around it with buckets of soil, and some men drove mule teams pulling timbers.

Hostetter continued. "If the water level gets much higher, that gate won't handle the pressure."

"And those people in Cibola will get their water."

"If they don't get out, those people could die."

Ben could see the fear in Hostetter's somber face. "Can you help them?"

Hostetter pointed to a wooden rod sticking out of the water. "That's my guide. I've made a notch in that rod every six inches. In two weeks the river has risen four feet. Another foot and I am evacuating the town. But unfortunately that's not enough."

"What do you mean?"

"I've been working with a lot of engineers and scientists, and we all agree that the water level of the Colorado hasn't been this high in hundreds of years. If this levee breaches, the whole valley will be flooded."

It was a sobering statement. Ben thought long and hard about it on the way back to town. Seeing these hopeful people work so hard, with so much will and desire, tugged at his emotions. He had no doubt that if that critical moment arose, Hostetter would do all he could to help them. Ben just hoped they would listen.

"About my time in Yuma," Ben said. "Would you believe me if I told you I was framed?"

"I might. Who framed you?"

"My boss. L. J. Gorum."

"That's all you need to say. He's everybody's boss, including mine, and the biggest, richest crook in the Southwest."

"I thought you worked for the government?"

"Gorum owns the government contract. He hired me."

"I see. Then you'll help me?"

Hostetter smirked and slapped him lightly on the shoulder. "Follow me."

Instead of going back to the office, Hostetter led Ben to a house and barn a block away. Inside the barn were three stalls, a buggy, a buckboard wagon, and several tools. Buckets and lanterns hung on the walls. Hostetter opened a stall door and led out a burro. He had made a slip halter with a rope and handed it to Ben.

"You'll need this."

Ben looked curiously at the burro, then watched Hostetter walk around the barn and gather more rope, a pickaxe and shovel, two buckets, two lanterns, and a block and tackle, and helped him tie them all to the burro.

"You'll be digging into several feet of sand. It's fairly easy digging, just a lot of it. Make sure you wear a clean neckerchief over your mouth and nose every day. It's salty as you go down, and you don't want that stuff getting into your lungs. You don't want it in your eyes either, so don't rub your eyes. When sweat runs down your forehead, dab your forehead, but don't wipe your eyes. Got it?"

"I got it."

"All right." Hostetter also tied a sack of oats to the back of the burro. "For your horse and the burro. They'll have nothing else to eat out there. Now, come inside and fill your stomach before you leave."

Ben thanked Hostetter for his generosity, then followed him into his house, a fairly new wooden cottage, painted white, with a front porch lined with gingerbread on the eave. They walked inside and both men removed their hats. The smell of a hot meal filtered through the air. Ben thought it might be stew, or soup. He immediately noticed a teenage girl wearing an apron and working in the kitchen. She poured water into a copper kettle and set it on the stove, then turned and acknowledged the men with a tender smile. She was a lovely young thing, Ben thought, with brown eyes and long auburn hair, the long bangs combed back and secured with an ivory comb. Before sitting at the table, Hostetter walked up to her and kissed her on the forehead.

"Bring us some coffee, will you, dear?" Hostetter said.

"Sure, Grandpa."

The two men sat at the table, and Hostetter reached for a platter of bread in the center. He tore off two pieces and handed one to Ben.

"Felicia, my granddaughter," Hostetter said. "She has been with me for three years now. Terrible tragedy when her parents died. But we are good for each other, I think."

Felicia came to the table with a plate for each of the men, and then delivered a small crock of honey and a dish of butter. Hostetter quickly spread some of each on a corner section of his bread and bit it off. Ben covered his entire slice with butter, then honey. Felicia came with two stone mugs and filled them with coffee.

Hostetter swallowed another bite of bread, then washed it down with a gulp of coffee. He smacked his tongue between his teeth.

"Those squatters out there," Hostetter said, between sips of coffee, "they're not much different than you. Some less than others, but for the most part they are acting on faith. They don't know the science of what they're doing, and neither do you. They just know they have no one offering them anything better."

Ben took a sip of his coffee and pondered Hostetter's statement. "Do you think I'm a fool?"

Hostetter grunted. "No, I understand. If I were in your shoes, or even like those folks out there, I'd likely be doing the same thing. I was lucky enough to stay with the army and learn a few trades. That experience landed me at the mines, and ultimately here."

"But you're helping me," Ben said. "If what Abel says is true, there could be a fortune under that sand. More money than this part of the country has ever seen. Don't you want a part of it?"

"No, I'm too old for a fortune. Riches come with too many obligations, and I don't need the pressure this late in life."

"Not even a commission? Or hush money?"

Hostetter grinned. "No, Winthrop was like a brother to me, and he wanted me to help you, so I will. But my grand-daughter there, I would like to do a lot more for her. Get her out of this godforsaken desert. If you do find your treasure, get her set up in the big city—San Francisco, Los Angeles, someplace where she can make a better life for herself, and that will be payback enough."

Ben took a good look at the young beauty, dutifully caring for her grandfather. "It's done," he said.

The two men finished a meal of beans and bacon, and

after another cup of coffee Ben bid his farewell. Hostetter followed him to the burro and to his horse in front of the office. Ben tied the burro's lead to his horse and before he mounted, Hostetter handed him a bottle of bourbon.

"For when it's time to celebrate."

Ben grinned and shook the man's hand.

"One more thing," Hostetter said, holding out a clenched left fist. He dropped the pendant into Ben's open hand. "I do believe this is part of a journey. The next part of that journey is with you."

Ben acknowledged Hostetter's sincerity with a nod, dropped the pendent inside a saddlebag, then mounted the black mare to ride. He touched the brim of his hat, then nudged the horse with his spurs and led the burro west toward the river. The tools and gear clanged as they went, and the people of Cibola watched him ride. What a spectacle he must be, he thought, riding into the desert chasing a dream. Then again, like Hostetter had told him, the reason for these folks being in Cibola was not much different from his, except they had reached their destination and his was still to be found. If it was even there at all.

Chapter Three

I T was a quiet evening save the music from the cantina and the distant calls of the Clapper Rail. Hostetter enjoyed his evenings sitting on the porch, smoking a cigar, and listening to the town wind down. It was a great place to relax and let his supper digest. With his cigar he also enjoyed a cup of coffee, which Felicia would bring to him once he was settled in his wicker chair. On this particular night, however, she was late coming, which was not like her. Hostetter also felt a peculiar strangeness realizing that he didn't hear her move about in the kitchen, cleaning up, as he usually did. To settle his curiosity he got up from the chair and walked inside. He stopped instantly once he saw her, a knife to her throat, tears running down her cheeks, and in the clutches of a man he'd never seen. The man sitting at his table, however, he knew well. Very few in these parts didn't know Paulson Duff.

Hostetter walked slowly toward the table. Duff had poured himself a cup of coffee and was stirring in a spoonful of sugar.

"What is this?" Hostetter said.

Duff grunted, then took a sip of his coffee. "The young lass makes a nice brew."

Hostetter studied the man holding his granddaughter. He was tall, almost lanky, with piercing blue eyes and wearing a thin black mustache. His hat was hanging on his back from a leather chin cord, and a tuft of his bangs had fallen down over his forehead. His face was well tanned from many days in the sun. Over a white shirt he wore a silky black-on-gray vest and on his hips a fancy rig of twin .45 Colts.

"I'm assuming you've never met Edgar Calhoun," Duff said.

Hostetter felt an instant fear rush through him. Not only was Duff a hard case, but Edgar Calhoun was Gorum's henchman. He was known all over the Southwest for his marksmanship, with both a rifle and a six-gun. Apparent now, from the looks of the Bowie in his hand, was that he was also very good with a knife.

Duff set the cup on the table and licked his lips. "How are you, Jeb? Looks like your project has the valley on its toes."

"Never mind the project," Hostetter said. "Tell me what this is about."

Duff stood from the table and picked up a pair of tan leather riding gloves from next to the coffee cup. He slapped them lightly in the palm of his hand. "We stopped and asked a few people about a man who came to town, riding a black horse with one white leg. Several of them knew just who we were talking about. Said he came here, and was seen talking with you."

Hostetter looked at Duff with contempt. "Yeah, so what?"

Duff laughed. "What did Ben Ruby want with you? Where was he going?"

"Why don't you ask him?"

"We could do that, but asking you could save us some time and tracking."

"Well you're out of luck, because I'm not telling you anything."

Duff took a deep breath, then shook his head. He stepped closer to Hostetter, put the gloves on, and when he was close enough, brought a roundhouse punch to Hostetter's cheek. The blow sent him to the floor and Felicia screamed in horror. Calhoun struggled to control her, covering her mouth with his free hand.

Duff leaned over. "Maybe you need some convincing. How's that for an appetizer?"

Hostetter said nothing, and Duff grabbed him by the shirt collar, picked him up, and delivered another healthy punch to the other side of his jaw. Hostetter fell into the table, causing the metal coffeepot and clay cup to tip and spill. He caught himself and looked up at his terrified granddaughter. She was a bit of a blur. The second one had been a harder, dizzying blow. He could taste the blood that now trickled down from his lips.

Duff grabbed him by the back of the collar again, turned him around, and placed the next punch directly on the nose. This time Hostetter fell backward on the table, tipping it over and causing the coffeepot to clang to the floor and the mug to shatter.

A dull and numbing pain shot through Hostetter's brow and made his eyes water. He tried to get up, but struggled. With both hands Duff grabbed him under his arms and lifted him up into a chair. Blood from his nose and mouth completely covered his chin and dripped onto his shirt.

Duff grabbed him by the hair, tilted his head back, and looked fiercely into his eyes. "Now, you can rethink my request. Or we can go another round if you like." Duff pointed a thumb over his shoulder. "Or we can start on her."

Hostetter blinked through his watery eyes at his frightened granddaughter, and the worst kind of fear overcame him. He knew there was nothing that he could do. He knew Duff, and he knew Gorum. Gorum provided much of the political influence on all the irrigation projects. He owned thousands of acres of land along the Colorado and Gila rivers and planned to profit greatly from the new agricultural commerce. He already owned the largest cattle operation in the valley, as well as two copper mines, and he had his sights set on the cotton and vegetable fields that were springing up along the canals. Hostetter, along with other area businessmen, knew that Gorum would be the only one who would profit from any of it. He was known as the tycoon, but his way of business was only good for him. He would exploit the labor as well as the land and product it provided. He'd already proved himself capable of that behavior in the mines and on the ranches. Why would he be any different on the farms? What was worse, though, for all involved, was that the law protected him, with legal and political influence all the way to Washington. This foray in Hostetter's kitchen would go ignored and uninterrupted.

Though he probably shouldn't be, Hostetter was a bit surprised that they were on to Ben Ruby. Did they know about the treasure? Was there a snitch in the prison that worked for Gorum? Did Ben talk too much? It was hard for Hostetter to guess, especially in this condition. One thing he knew, however, was that regardless of whether he told them what they wanted to know or not, he would be dead, Felicia would be taken to Gorum's ranch and become a servant, and eventually they would find Ruby and they'd take it all from him. Too much power. Too much influence. It couldn't be beaten.

"I'm not telling you anything," Hostetter said, wiping under his nose with the back of his hand.

Duff weaved the fingers of his gloved hands together and brought them to his chin. "That's unfortunate." He turned around and nodded to Calhoun, who brought the girl around the table. "Take her outside. Tell Redman to get the horses ready."

Felicia tried to squirm away from Calhoun. "No! Grandpa! No!"

"Please," Hostetter said, "please don't hurt her."

Duff took the knife from Calhoun and watched him drag Felicia screaming and crying out of the house. He turned back to Hostetter. "You have one last chance to tell me about Ruby. Why not make it easier on yourself?"

"I'm dead anyway. I'd rather die with the pleasure of knowing I made you work harder."

Duff laughed out loud. "So you think?"

Duff gritted his teeth and grabbed Hostetter by the hair, held up his head and swung the butt end of the knife into the side of his head. Hostetter fell to the floor, dazed and barely conscious.

Duff kneeled to the floor and grabbed him by the hair again. "Gorum said you're too valuable to the projects. I can't kill you. But just think—you'll be laid up awhile, sore and miserable. And you'll be thinking about that honey of a granddaughter, performing a different kind of service to old men!"

Duff laughed loudly as he let go of Hostetter. His boot steps beat the floor like a mallet, and he slammed the door as he left the house. Hostetter could barely move and could only breathe through his bloody mouth. He was amazed he was left alive, but he was sure they would have taken Felicia no matter what he told them. At least if he survived this, he could try to bargain with Gorum to get her back. He just hoped she could survive it, too.

He tried to crawl but he couldn't, nor could he muster the strength to get up into the chair. So he lay there on the floor, helpless. He couldn't stop thinking about Felicia. Ruby, well, he supposed he could take care of himself. But Felicia could not handle the servitude they would put her under. The loss of her parents had made her fragile, and the mental trauma would be more than she could bear. But how could he save

her? What could an old man under Gorum's thumb do? The
physical beating and mental pressure was more than his old
body and mind could handle, so he lay there on the floor in
a daze and searched for God.

AFTER A JOSTLING FERRY RIDE ACROSS THE COLORADO
River, Ben was glad to be on solid ground again. He rode
through a pass between the village of Picacho to the south
and the Palos Verdes to the north, until the setting sun made
the ranges brilliant behind him. It was difficult getting used
to the clanging of the gear tied to the burro, and after two
hours of riding he decided he had had enough of it and
stopped to make camp. The spot he chose was near a dry
gully along the eastern foothills of the Chuckwalla range.
It was quiet and out of the wind, which had picked up a bit
since he left Cibola. He unsaddled the mare and relieved the
burro of its cargo, tied the animals to a mesquite bush, then
poured some of the grain in a bucket and fed each of them.
They crunched heartily on the oats, and Ben couldn't help
but give each of them an affectionate rub on the neck.

While they ate, he roamed about and gathered mesquite
branches and ironwood. He started a fire with twigs from a
creosote bush, broken and clumped together, and before long
night was upon him and he was searching for warmth next
to the fire. Coyotes gave him the tone of the night by
announcing their nocturnal affair, and the shuffle of desert
mice often distracted him from his thoughts of what lay
ahead.

Once the fire had created a few glowing embers, Ruby
dug out his coffeepot, poured some water out of one canteen,
and prepared enough for one cup of coffee. Water had to be
used sparingly. Sure, he had three canteens, but he also had
a horse and a burro to share it with, and tomorrow he would
have to cross the Imperial Dunes, which were a good four
miles across and slow stepping. For his own food he brought

a good supply of beef jerky and dried fruits. It was quick and simple, with no need of preparation. His travels were only for a couple days. If they were longer, he would have brought some bacon, maybe some potatoes.

Food was plentiful along the river valley thanks to the irrigation projects. Though many newcomers were waiting on canal construction, a few had already made their own canals and started their own farms. One canal made a stretch from the northeast, from Blythe down into the valley near the dunes, constructed by a man named Bernard Cashman.

Ruby opened his saddlebag and grabbed the tin box. He flipped open the lid, shoved the pendant aside, and found the postcard. It was a bit sun-faded, the corners worn and rounded. He remembered back to that evening in prison when Abel had told him about Cashman. The tin box was open, the pendant lying on the table, and Ruby had picked up the card.

"That's another man you'll need to see," Abel had said. "He's your typical hard-ass. Loves money and abuses labor. Kind of like Gorum, but he's no tycoon. And when it comes to methods, Gorum would smash this guy with his pinky finger."

Ruby studied the address on the card. It was addressed Imperial Valley, which was a big area, but the canal only went to one place. "What does he have to do with the treasure?"

"On his farm you'll find an old man, Indigo Juárez." Abel had pointed toward the box. "There is a letter, from his daughter, Yudexy. She sent it to me a few years back, explaining how they went to work for Cashman."

Ruby had picked up the envelope, studied the handwriting, and noted the return address. It was postmarked Cibola.

He had read the letter that night, and he decided to read it again now by the light of the campfire. The envelope had yellowed, too, over time, but the letter inside was still a fresh-looking parchment. He unfolded the letter and leaned closer to the firelight.

4 September, 1902

Dear Mr. Winthrop,

I am writing on behalf of my father, Indigo. He has grown old and frail and is no longer able to provide for us. This forces us to work on the vegetable farm for Bernard Cashman. He is a wealthy man and has constructed a canal into the valley. It is hard work and the days are long. Indigo talks of you often and speaks fondly of the memories. I write to you only to deliver a reminder of his never-ending friendship with hopes that it brings to you a hint of happiness. We all wish you well and hope that you are at peace.

Regards,
Yudexy Juárez de Fernandez

Dado que no podemos conseguir lo que nos gusta, nos gusta lo que tenemos.

The closing proverb had stuck with him since he first read the letter, and it still affected him to this day. "Since we can't get what we like, we like what we have." According to Abel, Indigo's family had suffered for generations and they accepted whatever came their way. Throughout his life Ben had had to do the same thing, and he'd not been given much. Now he'd been delivered a wild dream, a treasure map in the form of a tin box of items. He'd never felt so unsure or curious about something like this, yet he'd never been so equipped to pursue it either. Many times he had thought about the length of his prison sentence. In and out in a few months, or a couple of years, he would have probably just gone back to work for Gorum and worked off his debt. But eight years was enough to spiritually recondition him and for him to connect to a different reason and persona. It was almost a naked feeling, to be so dedicated to a legend yet so uncertain. Meeting Hostetter had helped with the curiosity. He was a smart man, with a lot of common sense, and his support meant something to Ben.

Ben folded the letter, stuffed it back in the envelope, and returned it to the box. He poured the coffee into the tin cup and stared into the fire as he sipped. He thought about Gorum again, and the episode at the bathhouse. Duff was surely on his tail, just how close couldn't be calculated. Probably had the kid with him, too. Ben shook his head as he thought about the kid. The encounter in the alley proved one thing: the kid was green. Likely some young buck looking for work who found himself on Gorum's thug list because of his big size. Maybe he started as a cowhand, or in the mines, and got in a fistfight with a foreman and proved himself. That was usually all it took. Strength and a share of guts, and Gorum lapped them up like a hound dog over a skillet of gravy. Ruby had experienced it a few times but was smart enough to turn the other cheek when he really felt like belting a foreman in the mouth. But the kid was different. Put him in a new suit of clothes, fancy new hat, custom boots, and a fine Colt rig, and he was at your disposal. He would do well, too, with a shallow conscience, but one softhearted move and death would be at his doorstep. Ben would watch for that. With any luck he'd catch it, and then he might just get the best of them.

AS THEY RODE THE TRAIL DOWN THE ALLUVIAL FLAT, the half-circle sun hung on the horizon among plumes of coral clouds. Duff, sturdy and alert, rode in the lead on a tall sorrel. Redman rode drag on a black-and-white paint. Calhoun rode between them on a bay gelding, with Felicia slumped in front of him, her hands tied to the horn of the saddle. She had initially been behind him, but twice she jumped off and tried to run. The new riding position was

Duff's idea. He scolded Calhoun for allowing her to ride behind him in the first place. An experienced gunman should have known better. Listening to Duff, Calhoun put a strong arm around her waist and added a penalty of shooting her in the head if she tried it again. She hadn't tried thus far.

They rode off the flat and up to the crest of a bluff that looked down into a dry arroyo. Duff retrieved his binoculars and peered down.

Redman rode up next to him. "Shouldn't we be making camp?"

Duff lowered the binoculars and sneered at the kid. "We make camp when I decide its best, not you." He looked back down into the arroyo and tucked the binoculars into his saddlebag. "Ruby is down there. You boys take the girl and settle below that ridge north of us. No fire. I'll be there shortly."

"No fire?" Redman said. "How will we keep warm?"

Duff gazed over at Felicia and grunted a short laugh. "I'm sure we can find a way."

Redman gave a light heel to his horse and rode off. Calhoun followed him and held the reins in his left hand while his right arm stretched around Felicia's abdomen. Redman noticed that she shifted back and forth to the steps of the horse, when earlier she had been more firm and upright, so he knew she was tired. Calhoun had to have realized this, too, because he let loose of her and rested his hand on his thigh.

"What are you doing?" Felicia said. "Aren't you afraid I will run?"

"You aren't going anywhere," Calhoun said.

"You sound very sure of yourself."

"I'm not sure of much of anything, but I don't think you'd take the chance of getting shot."

"Maybe I don't care if you shoot me. Maybe I'd rather be dead."

"No, then you'd have tried already."

They kept riding a little longer, then Calhoun stopped short of the ridge and dismounted. Redman dismounted, too, and Calhoun handed him the reins of the bay.

"Go unsaddle the horses," he said.

Redman looked up at Felicia. "What about her?"

Calhoun glanced up at her, then back at Redman with a grin. "Unsaddle her, too, if you want."

Redman led the horses deeper into the arroyo and found a spot where he could hobble them. He walked to the side of the bay and reached up for Felicia. She leaned in to him and he lifted her and helped her to the ground. When she was steady on her feet, she faced him, only a few inches away, and she stared into his eyes. He stared back for a moment, deep into her brown irises that studied him as if she was interpreting a Bible scripture. He untied the thin hemp ropes from Felicia's wrists, then coiled the ropes and put them in a pocket in his trousers. She rolled her wrists and rubbed the joints.

"Do you really think he would shoot me?"

He turned quickly to the horse and started to loosen the cinch. She moved closer to him, to where he could see her from a peripheral view.

"I don't think you could," she said. "Have you ever killed anyone?"

He flipped the stirrup up and worked more briskly with the cinch.

She rubbed a hand down the gelding's neck. "I don't think you have."

He turned angrily to her. "You don't know a damn thing about me!"

She developed a slight smirk.

He took a deep breath and exhaled, then untied Calhoun's bedroll. He pulled it down and shoved it into her arms. He pointed below the ridge. "Take it over there."

"Where is your bedroll?"

"You don't worry about me. Now go on."

She kept looking at him, then slowly turned away, carrying the bedroll under her arm, a fearful look on her face.

Redman removed the saddle and set it over a rock. He grabbed the saddle blanket and flipped it a few times to get rid of the dust, then draped it over another rock. As he finished securing the hobbles on the two horses, Duff rode up the grade and dismounted. He nodded toward Felicia, who was on her knees untying the bedroll.

"Why isn't she tied up?" Duff said.

Redman looked over at her. "She's not going anywhere."

Duff walked up to Redman, close enough that Redman could smell his stale breath and see the tobacco stains between his teeth.

"You don't have the liberty to make those kinds of decisions, nor the intelligence or experience to ascertain what is best. Now you go over there and tie her wrists and ankles. And you do so with a swift effort. *Comprendes?*"

Anger boiled inside of Redman, but he held his breath and his tongue. He fished the rope back out of his pocket, then grabbed the long coil of rope from his saddle and walked to Felicia. He dropped to his knees in front of her, grabbed her wrists, and pushed them together. He wrapped the rope around them swiftly three times, then tied a double knot on the bottom side.

Felicia paid no attention to Redman's constraining moves and gazed at Duff. "Do you think he killed my grandfather?"

"I don't know," Redman said.

"I think he is heartless, but I don't think he is stupid. My grandfather is an important man. Murdering him would not be a wise thing to do." She turned her head back to Redman. "But you—I don't think you are like him. You are not heartless."

Redman pushed on her shoulders. "Lean back."

She only grinned at him. "You know I'm still a virgin."

Redman gazed at her in surprise.

"If it is to happen on this trip, I want you to be the first."

"You're talking foolish," he said.

"No—a fool would believe that I would be spared. I know where I'm headed and what is to become of me. My grandpa has warned me about Gorum and his men and the young girls he keeps as bond servants. If that is how I am to live the rest of my life, then I would rather look back at this moment knowing that it was you, rather than him. It will happen, right? Please give me that wish."

Redman pinched his lips and pushed her to where she fell on her back. He pivoted around and lifted her feet and tucked them under his arm. In one swift motion he wrapped the rope around her ankles, like roping a calf, and then tied them tight. When he stood to walk away, she stopped him with her soft voice.

"How can I cover myself tied up like this?"

He turned and looked down at her. She lay helplessly on her side. "You figure it out."

Chapter Four

❧

Right before sunrise Redman woke with an eerie feeling
that started with a sensation in his stomach and grew
to fuzziness in his head. He threw off the blanket and wiped
at his face with his bare hand, waking the muscles around
his eye sockets. He looked around and could faintly see their
horses in the predawn, each with a fetlock cocked forward
and in a peaceful rest. The desert around him didn't seem
to tell him anything about his feeling, but he looked to the
bedding beside him and jumped up when he noticed Felicia
missing.

He quickly looked where Calhoun had laid out his bedroll and noticed he was gone. He looked over toward the
horses and the bay was gone, too. Then he looked at Duff's
bedroll, a good thirty feet from his, and saw the silhouette
of the big man standing and removing his trousers. Redman
walked slowly toward him, and it all came clear when he
saw Felicia jump up, scream, and try to run. Duff held on
to the waist of his trousers with one hand and ran after her.

She didn't get far and he laughed as he caught her. She lay on the ground below him, her hands still tied, still dressed, the rope around her ankles cut, her hair in a disarray and fear in her eyes. Without hesitation, Redman pulled his Colt, pointed it at Duff, and cocked the hammer. Duff lost his greedy expression and turned instantly to Redman.

"Get away from the girl," Redman said.

Duff only stared, eventually producing a smirk and a light chuckle. "Well, well. Look who just signed his own death certificate." Redman stood firm while Duff buttoned his pants and took one step backward. "Now, you put down that gun and remember what your job is."

"No, I won't," Redman said. "Where's Calhoun?"

Duff spoke through his teeth. "Kid, I'm warning you. I will cave in your empty skull—"

"No!" Redman stood firmly and glared at Duff without blinking. "Now I asked you where Calhoun went."

"He went to scout the area, but he'll be back any damned second. You think you can take both of us, kid? You have the ambition of a fool."

"Back away from the girl or I make you dead. It's not a warning, it's a guarantee."

Duff grunted, nodded, and took another step back. "You really think you can get one up on me?"

"I already have."

Duff glanced down at the girl, then back at Redman. "Okay, greenhorn, what's your next move? Let's see where it gets you."

"Drop that rig, and the knife in your boot. Very slowly."

Duff was hesitant but eventually did as the kid said, unbuckling the gun belt and letting it fall to the ground. When he bent over and reached inside his boot for the knife, he rapidly flicked his wrist, sending the blade into Redman's shoulder. The kid's gun went off but sent a bullet out into the desert, ricocheting off a rock, and Duff quickly pounced on him and knocked the gun out of his hand. On his knees, the big man straddled the grimacing kid, picked up the gun, and put it in the waistband of his trousers. He smirked as he removed the knife from Redman's shoulder and wiped the bloody blade on the kid's shirt. Redman closed his eyes and sucked in a large breath and put a hand over the wound.

Duff stood up and glanced at the girl. "I'll deal with you later—trust me. But I've lost my will and we need to get riding. Go make some coffee. And don't think about trying anything stupid." He looked back at Redman. "Get our horses and get them saddled. As you've just found out, you will never have the sand to get the edge on me. So get used to it."

Duff turned and walked away, and Felicia immediately walked on her knees over to the wounded Redman. She lifted his hand away from the wound. "Let me fix you a bandage."

Redman pushed her away and rose to his feet. "I don't need your help."

She stood and grabbed his arm. He looked directly into her eyes. She smiled tenderly. "That was very brave of you. I will never forget it."

He looked at her a moment, then walked away from her, still holding his wound. Though her gratitude was felt, humiliation had still set in. It had all happened so fast. Protecting her was an immediate reaction, one that he couldn't control. Now he had to try to live with the consequences, and he knew, without question, that they would be brutal.

BEN HAD RISEN EARLY AND RIDDEN FOR FOUR HOURS along the foothills of the Chuckwallas, until the sharp-ridged peaks disappeared behind him and led to a crusty playa. The sky was cloudless, but it was a faded blue in the desert, dulled by the sun's reflection off the sandy desert floor. The mirage in front of him seemed to widen as he rode farther, intensified by the growing heat. The sun was still at his back, and he hoped it would stay that way until he crossed the dunes. He had been here once before, picking up a load of supplies at Temecula, and remembered how badly the heat radiated off the sand. It was like riding into a furnace, which one seemed to tolerate the first hundred feet or so, but after that came misery, and turning back was not any better an option than continuing on. Those images of the past quickly came back to him as the dunes started to appear—waves of cream-colored sand in a wide swath across the valley, as if God Himself had spread a patch of honey on the earth. Then again, Ben thought, as ruthless as the desert could be, maybe it was Satan's recipe.

The horse started to slow the deeper they got into the dunes, eventually high-stepping and towing the load of the burro, whose shorter legs had to move faster to keep up. Ben kept the mare moving, slapping her with the reins and only allowing an occasional rest for a sip from the canteen and a wipe of his sweaty brow. On normal terrain a horse could cross a four-mile stretch in an hour, but as slow-moving as it was around the deep bowls of the dunes, it would be at least two, maybe three hours to make this crossing. It all depended on the mare and the willingness of her burro counterpart.

But Ben was prepared for this trek and was nearly through it before high noon, when the sands began to break and occasional vegetation appeared. He stopped and gave the horses a rest, some water and a handful of grain, and for himself some beef jerky and raisins.

He figured to rest a good fifteen minutes or so before getting back in the saddle and heading north to the Cashman farm. He was near that point when he wondered if the heat had gotten to him. Usually it was the eyes that deceived someone under the intense sun, but in this case it was his ears. It was a whistle. Not like the whistle of the wind, but from the lips of a human. He turned and looked to his right, then behind him, and wondered if the eyes and ears had joined together in the desert prank. He led the horse and burro over the peak of a dune, and sure enough the image became clearer. No more than fifty feet away stood a canvas tent, a sorrel horse, and a man in all off-white attire and a straw hat, bent over, whistling. In most cases this was a cause to be leery, but Ben did not sense danger. He was continuing to lead the way toward the tent and to where the man stooped over a hole he'd dug, when suddenly the mare whickered and the man jumped back a good five feet, dropping a wooden clipboard into the sand. He looked up at Ben in fear.

Ben held up a hand. "Easy does it, pardner. Just didn't expect to run into anyone like this."

"That makes two of us," said the young man. Ben figured him to be early twenties, but wasn't quite sure of what to make of him. He wore bone-colored trousers and a matching shirt, almost the same color as his tent. His face was red from the sun, nose slightly burned and peeling, and he squinted his blue eyes as he peered through round wire spectacles.

"Goodness, you startled me." The young man got on his feet and retrieved his clipboard, magnifying glass, and pencil, and blew the sand off of them. He walked to Ben and offered his hand. Ben accepted the shake.

"Ben Ruby."

"Nice to meet you, Mr. Ruby," the young man said. "Francis Baker, UC–Berkeley."

"Beg your pardon?"

"I'm a college student—working on my master's degree. Work directly under Professor Andrew Lawson himself."

"Lawson?"

"Yes, you know . . . great discoverer of the San Andreas Fault? Branches run all through this part of California."

Ben glanced over at the tent, noticed the many tools outside, and then looked back at the hole Francis had dug and the shovel standing inside the hole. Ben nodded at the clipboard. "What do you have there?"

Francis clutched his clipboard, as if hiding something secretive. "Oh, this is just part of my research. Did you know this is an old seabed? Look here!" The young man jumped down in his hole and lifted up a wooden bucket filled with stones. He reached inside and pulled out a clamshell and held it under the magnifying glass. "Mollusk. Proof that they were once stranded here. I found more to the west near an old shoreline. Absolutely fascinating."

Ben scratched his chin. "Mollusk?"

"Yes, exactly. Intriguing, eh?" Francis dumped the contents of the bucket onto the ground. He ran his hand over the pile of sand, stones, and old shells, smoothed them out, brushed them off. He picked up a larger shell, blew the sand off it, and looked at it closely. "The sea life here must have been abundant at one time. I've seen all sorts of evidence. Sand and gravel bars. Beach deposits. Wave cuts in the rocks along the mountains. It's all very clear."

Ben studied him for a moment. "So you're saying that you have proof there that this area was once a sea?"

"There's no question. It's hard for the average man to believe, but to those of us more educated—or trained in what to look for—we can see all the signs. Funny though, even the Indians of these parts believe it to be true."

Ben had to take in a deep breath to make sure the sun wasn't playing tricks on him. The young man was certainly real, and the evidence in front of him couldn't have been any clearer. Now the question was whether or not he could trust this college boy. Questions began rolling around in Ben's mind, and though he was sure the kid would be happy to oblige, he thought it better to be little more hospitable. Ben reached in his saddlebag and grabbed the cloth bundle of jerky. "Are you hungry? I have plenty."

Francis licked his lips and looked at the bundle with anticipation. "Yes . . . of course. That would be very kind of you." He flipped the front of the tent open and set the clipboard inside. "Might as well come into the shade."

Ben nodded and tied the mare to a tent stake opposite the sorrel, then joined Francis inside. Though it was likely a custom-made tent, it reminded Ben of an army officer's, probably twelve feet square and waist-high on the sides before it tapered up to its peak. Though the student was its only occupant, Ben was certain it could easily accommodate eight, maybe ten, men. Due to this roominess, Ben was not surprised to see a wooden folding table not much bigger than a lap tray, a wooden camp stool that folded flat, and a lantern that hung above them.

Francis tied the flaps open to provide some light—an opening which faced the west. It was indeed a nice shady spot, with a gray flannel blanket on the floor where the two could relax and enjoy their lunch. Both men removed their hats. Francis ran a hand through long, blond bangs and flipped them backward over the sweaty ring formed by his hat.

Ben looked out the flaps to the western horizon, absorbing what he'd just learned.

Francis talked while he chewed. "So what's your destination out here, if I may ask?"

"I have some business at the Cashman farm, a bit north of here."

"Oh yes. I made a stop there on my way through. Not a very hospitable fellow. Wife's a bit of a nag, too. But I made my stay short and got right to my work."

Ben nodded. "Your work. It's very interesting."

"I love the mysteries of the earth. I wish I had time to explore them all in my lifetime. But I will have to be satisfied with those of California for now."

Ben tossed a handful of raisins in his mouth and then handed the sack to Francis, who poured some into his palm.

"This is kind of you to share. Been living off bacon, airtight beans, and old biscuits. Beats starving, but I'm growing a little tired of it."

"How long have you been out here?" Ben asked.

"Just got here yesterday. Plan to move on tomorrow morning."

"Where to next?"

"Back west, maybe south to Mexico. Need to find old shorelines on the mountains. That's where I'll find the travertine deposits. The subject of my thesis, you know."

Ben gazed out into the sun and at the mirage on the playa. "Shorelines. How long ago . . . did this sea exist?"

Francis rubbed his hands together and joined Ben at his gander into the desert. "Hard to say exactly, but most experts agree that it disappeared in the early 1600s. Fed by the Colorado River for over a thousand years, until it evaporated out."

"Evaporated?"

"Yes, that's the theory. A long drought, possibly, throughout the Rockies, light snowmelt. It would have to have considerable flow into the desert to avoid evaporation. You know, this heat evaporates water very quickly. If the inflow is light, then evaporation takes control."

"I see." Ben absorbed this new knowledge. "And what's this business about a fault?"

"The San Andreas. A fault line, where tectonic plates rub together. When they do, the friction causes earthquakes."

Ben knew the dizziness he felt now wasn't from the heat. "So how do you know all this?"

"Research, of course. Professor Lawson pioneered most of it. Some of the earliest information comes from the Spanish Conquest. But most of it comes from scientific research . . . from geologists like myself. My thesis, which is mostly why I'm here, will be on the formation of travertine on rock surfaces. More specifically, the role of the sun versus the cool nights in its formation. It's never been researched and I will prove it is essential."

"Rock surfaces," Ben said. "The rocks you found in that hole?"

Francis raised his eyebrows, as if embarrassed. "No, rock

surfaces on the mountain ranges I was speaking of—near the old shoreline. I'm doing this dig for fun. Always wanted to do a dig like this."

Ben pondered what he'd heard, realizing that Francis had a love for exploring. "This old sea—how deep would it have been?"

Francis answered instantly. "In its prime, three hundred feet. The old shorelines indicate thirty, maybe even fifty feet above sea level."

"So it's possible for ships to have sailed in those waters?"

"More than possible, it's very likely. The lake that was here was freshwater, but there was a winding inlet that led from the Gulf of California, and was no doubt navigable by ships."

Ben thought for a moment, wondering how much he should reveal to the student of science, but it didn't take long for him to feel a confidence in the young man and a need for his assistance. More so, however, it was a bit mind-numbing to discover Francis in this place, of all places, and to recall Abel Winthrop's mention of destiny. Could Francis be a part of it? The thought made Ben shiver.

"How would you like to join me on another dig—just for fun?" Ben asked.

Francis looked perplexed. "Join you?"

"What would you say if I told you I knew where an old Spanish ship was buried?"

"I'd say you were mad!" Francis laughed and nearly fell to his back. "Those crazy old tales. Not that it's not possible, but how would you ever know where to dig? It's such a crazy notion, Mr. Ruby. You seem like such a practical sort. Never would have thought that of you."

"Yeah, so you say. Well, never mind then." Ben felt an immediate regret. "I'm sure the horses have had a good rest. I best be on my way."

Ben had stood and stooped to exit the tent when Francis rose to his knees and grabbed his elbow.

"Wait," Francis said.

Ben turned and studied his retracting curiosity.

"Do you really think you know where such a ship may be?"

Ben nodded. "Let's just say I have a pretty good source."

Francis stood quickly. "Well, then. I suppose the travertine can wait."

Ben was amused at how quickly Francis scurried around and organized his gear. Ben helped him tear down the tent and pack to ride. To carry his equipment the student had built a travois out of pine lumber and a fisherman's net, which towed easily behind his horse, with short spoke wheels that he said came from a couple of high-wheeled bicycles he'd found in a scrap yard. Ben had seen travois before that were used by Indians, and they were much more primitive and dragged on the ground, but this invention was quite advanced, incredibly sturdy and still lightweight.

The Cashman farm was still a half day away, and Ben was certain the trip would seem to go faster with the student's company. He knew, too, that it would be a good time to ask more questions about the science and history that would hopefully back up the legend. His faith had been lacking up to this point, but it was somewhat restored now with his new acquaintance.

Just as they were about to mount to leave, Ben caught a glimpse of some movement east over the dunes. He reached into his saddlebag and grabbed a telescope and peered through at the image. Two riders, maybe three, but he couldn't make them out. They were following his trail, no doubt, which meant only one thing: Gorum.

"We have to get moving," Ben said.

"What do you see?"

Ben put a foot in the stirrup, lifted himself up, and swung over the mare. "Trouble."

The student mounted as well and in frequent glances looked nervously behind him and across the dunes as they rode northwest into the playa. Ben wondered if Francis had had any idea how dangerous it was for him to be out alone in this hellhole. The elements and the wildlife were a big threat as it was, but those following would stop short of nothing to get what they wanted, even at the expense of some harmless college student on a campout. Ben was thankful that he'd came onto Francis when he did and that he didn't ride past him. That danger was gone, and Ben hoped that he could protect the student from the new dangers that awaited them both.

Chapter Five

THE sun was fading far in the west before the terrain started turning green and the smell of water filled the evening air. The playa from the dunes on had been hard and crusty, with only occasional vegetation, like the typical amaranth, wild celery, bursage, three-awn, and tumbleweed. As they got closer to the Cashman farm, the newly constructed canals appeared, which fed the needlegrasses and bent grass that grew on the banks. Ben was amazed how much things had changed since he'd gone to prison. Nowhere this close to Yuma could one see so much green until now. It was intriguing, and he understood how it brought hope to the minds of many, but he couldn't help but think about men like Gorum who took advantage of such new techniques. Greed consumed men like him, which bred corruption and abuse of people.

Bernard Cashman was, in many ways, like Gorum, but he was not a killer. Word had gotten around that Cashman worked people hard and paid them little, was belligerent and unfriendly, but it was his wife, Verona, who ruled the roost. Gorum was not the type to ever let such a thing happen and would strike a woman without hesitation for talking back to him, but on the Cashman farm Verona was the water that put out the fire. Whenever the flames got too high, she met them without challenge. Who was to say what her husband would be like without her, but as far as the people who worked at the farm were concerned she was a blessing.

Before long the grasses along the banks of the man-made canal turned to planted fields with occasional workers, native men and women wearing straw hats, white cotton clothing, and sandals, who stopped their labor to acknowledge the presence of the visitors. The workers carried large canvas shoulder bags that held the waste of unwanted weeds that could suffocate the desired plants if not removed. The planted fields stretched for at least a mile on each side of the canal, which was a consistent one hundred and fifty feet wide and would have been easily mistaken for a river by the untrained eye. Amid the fields were several rectangular wooden buildings and a larger adobe home with a roof covered in red clay tiles. The closer Ben and Francis got to the buildings, the more the workers seemed to react, especially those with children, who tried to contain them from running to greet the visitors. The older ones couldn't be stopped, such as the young barefooted boy who ran up to them in soiled, white cotton attire, teeth aglow in the fading sunlight. Ben and Francis kept riding as the boy jogged beside them.

"*Hola!* My name is Raul. I am happy to be at your service. And I am not too proud to accept tips if you think my service is good."

Ben smiled at the assertive lad, who quickly turned his attention to Francis. "You are back, *señor*. Did you have a nice visit to the desert? Do you need your clothes washed? Your boots polished? The desert is harsh on such things, you know. I will fix them up again as good as new!"

"No, thank you, Raul," Francis said. "But I'm sure Mr. Ruby

would be as obliged as myself if you took our horses and burro and watered them and gave them some grain."

"*Sí*, but the proprietor would not be happy if I gave water away. You will need to pay in advance."

Ben glanced at Francis in disbelief. "Is he serious?"

"I'm afraid so," Francis said.

Ben nodded toward the canal. "All that water, more than enough for a world of horses, and he won't share it?"

"He paid for the labor that brought it here, so he feels entitled."

Ben shrugged. "I suppose I can't argue there."

"No, and arguing about it wouldn't help. Our canteens— don't expect to fill them either without payment. You could be dying of thirst and it wouldn't matter."

Ben sighed. "What's the world coming to?"

They continued riding, Raul tagging along at their side until they reached the courtyard in front of the adobe, which presented an array of several white and red chickens roaming about and pecking the ground. The men stopped at a hitching rail. A wooden pail hung on a peg above a water trough. Ben chuckled a bit after reading a sign nailed to a post that read:

WATER .50 CENTS PER PAIL
PAY FIRST, DRINK LATER
NO CREDIT

As they stepped down from their horses, a sharp voice came from across the yard, from a portly, middle-aged man in tan trousers, white shirt, and a straw hat. He stomped as he walked, pointing a finger. "Keep those animals away from that water!" When he got closer, he glared at Ben with sage green eyes that didn't blink. "No water before payment."

Ben pointed a thumb back over his shoulder toward the sign. "Yeah, mister. I can read."

The man stopped and put his hands on his hips, studying

his new visitor. "I'm Bernard Cashman, not 'mister.' I'm the owner and proprietor of this farm. Nothing goes on here without my knowing." He shifted his gaze to Francis. "You again. And you come back bringing another freeloader?"

Ben held up a hand. "Now, wait just a minute here." Ben opened a saddlebag and reached inside the tin box and grabbed two silver dollars. He handed them to Cashman. "Not here for handouts. I'll gladly pay my way, and his. Here's enough for four buckets. Three for the horses and mule, and one from your fresh barrel over there for our canteens."

"Fresh water is fifty cents more," Cashman snapped. "What do you think I'm running here? A free-for-all?"

Ben grabbed another silver dollar from the saddlebag and flipped it in the air. Cashman caught it with ease. "Keep the extra fifty cents—consider it a token for your having such a kind greeter." Ben winked at Raul.

Cashman's eyes shifted back and forth and he cracked a fake smile. His arms moved from his hips to a quick clap, then above his head motioning to Raul. "What are you waiting for? Take care of these men and their horses! Fetch the water that they've paid for so willingly!"

Ben and Francis handed Raul the reins, and after Ben grabbed the tin box from the saddlebags, Raul nimbly led the animals away. Ben took two steps toward Cashman. "Name's Ben Ruby. I'm looking for Indigo Juárez. I was told he lived here."

Cashman glanced at the box and grunted. "What do you want with that dried-up old prune?"

"We have a mutual friend."

The proprietor looked him up and down. "Yeah, I bet you do."

At that moment a heavyset woman stepped outside from the adobe. She was a bit taller and even heavier than Cashman, big-boned, with broad shoulders, wearing an ankle-length, light blue cotton dress and a white apron. Her graying hair was up in a bun, and unlike many of those who lived and worked at the Cashman farm, she had a complexion that was a milky white. The flesh under her gray eyes sagged, as did a ridge under her chin. A bit of dark facial hair was visible on her upper lip. She wiped her hands on her apron as she stepped closer to the sunlight, but never completely out of the shade.

"Did you bring him any tobacco?" she asked, her voice deep and authoritative.

Ben and Francis removed their hats.

"Ma'am?" Ben said.

"That old Indian. He could stand some new tobacco."

"No—no, ma'am, I didn't. But if there was a place to buy some, I'd be happy to do so."

"Yes, there is a place," she said. "But unfortunately you were probably just there." She studied him a bit. "Name's Verona Cashman. That dumpy fella there is my husband. Says he runs the place, but I beg to differ."

Ben and Francis glanced at her embarrassed husband. For Ben it was easy to tell the man had no will to defend himself.

"I suppose you'll be needing a place to stay," Verona said.

Ben fumbled with his hat in front of him. "Just for the night, ma'am. Due to the price of your water, I'm afraid to ask the cost of boarding."

"Don't worry yourself none about that. You keep that old Indian away from our garbage pile and that'll earn your keep." She took a deep breath, then put her hands on her hips. "What's your business in these parts? I have to ask, you know. We own much of the land around the canal, from here to Blythe." She pointed a thumb at Francis. "Are you like that fella there, looking for answers in rocks?"

"Oh, I'm not much of a scientist. Indigo and I have a mutual friend. Just making a personal call."

"Very well, then. You'll find his shelter on the north end of the bunkhouses. He's the primitive sort."

Ben was amused by the woman, and he took a bit of a liking to her. "So I hear."

Ben and Francis donned their hats and walked down the dusty lane to the bunkhouses. Unlike the white adobe ranch house, the bunkhouses were fairly new lumber structures, pine-boarded and shingled with cedar shakes. There was a solitary window on each side of the buildings, but none with glass; each was covered with some sort of cloth. Like the windows, the doorways were protected by a quilt or woolen blanket. Occasionally a swarthy face would peek out at the visitors. At the end of the lane they came to a shelter, no more than twelve foot square, made of a hodgepodge of cedar logs and lumber, a roof thatched with straw and mud, and white cloths covering the openings. Ben knew this had to be the primitive structure so many had spoken about. As he stepped up to the front, he examined the burlap covering and wondered how to announce his presence. Since he saw nowhere to knock, he decided just to yell.

"Uh, howdy! Indigo? Are you in there?" He looked at Francis and shrugged.

The response from inside was immediate. "*Sí, mi amigo.* Come protect yourself from the sun."

Ben pulled back the burlap flap, and he and Francis ducked as they entered the shelter. It took a few seconds for his eyes to adjust to the darkness, and he could smell the smoke of foul tobacco. In the dimness he made out the skinny old man sitting in a rocking chair battered save for the arm rails partially covered with a frayed quilt. The old man wore denim dungarees, tied with ropes at the cuffs, and leather sandals on his feet. His shirt was faded red cotton with a pocket on each side of his chest. His hair was gray and white and combed back into a ponytail. Ben had never seen a face look so old and furrowed, and eyelids so squinted and narrow—so much that he couldn't make out the color of the man's eyes. The old Indian puffed on a pipe, and once he'd acknowledged Ben's presence, he leaned a bit forward and tapped the pipe on the side of the chair, then stuck it in his shirt pocket.

He gave Ben a good look, then raised both hands above his shoulders and looked up toward the top of the shelter. "The gods told me that a great visitor would come my way. Once again they are faithful to their word."

"I am indeed a visitor," Ben said, "but I'm not sure how great I am." Ben felt a bit sorry for him, especially after the old man smiled and revealed only three, badly stained teeth—one on top, two on the bottom. Indigo slowly extended his wrinkled right hand and joined it with Ben's. The old man's grip was gentle but firm. "Nice to finally meet you, sir."

Ben knelt to a reed mat in front of Indigo's chair and rested on one knee. Francis kept standing behind him. Ben opened the tin box and produced a leather medicine bag that jingled as he dropped it into the palm of his hand. He gave it to Indigo.

Indigo did not need to look at it long before he nodded. "Ahh, you knew my friend Abel."

"I spent some time with him—he gave that to me on his deathbed. Before he passed, he said this would give me good medicine if I walked the right path. He said you had told him the same thing, but he walked the wrong path."

Indigo nodded, handed the medicine bag back to Ben, then retrieved the pipe from his shirt pocket. He pinched a chunk of used chewing tobacco out of a tin can beside his chair and stuffed it inside the pipe bowl. He grabbed a red-tipped match from his other shirt pocket, struck it on the arm of the chair, then sucked the flame into the bowl. Intermittent puffs of a putrid-smelling smoke rose above him and wove their way into the thatch.

Indigo relaxed back in his chair. "This is true what Abel said. And now you are out of the prison and wanting to walk the right path."

Ben nodded.

"And this is why you come to me?"

"Not exactly." Ben glanced nervously at Francis. "Abel also told me about a story you once told him, of an old ship buried in the dunes."

"I have told that story to many people. Many who laugh."

"Yes, well, sir, I'm not laughing. I'd like to hear the story, and I'd like to find that old ship."

Indigo nodded and held out a hand. "Then join us for supper, and tonight I will tell you about the People."

The flap of the shelter opened and Ben turned to acknowledge the visitor. He was not prepared for the sensation that overcame him—the stopping of his breath, the tingle in his stomach. He quickly removed his hat. Yudexy Juárez stepped inside the shelter carrying a basket lined with a white cotton cloth and filled with bread, cheese, and a tube of sausage. The bangs of her long, raven hair were tied at the back of her head, exposing her ebony eyes and tanned complexion, which gave a sharp contrast to her white cotton dress. When she noticed Ben, she stopped in her tracks, as if she, too, had a moment of similar enchantment.

Ben fondled his hat with both hands as Yudexy stepped shyly around him and Francis. "*Con permiso, señor.*" She set the basket of food on a table next to Indigo's chair.

"I hope you have brought enough food for our guests," Indigo said.

"*Sí,*" Yudexy said. "There is plenty." She shared an affectionate smile with Ben.

Indigo glanced inside the basket. "The bread and cheese will do, but I am sorry that all we have for meat is this reverse intestine."

Yudexy let out a short gasp. "Papa, do not say such things. You should be grateful that we have food to eat."

Francis grunted. "Reverse intestine?"

"They use the intestines of pigs and deer to hold it all together," Indigo said. "They grind up the parts that no one else will eat, mix them with pig fat, run it all through a grinder again, then shove it all in the intestine. What I wouldn't give for a slice of backstrap."

"Papa," Yudexy said, "you couldn't even chew a piece of regular meat if you had it, so stop complaining."

After a teasing sneer, the old man winked at his daughter, then acknowledged his guests once again. "She is beautiful, just like her mama, but even a strong-willed woman like her would have forbidden such food at our table."

Ben nodded at his pipe. "What about your tobacco? Would she have approved of that?"

"Why would she have to? She did not smoke it."

All of them chuckled at the old man's wit. Ben quickly understood what Abel liked about Indigo. There was nothing dry or perverse about him. He was a genuine soul and Ben felt an immediate bond.

"I will go get us some water," Yudexy said. "Please, *señores*, make yourselves comfortable." She kissed Indigo on the cheek, then walked nimbly out of the shelter. Ben watched her walk out, and as much as when she walked in, his heart felt as if it was beating fast. He slowly put his hat back on, only tilting it back in a more casual way—as if just to find a place to put it rather than wearing it.

"She is a widow, you know," Indigo said.

"Beg your pardon?" Ben said.

The old man struck another match and winked at Ben as he sucked the flame into the pipe. It was true, Ben thought, he was wise beyond his years. And he had many of them.

Chapter Six

THOUGH Indigo had griped about the sausage, the meal really wasn't half-bad. The meat was sliced thin, had a smoked flavor, and was a bit spicy, and it was eaten with the bread, which was fresh and still warm. Yudexy brought in a crock of honey butter for the bread, and another wooden bowl filled with fresh strawberries. She put raw spinach in a larger wooden bowl and crumbled goat cheese over it, added sliced tomatoes, chopped white onions, then topped it off with a spicy vinegar dressing. Ben had never seen anything like it. Not only the salad, but he watched Yudexy take such a pride in their meal, amid a setting so simple. She'd also taken the time to place candles sporadically around the shelter, adding a dim light and pleasantness to the atmosphere. Though it was not a great feast, it was very satisfying, and Ben could not remember ever feeling so comfortable and relaxed during and after a meal.

They all sat on the floor, on mats made of woven reeds, circled around the food, which was all placed on a blanket in the center. Raul had joined them, and Ben was pleased to know that he was Yudexy's son. The boy made frequent glances at Ben, which Ben understood to be youthful curiosity. Yudexy, too, exchanged a few glances with Ben, which began with a shy smile and always ended with her picking up a bowl of something and offering Ben more. At first he could easily accept, until he was too full for another bite and had to decline. He hoped to learn more about the boy and his mother, but the conversation around their supper stemmed more from the excitement of Francis's expeditions and ultimately to the years Ben had spent with Abel Winthrop.

Raul extended his curiosity further. "Why did you go to prison?"

"Raul!" his mother said sharply.

"No, it's fine," Ben said. "You all have a right to know."

"But not now," Yudexy said. "It's time for him to go to bed." She grabbed Raul by the arm and lifted him.

"Aw, Mama!" he complained.

"*Vamanos*. Say good night to Señor Ruby."

"Please," Ben said, "call me Ben."

"Good night, Ben," the boy said. He said good night to Francis, hugged his grandfather, then quickly snatched a strawberry, shoved it in his mouth, and ran from the shelter. Yudexy took a deep breath and rolled her eyes. "He is a lot to handle."

"I can see that," Ben said.

Yudexy rose to her feet. "I should probably go, too."

Ben quickly stood as well. "Let me walk you."

Without much hesitation, Yudexy accepted, and not with words, but with a gentle smile and slight nod.

THEY WALKED IN THE NIGHT AMONG THE BOARDING shacks, which cast very little light from within. Yudexy explained that Cashman would not supply them with oil for their lanterns, that it was too expensive. One day, when he'd been in Yuma, he brought back a surplus of candles that he bought for pennies on the dollar, so that was their only source of light. They had enough candles to last a decade.

The faint ripples from the flowing canal water could be heard, along with the frogs that sang their evening song. The smell of turned soil and vegetation was also a new sensation that Ben would have to grow accustomed to.

Yudexy wrapped a blue knitted shawl around her shoulders and clutched it together in the front. Ben was thankful for the appearance of a half moon, which shed just enough light for him to see her.

"This is quite a setup here," Ben said.

"It has brought much needed work. My papa would prefer only to complain, but we would be cold and hungry without it."

"I'm sure he just misses the old ways."

"Yes, you are right."

There was an awkward silence as they kept walking, with occasional glances that drew Ben more into the person beside him. He had seen many beautiful women in his lifetime, but there was something about Yudexy that put her above them all. He supposed it could be her black hair. He'd always had a special attraction to brunettes. Or maybe her figure, which wasn't quite slender, but a little curvy, in all the right places. But he was sure it was more than that. It was more her style. The way she nurtured her father and paid attention to the smallest detail. She was mature and prone more to reality than fantasy. This was it, no doubt, along with the essence of a good mother.

"Raul," Ben said. "He's quite a boy."

Yudexy sighed. "Oh, I don't know where he gets it."

"If you don't mind me asking, what happened to his father?"

"He died two years ago."

"I'm sorry to hear that. What happened?"

She clutched her shawl tighter.

Ben felt regret for asking. "You don't have to talk about it."

"No, it's okay. They were working on a temporary dam while building the canal. They used heavy timbers to hold back the water, and the river was flooding and caused the dam to collapse. The timbers fell down on him."

"That's terrible. I'm sorry to hear that."

"It's not been easy—not having a man to provide for us. I've been lucky that Señora Cashman pays me to work in the fields and sometimes in her home, cleaning or canning. But I am more concerned about Raul. It's tough for a boy to grow up without a father." Suddenly she chuckled. "When he gets in trouble, his grandfather calls him 'half orphan.'"

Ben laughed, and he admired how her face seemed to glow when she was amused.

"Raul seems like quite an enterpriser. Does he get that from his father?"

"Oh no. His father was a very quiet man. Only spoke when it was absolutely necessary. When Raul got out of line, all his father had to do was look at him in his own stern way and that was it. Now, when he gets out of line with me, he seems only amused when I scold him."

"Does that bother you?"

She thought for a moment. "Not really. I don't want to dampen his spirit. He is what he is."

"Maybe he gets it from his grandfather?"

Yudexy smiled. "Yes, I suppose you're right."

They stopped walking in front of one of the boarding shacks, and Yudexy turned to face him.

"This is my place. Thank you for walking with me."

Ben was not happy that his time with her was over, so he absorbed all he could of her face, the oval contour, the way the moonlight glistened in her raven hair, but most of all how she looked at him.

He removed his hat and made a slight bow. "Good night, ma'am."

"Please, call me Dexy."

"All right. Good night, Dexy."

She smiled at him and turned and walked away. He watched her all the way to the door, until she turned her head back and gave him one final smile—one that would surely last until morning.

ON THE WAY BACK TO INDIGO'S SHELTER BEN WAS greeted by a frisky white puppy. It came out of nowhere, it seemed, wagging its tail and turning in circles. Ben was quite taken with it, and he squatted and petted its head and scratched its ears. The pup rolled to its back, and Ben rubbed its pink belly and saw that it was a male. He figured it to be about three months old.

"So what are you doing out and about, little fella? Up to no good?"

The pup jumped to its feet and let out a short bark, then ran to a nearby shack and crawled through the blanket-covered doorway. The shack seemed abandoned, and out of curiosity Ben decided to follow the pup. When he got to the doorway, he pulled the blanket aside and could barely see the stacks of crates in the light from a moonlit window. He reached in his pocket and found a match and struck it on the dry wood of the doorjamb. He held the match closer to one of the crates and read the word CANDLES stenciled on the side. He held the match higher and noticed that the room was full of similar crates, and ones farther back were labeled DYNAMITE. Ben shook the match out quickly and stepped back outside. Perhaps it was only natural, he thought, to feel so content and comfortable one moment, then the next be reminded of the one thing that had caused him the greatest pain of his life. Somehow, he figured, he would find a way to put it all behind him.

BACK AT THE SHELTER BEN FOUND INDIGO ONCE AGAIN in his chair smoking his pipe, and Francis lying on the mats, laughing and holding a tin cup.

"Ah, Ben," Francis said, holding up the cup. "The old man broke out the agave."

Ben sat down next to him, and Francis grabbed a clay decanter and another cup, filled the cup half-full, then handed it to Ben. He accepted it with caution.

"This is the real juice," Francis said, holding up his own cup and nodding to Indigo. "*Tu salud!*" He took a healthy drink, then smacked his lips. "Made authentically by the People from real blue agave. The old man told me so."

"You better go easy with that," Ben said.

"Ah, it's no big deal. Try it!"

Ben took a sip, then smiled at the old man.

Francis laughed loudly. "You see? I've sampled quite a bit of tequila in these parts, but none as good as this."

Ben took another sip and agreed that it was quite original. He'd normally associated drinking with trouble, but he thought that a good social drink in a safe atmosphere couldn't hurt anyone. So maybe this wasn't a bad time for one.

"Mezcal," Indigo said, tapping his pipe on the rail of the chair. "There is this saying: *Para todo mal, mezcal y para todo bien también.*"

Francis leaned toward Ben. "Sorry, but my Spanish is a little rusty."

Ben swallowed another sip. "He said, 'for everything bad, mescal, for everything good, too'."

"Hmmm. Have to ponder that one over another."

Ben was amused by Francis and worried at the same time. He'd seen ranch hands get ahold of mescal and suffer the sudden aftereffects when they realized a day later how quickly it can sneak up on a person.

It was too late now, Ben thought, and regardless of the student's state, it was time to relax. Without invitation or warning Indigo proceeded to entertain them with a story. Getting their attention was not difficult, considering the way the old man looked above his head and waved his hands.

"The gods said it was time to rest and to leave the land in their hands. It was midday, and to the east there was sunshine, but in the west a great dark cloud came over the village. The women gathered their children and secured them in their huts. The men worked feverishly to make sure the huts were strong and could withstand the storm. For the rest of the day and all through the night the wind blew with great force. Along with the whining of the wind we could hear the sand beating against the huts. The women slept with their children while the men stayed awake to tend to the huts if needed. We knew that when the gods were through with the land, there would be a great transformation and it would not be without purpose.

"By morning the storm had stopped. The men had to dig through great drifts of sand to get out of the huts. Once they were through, all of the men, women, and children roamed to see what the gods had done. We could no longer recognize our land. It had a new face. As we walked down from the foothills, we could see something strange in the valley. There, in a wide open space, were vultures, perching on the mast of an old ship, sticking six feet out of a dune. We all knew what to make of it. We had all heard the legend. The Spaniards had come and tried to take from us, but the gods protected us, and for two hundred years the remnants were buried in the dunes. It was a reminder from the gods that many will come to take from us what is ours, and even though they may succeed for a short while, in time the gods will return to us our birthright."

Ben was feeling a bit numb from the mescal, but no more numb than from what was being revealed to him. He'd had his doubts, but Abel was right. The old man knew where the ship was.

THEY LOOKED OUT OVER THE RIDGE AND INTO THE valley for several minutes before the sun set, while Duff contemplated going in at night. After he consultated with Calhoun, however, they both felt it best to wait, since they no longer could trust Redman. The Cashman farm was new terrain, and they were too unfamiliar with the layout. It would be best to surprise the farm at daylight.

Redman made a bandage out of a cloth sack he'd been using to carry food in his saddlebag. He filled a tin cup with water and placed it in the hot coals of the campfire. Once the water came to a boil, he soaked the cloth to sanitize it. He sat bare-chested next to the fire holding the cloth against the wound, occasionally grimacing at the dull pain.

Duff lay on his side staring into the fire and chewed on some jerky, with Redman's own six-gun lying by his side. Calhoun sat on a boulder not far away cleaning the dust out of his Colts. Both of them exchanged hard stares with Redman.

Felicia was not far from Duff, lying on her side, hands and feet tied, her long, auburn hair nearly matted and in disarray as she tried to rest. Redman couldn't deny that he worried about what would happen to her. Women had showed him attention before, but he'd never really courted anyone. The men who worked for Gorum accompanied him to saloons and bought him whores, but not until now had he realized how different it was having real affection for someone. He tried not to think about what she had said, about her wanting him to be the first, and the guilt that it had laid upon him. The problem was he couldn't stop thinking about it. Tonight could be the night, he thought, when Duff invaded more than her body, but her soul and will for life.

He glanced over at Calhoun, who had popped out the cylinder of one of his Colts and removed the bullets, and now blew through the openings. Hopefully Duff wouldn't try anything with Calhoun nearby. No, it was too risky to take a chance.

Redman stood and started to walk into the darkness, and Duff immediately grabbed the Colt and pointed it toward him.

"Just where are you going?" Duff asked.

"I have to relieve myself."

Duff thought for a moment, glanced at Calhoun, who shrugged, and then Duff put the pistol back down. "Don't take too long."

Redman walked out into the darkness and looked for the horses. If not for the reflection of the soft moon that was intermittently hidden by drifting clouds, he wouldn't have been able to see the men. He glanced back to see if they were watching him. Duff still stared into the fire, but Calhoun occasionally looked his way. When Calhoun noticed Redman near the horses, he stood from the rock.

"Hey what are you doing?" Calhoun said. Duff turned to look as well.

Redman unbuttoned his trousers and squatted behind the horse. "Just want some privacy."

He kept a watchful eye on both men, and eventually Duff turned back around and Calhoun sat back down and went to work cleaning his other gun. Redman knew it was now or never, so he kept squatting and reached over to the hobble on his horse's legs and started to loosen it. The soreness from his shoulder wound caused him to grimace, but he would have to deal with the pain. The horse whickered from the movement of his arm, and that got Calhoun's attention. Redman pulled his hand back quickly, and when Calhoun looked away again, Redman went back to work. To lessen the likelihood of the horse wandering off, Redman left the loose hobble on its legs to make it think it was still tied. For safe measure he checked the hobbles on the other horses. They were good and tight, and that would buy him time.

He stood and buttoned his trousers, still keeping an eye on the two men. He quickly reached into his pocket and retrieved the fancy pocketknife that Gorum had given him for Christmas. Duff must have forgotten or never thought to ask for it. Gorum had given one to all his employees, including Duff. They were a popular item in England and had made their debut in America with a company in Pennsylvania. It was like Gorum to stay on top of such things, but very few people had pocketknives, and Redman's concern now was whether or not Felicia knew how to use one.

As he walked back to the camp, he made a slight detour and walked between Duff and Felicia. He walked a little closer to Felicia, held his fist out slightly to his side, and dropped the knife near her tied hands. Though surprised, she quickly grabbed it and held it in her fist.

Redman sat back down and stoked the fire. Duff and Calhoun still seemed relaxed and oblivious to anything he had done. Now he and Felicia just had to wait for the other two to go to sleep—for the right opportunity to break away. Redman had to protect her from these men, even if it cost him his own life.

Chapter Seven

"RUN!" Redman yelled, which startled Duff enough that he jumped wide-eyed from his bedroll only to catch two handfuls of campfire ash in the face. It would not deter him long, but it was enough to get by him, and for Redman and Felicia to get to the horse while Calhoun figured out what was happening and drew his gun. Redman hoped that it would be too dark for Calhoun to shoot, but that didn't stop Calhoun. Bullets were flying before they even mounted the horse, but even a skilled gunman would have to be extremely lucky to hit a target he couldn't see. Plus, Calhoun wasn't dumb. He wasn't going to risk hitting their horses. At least Redman was banking on that.

He helped Felicia up onto the horse's bare back, kicked the hobble loose, then jumped on himself. Duff yelled in the background, calling for Calhoun to kill them, but the gunman argued that he couldn't get a clear shot. Redman reached around Felicia, grabbed on to the horse's mane, grimacing from the shoulder wound, and kicked and hollered feverishly. "Yah!" he yelled, and the paint whickered and galloped into the darkness.

Two rapid shots rang out and Redman felt a burn on his right thigh. He winced and reached down, but it was only a graze. He kept kicking and hollering, holding on to Felicia with one arm, the mane with the other hand, and in just a few moments he realized that they had broken free. For how long he wasn't sure, but at least they now had the chance he'd longed to have.

DUFF TRIED NOT TO RUB AT HIS EYES, AND HE KNEW HE was worthless to help. He yelled at Calhoun. "Go after them!"

"Why rush?" Calhoun said, holstering his gun. "There is only one place they can go. Let's gather our wits and go down there and get them all."

"You're right," Duff said, blinking his sore eyes. "Get me some water."

Calhoun brought him the canteen, and Duff poured water into his hand and splashed it over his eyes. Before long he'd blinked enough to see clearly, and he wiped his face clean.

"Let's saddle up," Duff said. "I'm gonna kill that son of a bitch."

Calhoun grunted. "And the girl?"

"Oh, I've got plans for her, too."

THE CONSTANT JOLTS OF THE GALLOPING HORSE CAUSED Redman's shoulder wound to open and bleed, as well as augment the pain. They were lucky, however, that they didn't have to guide the horse and all they had to do was hold on. The horse had a more sensitive nose than humans, and Redman figured since he could smell the water he was sure the paint could, too.

In less than thirty minutes' ride they were among the boarding shacks and could see a dim light in an adobe.

Redman figured it to be about three A.M., which would work in their favor. The longer the darkness, the more time they had to find shelter. Because of this newly felt safety, he slowed the paint to a lope.

"Do you think they're right behind us?" Felicia said.

"If not, they will be real soon. We have to get help."

Redman kept wincing from the pangs of his wound and he felt dizzy. The horse slowed to an easy walk as they approached the adobe. The paint went immediately to the water trough and started drinking.

"I need you to help me down," Redman said.

Felicia looked behind. "Oh God, you're bleeding!" She climbed down quickly, then held out her arms for him. He slid off much more slowly and put his good arm around her as he walked. He limped a bit, then looked down at the bullet graze on his leg. There was a lot of blood there, too.

"What happened to your leg?" Felicia said.

"Don't worry it's just a graze."

Felicia helped him to the large wooden door of the adobe and beat on it frantically. "Help! Help us please!"

She kept pounding, and eventually the door opened and Bernard Cashman looked out.

He held a lit lantern above him. "What do you want?" Cashman said.

"He's hurt," Felicia said. "We need help."

"There's no doctor here. Now, go on—get off my property! And get that horse away from my water!"

Before he could slam the door in their faces, a hand came forward and opened the door wider. It was Verona in a long, white nightgown. She took the lantern from her husband and took a good look at the visitors.

"Please help us," Felicia said.

"Bring him inside," Verona said.

Bernard bit his lip and backed away.

Felicia helped Redman to a chair near a dining area. Verona came closer with the lantern. Redman tried to focus his watery eyes. He could see well enough to tell that, compared to many houses he'd seen, this house was a palace. The floors were wooden and varnished, covered in places with fine woven rugs and furnished with plush chairs and a sofa. Smaller tables lined the walls and were decorated with native pottery and European vases. Larger pots were spaced out on the floors near the walls and each filled with some sort of flowering plant or cactus. Framed family portraits hung on the walls, as did older daguerreotypes. The table and chairs in the dining area were made of a sturdy, dark stained oak and were the only items that seemed more practical, save the cast iron cooking stove and the woodpile next to it.

"Bullet wound?" Verona asked.

"No," Felicia said. "It's a knife wound. But the wound on his leg is from a bullet."

Verona held the lantern down low to examine the leg wound. "Bernard, fetch me Dexy. Tell her to boil some bandages. And go tell José to take care of their horse."

Bernard stepped forward angrily. "Who is going to pay for all this?"

Verona stood firmly, held up the lantern, and glared at him. "You are! And if you don't do it promptly, you will not be sleeping in this house again."

Quickly defeated, Bernard stomped away and Verona turned back to the business at hand. Though Redman had never really been in this kind of situation before, he'd never expected that an experience like this would include the care of such a spirited woman.

"Help me get him into a bed," Verona said. "We have to get his clothes off and clean those wounds."

Felicia knelt by Redman's side and ran her hand affectionately across his forehead. "You see, it's going to be okay."

Redman smiled at her and suddenly realized it was the first time he'd ever done so. Even through her soiled face and matted hair he could still see her natural beauty. Her smile and the way she looked at him were nearly enough to heal his wounds.

After they helped him into the room and got him into bed, Felicia had the duty of removing his clothes. Verona instructed her to cut them off, that it would be easier and less likely to infect the wounds.

"Let me get you a knife," Verona said.

"No need," Felicia said, revealing the pocketknife clutched in her fist.

"Good enough," Verona said. "I'm going to get my medical bag and see about getting those bandages."

"Wait a second," Redman said. "You have a medical bag?"

"My dear, we are one hundred miles from the nearest doctor. I have fifty people to look after here, and if I didn't do the doctoring, then no one else would." She winked at him, then left the room.

Redman gazed at Felicia with rheumy eyes as she pulled out the longest blade of the knife and started cutting at the neck of his shirt.

"I'm glad you knew how to use that knife," Redman said.

Felicia continued to cut on the shirt all the way to the bottom, then at the sleeves. "You're forgetting," she said, "that my grandfather worked for Gorum, too. He was also on his Christmas list."

Redman found another smile for her, and though he thought it should have been awkward, he loved her touch, even though it was with a knife. How ironic, too, he thought, that he helped save her from getting her clothes torn off, and the result would be her removing his in a similar fashion. He was just thankful that now the intent was different. He wasn't yet embarrassed, and even if he was, he thought, he didn't have the energy to stop her.

A minute later Verona walked in carrying her medical bag and wearing round, wire-frame spectacles. She set the bag on a lace-covered table next to the bed, opened the bag, and retrieved a brown glass bottle, a spoon, and several white cloths. She grabbed the glass bottle and removed the cap, then poured some of the contents on the spoon.

Redman's eyes got a little wider. "What is that?"

She lowered the spoon down to his mouth. "It's laudanum. It will help ease the pain."

Redman opened his mouth and Verona tipped the spoon inside. He wasn't prepared for the bitterness and wished he'd have held his breath before he swallowed. Verona set the spoon on the nightstand, then grabbed several of the cloths. She obtained another, much larger bottle from the bag, with amber liquid swishing inside its clear glass.

"Now this, I'm sure a young cowboy like you is much more familiar with."

"Whiskey?" Redman said.

"That's right."

"But don't go getting all excited, it's just for cleaning, not drinking." She took several of the white cloths and held them to the end of the bottle, tipped it up, then set it back down by the bed. She dabbed the cloths on the shoulder wound and Redman instantly winced and sucked in a long breath.

"Just a little angel kiss," she said. After the cleaning, she looked over the wound carefully. "Yeah, looks pretty clean—missed the collarbone. There'll just be a lot of soreness for a while, but you'll heal up."

She grabbed some fresh cloths and repeated the treatment to the shoulder. The second cleaning didn't have near the sting as the first. Once satisfied, she reached for yet another cloth and tipped up the bottle, then looked down toward his leg. "Now roll yourself over."

He glanced at Felicia. "Cover your eyes."

Redman rolled as Verona instructed, and she peeled back the bedclothes, exposing his white, freckly backside. She rubbed more than dabbed this time, and though quite painful, it didn't have near the jolt as when she touched the gaping shoulder wound.

Redman held his breath as long as he could and felt instant relief when she stopped rubbing.

"All right, pardner," Verona said, studying her work on the wound. "Now let's get you bandaged up."

Verona hesitated a second, then handed Redman the bottle. "What the hell," she said. "A little sip might be good for the soul."

Redman gladly accepted and tipped the bottle to his lips.

Felicia responded in awe as she looked at the bloody cloths. "I'm not sure I could do that."

"It's not that difficult," Verona said. "I just pretend the wound is my husband, that way I'm not stingy with the amount I apply."

Felicia laughed and grabbed Redman's hand.

Yudexy entered the room with a wooden bowl of steaming white cloths. She did not look at either of them directly in the eyes or ask any questions; she just set the bowl next to the medical bag and removed her shawl.

Verona looked in the bowl. "Perfect. Dexy is my assistant in medical matters. She knows exactly what to do. Now, while she's fixing you up, why don't you both tell me what the hell is going on."

Redman nodded to Felicia, and she filled them in on all the details. When she mentioned Ben Ruby's name, Yudexy stopped working. She listened intently, and when Felicia finished she expressed her concern to Verona. "Those men could be here any minute. We must warn Señor Ruby."

"You're right," Verona said. "I'll finish up here. You go."

"*Gracias, señora.*" Yudexy wrapped her shawl around her shoulders and quickly left the room.

Verona put her arm around Felicia. "Don't you worry none, honey. We'll do all we can to help you." She gave her a pat on the back and walked to the bowl of bandages. Yudexy had cleaned around the wounds very well and had made a good start on the shoulder bandage. Verona continued wrapping the long cloths around Redman's armpit and over his shoulder. She nodded at Redman. "And you, young man, are a brave one. I'm proud to have you here."

"Thank you, ma'am," Redman said. "I sure hope we didn't bring you more trouble."

"You don't worry about that. You just lie here and rest. We'll deal with those boys when they come. They may be tough ol' birds, but they've never had a run-in with an old Irish lass like me."

Redman appreciated her humor. "I'm sure you're right, ma'am."

IT WAS STILL AN HOUR FROM SUNRISE AND THE MOON was gone, but Yudexy was all too familiar with the paths at the Cashman farm and she had no problem finding Indigo's shelter in the dark. She ran barefoot down the path and passed all the boarding shacks. The white pup came racing from the storage building and barked from the excitement of her running.

"Shush!" Yudexy said while the pup ran at her feet. Her voice only made him bark louder. "I said hush, *perrito!*" Yudexy approached the shelter, and as quick as she stopped running, an arm reached out and grabbed her around the waist. She gasped, only to have another hand come around and cover her mouth. The pup stopped at her feet, sat down, and looked up at them all, panting and wagging its tail.

"Where you going in such a hurry?" Calhoun said. His hot, rank breath warmed her ear.

Duff came walking out of the darkness, stooped, and picked up the pup. He rubbed its head and ears, and the pup reached up and licked his chin. "What a pair you are," Duff said, looking at Yudexy. He nodded toward the shelter. "Are they in there?"

He sat the pup down and kicked it hard. It yelped and cried continuously as it ran for cover.

Duff drew his gun and peeked inside the shelter. He lit

a match on one of the lodge poles and held it out in front of him. He shook out the match and sneered back at Yudexy. "There's nothing in there but an empty rocking chair." He grabbed her by the hair. "Where are they?"

Calhoun removed his hand from her mouth.

"I don't know," she said. Suddenly she caught a glimpse of Raul peeking around the corner of the shelter. She hoped he understood the danger and would stay far out of sight.

Duff pulled her to him and he glared down at her. "You were running out here in the middle of the night. I doubt you just had to go relieve yourself. Now, you know who I'm looking for and I want you to take me to them now. *Comprendes?*" He pulled harder on her hair, and she let out a short cry, then nodded.

Calhoun let loose of her, only keeping a firm grip on her arm as she walked out in front of them. She hated to lead them to the adobe, but she really had no choice. These men were brutal, she could tell, and how amazing it was that Redman and Felicia had had the determination to get away from them. There was no doubt that if they didn't get what they wanted, they would kill her and the others, too. She was thankful that her father had taken Ben and Francis away. She was sure he sensed the danger, a special gift he had had since he was a child. The best hope she had was that Raul had seen her and would go find Ben. Beyond that there was nothing to do now but pray.

Chapter Eight

B EN woke in a sitting position against a rock wall, his head throbbing, and to a blurred vision of Indigo holding a cup up to his mouth.

"Drink," Indigo said.

He did as the old man said and took in a healthy swallow of a thick, bitter, almost rotten-tasting concoction. It was only seconds after he swallowed that it all came back up and he leaned over and vomited into the rocks. There were several heaves before he had the strength to sit back up and even begin to calculate where he was and what it was all about. He looked around and saw a campfire, blankets on the ground, his hat and canteen. They were in a gully with boulders all around them and, above the rock confine, a hint of the sunrise. To his left he saw Francis, also leaned up against the rock wall, and Indigo held the cup to his mouth. The results for Francis were the same. Ben tried to stand, but an immediate dizzy feeling sent him back to the ground.

He leaned against the rock wall and took a deep breath. "How did we get here?"

"There are men looking for you," Indigo said.

Ben saw a canteen on the ground near his blanket, and he rolled to his knees and grabbed it. He rinsed his mouth out and spit.

Francis rose up and moaned. "Dear God, what is happening?"

The sound of someone running from outside the gully got their attention, and before Indigo could rise to his feet, Raul came racing into the camp.

The boy had a fearful look in his eyes and he stammered between long breaths. "There are men here! They have Mama!"

Ben slowly rose to his feet and put a hand on the rock wall to maintain his stance. "How many men?"

"Two," Raul said. "They both have guns and they took Mama to the adobe."

"It has to be Gorum's men," Ben said. "I will go."

"But there are more," Raul said.

"What do you mean 'more'?"

"Another man, and a girl. He is hurt and they came for help."

"Did you catch their names?"

"Only one—the girl. Felicia."

Ben ran his fingers through his hair and leaned over and grabbed his hat.

Raul walked up to him and looked at him with woeful eyes. "What are you going to do?"

It was a fair question, and not until the little white pup came running into camp did the answer come to him.

"Raul, you stay here with your grandpa. Francis, come with me."

"No!" Raul said. "Let me help you."

Indigo put his arm around Raul. "Do what he says, my

son. Stay with me. We will stoke the fire and talk to the gods."

Francis was slow getting to his feet. "I hope I'm not more of a hindrance than a good help."

Indigo put a hand in the air. "You've had the elixir, you are no longer under the spell of the agave."

Francis put a hand on his forehead and took a deep breath. "Yes, that must have been the bad of it."

IMMEDIATELY FOLLOWING BERNARD CASHMAN'S protest of their presence, Duff pounded his fist against the side of the proprietor's mouth, sending him crashing into the dining table and landing on the woodpile near the stove. Verona quickly went to his aid, but he rolled stubbornly and wiped the blood from his lips. Verona helped him up into a chair, then looked sternly at the men.

Calhoun held Yudexy with one arm around her waist and a gun pointed at her head, a haughty grin on his face.

"I know who you are," Verona said. "You've been here before. You work for that greedy Gorum who has been trying to buy us out."

Duff laughed out loud and took a good look around the room. "Nice place you have here. Must be good money in fruits and vegetables." He stopped at a pot of geraniums and picked one of the red blooms. He held it up to his nose and sniffed. "Ahh, how pretty," he said, then dropped the flower to the floor and mashed it with his boot.

He continued to walk around the room, and when he got closer to Verona he saw that she was almost as tall as he was. He looked her directly in the eyes. "My sixth sense tells me you have visitors. Where are they?"

Verona only stared at him and gave no answer.

"I see how you want to play. Okay, but let me enlighten you on something you may not know. There's a man visiting here—Ben Ruby. He just spent a long eight years at the Yuma prison. While in that prison he learned of something very valuable, and when he was released he aimed to find it. Since he came here, I can only presume that whatever he is after, it is here. Did you know you have a thief among you?"

Verona studied his smirking face. "How do you know this?"

Duff held out his arms at waist level. "Come on . . . who do you think you're talking to?"

"There's nothing here worth stealing," Verona said.

Duff gazed around the room. "I see plenty of value right in front of me!"

Felicia came running into the room. "That is not true!" Redman came limping behind her, a blanket wrapped around him crossways, a bloody spotted bandage on his bare shoulder.

Duff put his hands together in a praying position. "Ahh, our little prize reveals herself." His grin turned to a hateful glare as he drew his gun and aimed it at Redman.

The main door to the adobe flew open, and Duff quickly turned and pointed his gun in that direction. Calhoun backed against the wall and pulled Yudexy with him.

BEN WALKED INTO THE ROOM, HIS BOOT STEPS AND jingling spurs the only noises that could be heard. He quickly assessed the situation—Yudexy and Calhoun, Felicia and Redman, and Bernard and Verona—then looked directly at Duff, who still pointed his gun at Ben.

"No, he's right," Ben said, looking at Verona. "I'm only here for one thing."

Felicia tried to run to him, but Redman grabbed her arm and stopped her. Ben hoped that she would keep quiet and follow his plan.

Duff lowered his gun and laughed. He turned to Verona. "Did I not tell you?"

"I have what you're looking for outside. But the deal is you let everyone go, then it's yours."

Duff stepped closer to Ben. "What makes you think you can call the shots?"

"I have ten Mexicans out there with rifles surrounding the house. Any one of them can shoot a coyote in the eye at three hundred yards, so the chances of them hitting a husky bastard like you at fifty feet are pretty damned good. So you're asking why I'm calling the shots? That's why. You bring everyone into the courtyard where they can see. There's a wagon parked outside full of dynamite. It's payment in full. You release Yudexy and hold no one else hostage, then they'll let you drive away with the dynamite."

Bernard rose quickly from the chair. "My dynamite? What the hell do you think you are you doing!"

Verona grabbed her husband's arm. "Just let it be."

Duff glanced at Calhoun, who instantly started laughing. Duff followed suit and clapped his hands. "This is all very clever of you. But you're forgetting something."

Ben knew what Duff was referring to, but he decided to play dumb. "What am I forgetting?"

Duff took two steps closer to Ben. "Come on now. I know you're not that forgetful." Duff swung his fist into Ben's abdomen. Ben groaned and clutched his stomach and fell to the floor. Duff grabbed him by his shirt collar, lifted him back up, and breathed his sour breath into Ben's face. "Ten thousand in gold! Either you produce it, or people in this room start dying. And we start with her!"

Duff pointed at Yudexy, who looked fearfully back at Ben.

"All right," Ben said, wincing. "I'll lead you to it."

"Yeah you do that." Duff pushed him to the door. "*Vamanos!*"

Ben led them all into the courtyard in front of the adobe, to where the buckboard was parked loaded with wooden crates. Two mules were hitched to the wagon, and José, one of the farmhands, stood next to them pointing a rifle. José wore a straw sombrero and a white cotton shirt. He was not tall in stature or large in girth, but he bore the stare of a serious man.

Ben looked around the courtyard and Duff followed his gaze. The farmhands were positioned about, pointing rifles, just like Ben had described. Most sat one knee near the corner of a boarding shack, while two others lay bellied up on the roofs, and one on the roof of the adobe.

Duff walked up to the wagon and peered into the back. He lifted one of the lids off the crates. He closed the lid and turned back to Ben. "Okay, now where's the gold?"

"I'll take you to it."

Duff drew his gun, cocked it, and pointed it at under Ben's chin. "No, prison boy, you tell me where it is."

Ben nodded toward the storage building that stood a good hundred yards away. "In that shed. Behind some crates they keep a safe. Winthrop told me about it. I've already opened the door. There's more than ten thousand in it. Take it all, just let them go."

Bernard tried to walk toward them. "What the—"

Verona stopped him again. "Just shut up, Bernard."

Duff studied the shed for a moment, then turned back to Ben. "You stay here."

Duff walked slowly across the dusty courtyard toward the shed. Ben glanced at Calhoun, who watched Duff intently while still keeping a firm hold on Yudexy. Ben then searched for Francis, and found him peeking around the corner of a boarding shack fifty yards adjacent to the shed. Ben gave him a nod and Francis responded the same, then disappeared.

No one could see the look in Duff's eyes when he walked inside that shed, moving crates around looking for a safe that wasn't really there, or how his look must have changed when he saw the three sticks of dynamite come flying in the window, tied together and lit with a short sparkling fuse. All they could see was a once perfectly rectangular building suddenly and loudly explode into a ball of flames and flying splinters. Only three people knew to expect it. Ben and Francis, who Ben hoped was able to run far enough away and avoid injury. The third man was José, who through it all kept his rifle sights on Calhoun. And lucky enough it worked just as planned. Calhoun was so surprised by the blast and the fate of his comrade that he let go of Yudexy—who got far enough away from him that Jośe could get a clean shot.

Once he realized the tough spot he was in, Calhoun made a run for it. Ben put a hand out to José. "Let him go."

José lowered his rifle, and they all watched Calhoun jump on his horse and gallop away, racing out between the boarding shacks and toward the eastern mountains. Ben could see that Bernard Cashman was less interested in Calhoun and more interested in the fate of his shed. The proprietor ran into the courtyard and got as close as he could to the burning rubble, both hands on top of his head, his eyes glaring in anger and disbelief. He turned back toward Ben, but before he could make any charges, Verona quickly intervened.

"Bernard," Verona said, "we have a mess to clean up. Why don't you gather up a crew and get at it."

Bernard pointed at Ben. "He will clean it up! And he will pay for its repair!"

"He and many others already have paid for it," Verona said. "Now, unless you want to eat and sleep in a bunkhouse, I suggest you get at it."

Bernard huffed and glanced back and forth between his wife and Ben, but it didn't take long for him to do exactly as she'd said.

Just as Bernard stomped away, Felicia came running to Ben and met him with an embrace.

"Ben—my grandpa," Felicia said. "They beat him terribly."

Ben held her by the arms. "We'll get him help."

Redman, still wrapped in a blanket, limped up to them with the help of Yudexy.

Ben acknowledged his bloody bandage. "I guess you're with us now."

Redman nodded. "I have been since the beginning."

Ben smiled, reached forward, and shook his hand firmly. "Looks like you're in no shape to ride. We need someone to take Felicia back to Cibola and check on Mr. Hostetter."

"I will go," Yudexy said. "I have medical abilities."

"She does at that," Verona said. "Mr. Redman can stay in the house until he heals up. I'll send José with them. They will be safe in his hands. "

Ben shook José's hand as well. "Thank you."

"*De nada*," José said.

"Mrs. Cashman," Ben said. "I'd like to pay for rebuilding the shed. I can have José pick up the materials while he's away."

"You will do no such thing," Verona said. "It's not the first time Duff has been out here harassing us. It was worth it to see him gone. José can pick up the materials all right, but on my bill."

"If you say so," Ben said. "But I'd also like him to pick up some lamp oil and lanterns, if it's okay. All the candles in that shed are now a puddle of wax."

Verona scratched her head. "Candles?"

"Yes, that the workers used for light," Yudexy said. "It would be better if we had lanterns."

"I guess I need to get out of the house more," Verona said. "I had no idea that all you had was candles. I swear, that husband of mine squeezes his pennies so tight the Indian farts." She turned to José. "José come with me. You have some shopping to do."

Ben and Yudexy watched them walk away, and Felicia helped Redman back to the adobe.

Ben put his hand on Yudexy's shoulder. "Are you okay?"

"Yes," she said, followed by a deep breath.

"Some turn of events, wouldn't you say?"

She looked at him affectionately. "I'm just glad you're okay."

He held her hand. "We're all okay now."

Francis came sidestepping across the courtyard taking a good look at the damage he had done with the dynamite. He stopped midway between the burning rubble and where Ben stood, mouth slightly agape.

Ben walked up to him. "You all right?"

Francis looked ghostly, staring into the fire. "I just killed a man."

"It was either kill or be killed," Ben said. "I knew him. Duff would have stopped at nothing to get what he wanted."

"I suppose you're right." Francis looked down at his feet. "It's just not a good feeling, that's all."

"I understand," Ben said, putting a hand on his shoulder. "But look at it this way, you saved all our lives. You're a hero."

Francis looked perplexed. "I am?"

The two men smiled at each other. "Come on, college boy," Ben said. "We have work do to." Ben put his arm around Francis and they walked toward the smoldering remains. It was just one battle won, Ben thought. Duff being gone was only one knight off the chessboard. There were still many pawns, and there was still the king.

Chapter Nine

GORUM'S office was on the third and top floor of the Yuma Hotel and was considered the most awesome site in the city. To be invited to his office, to do business, or just to visit, was a great treat. Nowhere else within hundreds of miles could one go to see the luxuries that only the tycoon could afford. Three of the walls of his office were lined at the bottom with all-walnut woodwork, and above a chair rail was a maroon, velvet-flocked wallpaper brought in from New York. Along those walls were the finest furniture imported from England, such as the washbasin and gold velvet sofa; a crystal whiskey decanter and glasses from France; and a mammoth Swiss grandfather clock that nearly reached the ten-foot ceiling. The fourth wall was completely covered with bookcases. In those cases were hundreds of volumes of books, ranging from the expeditions of John Wesley Powell and Kit Carson, to fiction by James Fenimore Cooper and Herman Melville and the poetry of Walt Whitman and Alfred Lord Tennyson. The books, many said, were the most impressive items because they represented the level of intelligence that Gorum had. Gorum had hoped for that reaction, because in fact they were there mostly for intimidation. A librarian from New York had been hired to purchase the volumes, ship them to Yuma, and properly organize them in Gorum's personal library. With the exception of finding a poem to copy and send to his daughter for her birthday, he'd never cracked a cover.

Gorum's desk was also built of walnut, eight feet long and covered with stained leather that was tucked and tacked on the edges of the desktop. His high-back chair was built on a swiveling pedestal and upholstered with the same gold velvet as the sofa. That was where he was sitting when Calhoun came up the outside iron staircase and beat frantically on the door. Gorum drew back the sheer drapes along the window to see who it was, then went to the door and let him in.

Calhoun was breathing hard from running. He knocked his hat back and let the chin cord catch it. He stood there panting, with his hands on his hips.

"What?" Gorum said.

"Duff's dead."

Gorum only stared as the fury built up inside him. But he kept his cool.

"He walked into a trap," Calhoun said. "I was lucky to get away."

"Where?"

"At the Cashman farm in the valley. Ruby made up the whole scheme. I had ten guns on me. There was nothing I could do."

Gorum nodded and paced the floor in front of his desk. "What about Redman?"

Calhoun hesitated. "He turned on us. He's laid up, but he's with them now."

Gorum walked to the decanter and poured a glass half-full of whiskey. He drank it down in one big gulp, then turned back to Calhoun.

"Did you find anything?" Gorum said.

"Just the dynamite."

"Dynamite?"

"Ruby had a buckboard full of dynamite ready for us. But Duff asked for the gold. That's when he walked into the trap."

Gorum pondered a few seconds. "That was foolish of him."

Nothing more was said as Gorum walked back to his desk, and then he turned and pulled back the curtains and stared out into the sunny landscape of Yuma.

"Do you think there was any gold?" Gorum asked.

"No, sir," Calhoun said. "Not there anyway. I think Ruby was just trying to get rid of us."

Gorum nodded. "Get my horse ready."

"Sir?"

"We're going to take a ride out to the Cashman farm."

"Do you want me to get some more men?"

"No. This is not a game of muscle. It's a game of wits. Ruby might get the edge on Duff, but he'll never lure me into a trap."

Gorum walked closer to the gunman, and their faces were less than a foot from each other. Gorum grabbed him by the neckerchief, pulled him even closer, and spoke through clenched teeth. "Redman is dead!"

Calhoun showed no fear. "My pleasure."

HOSTETTER HAD MANAGED TO GET HIMSELF SOME water from a pitcher near a washbowl and crawl to his bed, where he spent the better of three days before Felicia found him there. She held him tight and cried. "I'm so sorry, Grandpa."

Hostetter coughed and spit blood into a porcelain bowl beside his bed. His lips were swollen and the cuts were dry, and whenever he moved them they bled. He couldn't breathe through his nose and was sure it was broken. One of his eyes was swollen completely shut, and his whole body felt sore and battered. Though he was happy to see his granddaughter home safe, he didn't have the strength to embrace her.

"Water," he said.

Yudexy found the pitcher of water and brought it to his bed along with a cup. Felicia tipped the cup to his mouth and he took in small sips. Yudexy cleaned his wounds, and Felicia warmed him some beef broth and brewed hot tea to help him regain his strength. He slept for another whole day before neighbors and coworkers started showing up to check on him. Though all expressed genuine concern for his condition, they were more worried about the rising water levels of the Colorado, which could force them all from their homes. The town of Cibola was facing great danger, and they needed their chief engineer to help decide what to do.

Felicia would not let them bother her grandfather with these worries until he had more strength. After he woke from his long rest, Yudexy checked his wounds and Felicia fixed him more broth. He rose up to his elbows and closed his eyes from the dizzy feeling.

"Not too fast," Yudexy said. She grabbed another pillow and put both of them at the head of the bed. She helped him lie back down, but now propped up a bit.

After a few seconds to regain his composure, Hostetter looked at both of them. He held Felicia's hand tight, then glanced at Yudexy.

"Ruby?" he said.

"He is fine, señor," Yudexy said.

Felicia held his hand with both of hers and leaned closer to him. "The man that did this to you is dead."

Hostetter nodded and closed his eyes for a moment. When he reopened them, he gazed around the room. "We got to get out of here." His voice was slow and gravelly.

"No," Yudexy said. "You must rest some more."

"You don't understand," Hostetter said. "I may have had

my eyes closed, but I've heard the people coming here. That dam is going to break and we have to get out of here. And Ruby, he may have gotten rid of Duff, but that will just make Gorum angry. No, now he has two more things to worry about. Gorum and the Colorado River, which will soon be carving a new path into the valley."

Felicia kissed his hand. "But you can't travel, Grandpa."

Hostetter coughed hoarsely. Felicia gave him his cup of water.

"In my barn there's a wagon," Hostetter said. "Fix me a bed in the back. Help me to it and take me to Ruby."

Felicia and Yudexy looked at each other solemnly.

Hostetter let out another light cough but refused a drink. He cleared his throat. "Felicia, go to my foremen. Tell them I said we have to evacuate the town. And do it quickly. We don't have much time."

A DAY LATER THE WORKERS AT THE CASHMAN FARM retrieved the charred, gory remains of Duff's body and gave him a proper burial. Regardless of his enemy status, they remembered their Christian belief, made the cross over their chests and prayed for his soul. After the quick interment, they gathered up all the debris from the shed and added it to the burning remains, of which in a few hours there was nothing left but a pile of smoldering ash.

Ben and Francis spent a better part of their day helping the workers and then decided it was time to meet with Indigo at the shelter to prepare for their trip back into the desert. On the way to the shelter they heard the sound of children laughing and eventually saw Raul and others swimming in the canal. They walked up to the bank of the canal to observe their playful behavior and were quite amused by their brown bodies bobbing up and down as they splashed water in each other's faces.

Raul noticed Ben and Francis, waved his arms, and called out to them. "Señor Ben! Señor Francis!"

Raul held in his hand a red object that Ben couldn't identify. "What do you have there, Raul?"

Raul held the object with his finger tips. "It's a handkerchief full of stones! Watch this!" Raul tossed the object into the air and it fell quickly, sinking into the canal. Raul took a long deep breath, then dove under the water. He was gone for nearly a minute, and Ben and Francis looked at each other with concern. Before they could contemplate intervening, Raul came back up holding the bag in the air and smiling.

Ben expressed his astonishment with a long exhale, and both men applauded the boy's performance.

"How deep is the canal?" Ben said to Francis.

"Forty—maybe fifty feet in places."

Ben raised his eyebrows. "Wow. The kid has some set of lungs."

"You're not kidding there," Francis said.

WHILE INVENTORYING THEIR EQUIPMENT, BEN REALIZED how serendipitous it was to have run into Francis. Not only would his tent come in handy as their shelter, but more so, he was an educated geologist, with maps, charts, digging tools, and expertise in the subterrain.

Later in the shelter that night, Indigo told the story of the earthquake in Imperial Valley, during the days of the Spanish Conquest, similar to how Abel had told it to Ben. Only it was much more intriguing coming directly from the source, and Ben wasn't the only one intrigued. When Indigo finished with the story, Francis seemed somewhat awestruck.

"Now I must go," Indigo said.

"Where are you going?" Francis asked. "To talk to the gods?"

"I guess you could say that," Indigo said. "I have to take a dump."

Ben laughed under his breath as Indigo walked out of the shelter. Francis, oblivious to any humor from the old Indian, swiftly fetched his bags and rummaged through his belongings. When he found what he was looking for, he brought a rolled document and set it between him and Ben. Ben held a candle as Francis unrolled a newer-looking map, printed professionally and not hand-drawn. The scholar adjusted his spectacles, then ran a finger from the top of the map down to the center, stopping on a point marked with an "X."

"Incredible," Francis said.

"You find something?" Ben said.

"This is a map of the San Andreas Fault created by Professor Lawson. It ends in the general area that Indigo mentions, and then joins other, smaller faults."

"What are you saying?"

Francis looked up at Ben over his spectacles. "This means that Indigo's story has merit."

A broad grin grew on the student's face as he went back to his bag and produced his journals. He thumbed through them rapidly, scanning the text with his finger and mumbling the words, until finally he stopped and brought one of the journals to Ben.

"Here it is," Francis said. "The Salton Trough consists mostly of Quaternary alluvium and lake sediments."

"But you already knew it was an old lake bed."

"Right. But its being from the Quaternary Period tells us that it occurred in our era. Some geologists believe that the Salton Trough was formed by continental drift."

"Drift?"

Francis put both of his hands palm-down on the blanket between them. "You see, there are theories that tectonic activity caused the continents to form." He moved his hands in opposite directions, rubbing them together. "The plates rubbing together are what cause earthquakes. When the plates drift apart, the continent separates."

"What does that have to do with us?" Ben said.

"Think about it! I personally know geologists who believe that Baja California was once connected with the main continent and not a peninsula. Indigo said the land broke apart and the sea drained from the valley. The theory of continental drift explains exactly that occurrence! Now, it technically could take thousands of years for it to move as far as it has, but it would be a series of many earthquakes that could cause it. This could have been one of them. What I'm really saying, Ben, is that Indigo's story could be true."

"Could be?"

"Remember, he does like his mescal, and I'm sure his ancestors did, too."

Ben grunted. "You got a point there. So what do we do next?"

"The hard part—we find the spot to dig." Francis pointed farther down in the journal. "Here I have noted that periodic surveys discovered mostly sediments from the Colorado River, such as silts, sands, and gravels."

"Is that good?"

"That means easy digging, my friend. We aren't blasting rock to get where we want to go. Just shovels, buckets, and ropes."

"I see your point."

Francis closed the journal. "Now the question is, where?"

"I can get us real close," Ben said. "We just have to have Indigo take us there."

"But you must be realistic. This is one hundred times harder than finding a needle in a haystack. It's a vast area out there. We have to be right above it and we can't miss. Or else we'll be digging fifty-foot-deep holes all over the desert."

"That's where you'll have to trust me," Ben said.

Francis took a deep breath and stuffed his journal back

in his bag. "I've come this far. Might as well go the distance."

The scholar yawned and stretched his arms, then lay back in his bedroll. It was only a matter of seconds before he was breathing heavy and snoring.

Ben reached behind him and grabbed his saddlebag. He retrieved the tin box and laid it in front of him. Holding a candle at chin level, he opened the box and inventoried all the items—the medicine bag, the silver pendant, the letter—and then found the page from *The Farmer's Almanac* and the compass. The page had yellowed from age and was ragged on the edge from being torn out of the book. It contained specific information that Abel had wanted, most specifically the position of the sun, its azimuth and altitude. There was a table of numbers and one number in particular, 55, was circled. The compass had a brass casing and a white face with gold and black letters. The needle was black with a red tip.

"This is not a basic military compass," Abel had said. "It's a naval compass. Beside the directional coordinates are degrees of azimuth. It's fairly simple, really. A circle is three hundred and sixty degrees. Zero, or three-sixty, is due north."

Abel had turned the compass until the needle pointed due north, then he pointed to a mark of red enamel on the side. "Here by the mark is fifty-five degrees. I put the red mark on it so I wouldn't ever forget it."

"What is at fifty-five?" Ben had said.

"Indigo showed me where he was standing when he saw the tip of the mast. From that point, if you point the compass due north, and follow the plane of fifty-five degrees, that is in line to where the ship was."

Ben had thought for a moment. "But wait a second, Indigo was just a boy. How did he know the azimuth was fifty-five degrees?"

Abel smiled and patted Ben on the shoulder. "Ah, you're a smart man, Ben Ruby." He grabbed the page out of *The*

Farmer's Almanac and laid it out so they both could read it. "This shows the times of the sun's position during the last week of June. Indigo remembered the time of year because his village was preparing to plant crops, and this was when they did so. He said the sandstorm was in late June, at the beginning of the monsoon season. Do you follow me?"

"I follow you," Ben said.

"The position of the sun changes from day to day, but it is consistent throughout the year." Abel pointed to a column of numbers. "In this column is the azimuth, and here are the corresponding times of the sun's occurrence. Indigo said that they came out of their tents about an hour after sunrise and that the mast was directly under the sun. Note here that sunrise was at five thirty-seven. The azimuth of the sun at six thirty was—"

"Fifty-five degrees." Ben looked at Abel and smiled.

Abel laughed out loud. "Pretty clever, eh?"

"Yes, it was." Ben scratched his chin. "So from the foothills where their camp was, you've identified the precise direction."

"Yes, you got it."

"But how far out?"

Abel had lost his entire grin then and had taken a deep breath. "That's where it gets a little more tricky. The only thing I have to go by is something else that Indigo told me."

"Which was?"

"He said that the mast was exposed for several days before the winds covered it up again. During that time the children would play on it—climb and swing on it like a bunch of monkeys. But the one thing he said that could help was that he'd race the other children to the mast from their camp. He may be a bit boastful, but he said he always won. It intrigued his mother to watch him race. When he started running she would put two handfuls of corn in a bowl, and by the time he reached the mast, it would be ground into flour."

Ben had nodded and breathed deeply. "That's not much to go by."

"You're right," Abel had said. "But with enough faith, this knowledge could be all you need."

Chapter Ten

THEY awoke at sunrise, and Raul helped them pack the travois, the burro, and their horses. He put a blanket on another burro for Indigo to ride. The boy was very helpful, and as Ben watched him work, he was reminded of the story of Indigo's childhood.

After they helped Indigo onto the burro, the old Indian summoned his grandson. Raul looked up at the old man, who was now wearing a wide sombrero.

"Go get my tobacco," Indigo said.

The boy quickly ran toward the shelter, and as Ben watched him, an idea popped into his head like an epiphany.

He turned to Indigo. "Do you have any corn?"

"*Sí,*" Indigo said. "Hanging in the food shed."

Raul returned at a sprint and handed the tobacco to Indigo. The old man stuffed it in his shirt pocket.

"Raul," Ben said. "How would you like to go with us?"

At first the boy seemed astonished. "Really, Señor Ruby?"

"That is if it is okay with your grandfather, of course."

Raul looked up at Indigo on the burro, his hands in a praying position. "Please, *abuelo*, please?"

"*Sí*, since Señor Ruby invited you."

Raul's smile made even the desert seem brighter.

"You can ride with your grandpa," Ben said. "But before you climb aboard, I'd like you to go to the food shed and fetch me six ears of corn. Find an old feed sack to put it in."

Raul shook his head, "But, Señor Ruby, I am not allowed in the food shed."

Ben looked at Indigo to intervene.

"This is true," Indigo said.

Ben thought for a second. "Okay, I'll do it. But go to the shelter and fetch me a wooden bowl, would you?"

Raul smiled. "*Sí*, Señor Ruby!"

Ben had to think for a moment on how to get the corn. He couldn't just walk into the food shed and take it. Since he'd been accused of being a thief, he wasn't about to raise doubts in anyone, including himself. The corn belonged to the Cashmans, and being that the real power of decision rested with Verona, he knew she'd be the one to ask. And he was right. She gave him permission not only to take as much corn as he needed, but to help himself to any of the other provisions he thought he might need. He found six ears of dried corn hanging on a wall and stuffed them in a cotton seed sack. As he was leaving the food shed, he noticed several mortar bowls and wooden pestles setting on a table under a window. He looked at one of the pestles a moment, then grabbed it and put it in the sack with the corn. She had said "anything he might need," he thought.

Indigo led them southwest into a long gully between the Orocopia and Chocolate Mountains and eventually out onto the crusty playa. The valley was flat for nearly as far as the eyes could see, with little vegetation and only a fuzzy image of the Santa Rosa Mountains due west. Those were the mountains, Indigo said, where he lived as a child and raised his own family, many moons ago.

They headed straight west across the playa, riding side by side, with Indigo and the boy between Francis and Ben. Besides the pack burro, each horse was loaded heavy with items needed for the camp and excavation. Raul, riding behind his grandfather on the burro, had grabbed his own sombrero before leaving. In the earlier part of the journey the hat hung on his back by the chin cord, but now, on the sunny playa, it rested purposefully on his head.

The consummate storyteller, Indigo entertained them with tales of his youth, of his mother and father, and their mothers and fathers.

"It was a hard life," Indigo said, "but it was a good life."

"What was good about it?" Ben said.

"The freedom," the elder said. "Freedom to hunt. Freedom to come and go. Freedom to be what the People were born to be."

Francis interjected. "But at least now you have continuous food and shelter. A way of living for you and your family."

"It is a way," Indigo said. "Just not the way of the People. It's been this way as long as the earth has existed. Man will come and try to take what is not his to take. He tries to control the earth, but the earth always wins. Always, in the end, the People get it back."

"But that doesn't explain," Ben said, "why you and your family are living on the Cashman farm. They don't expect to be giving it back anytime soon."

"The time it takes is for the gods to decide," Indigo said. "Just like you, Señor Ruby, who goes to prison for a short time. Your life is taken away, but sooner or later you get it back."

Ben shrugged. "What about the ones that are in for life and don't get it back?"

"Not everyone is meant for a life on this earth."

The old man's wisdom was a lot to absorb. They rode in silence for a good hour before they stopped and drank from their canteens. After they started riding again, Francis shifted the attention to Ben.

"So tell us, Ben. Have you always lived in the Southwest?"

"No, I was born and raised in Missouri," Ben said. "My father was a Union officer. He was killed at Bull Run while I was still a baby."

Ben wasn't sure what they wanted to know, but he told them about all he wanted to tell them. Growing up in Missouri wasn't his fondest memory. He didn't remember his father or what life was like before he went off to war. All he could remember was the man that courted his mother when Ben was still a baby, married her, and raised him and his three stepbrothers. It didn't matter that he was the oldest and the best worker on their Missouri farm, Ben was unfairly treated, and at times beaten, during his entire childhood. The man could never love him like his own. For that reason, at age sixteen Ben left home for Kansas City, where he worked in the stockyards seven days a week. One day he saw an ad in the *Kansas City Times* for business opportunities out west in Tombstone, Arizona. He worked another week to earn enough money to head down the Santa Fe Trail, and within a few weeks he was working on a ranch as a cowhand.

The stockyard was miserable work, but the ranch life was truly Ben's favorite. He enjoyed riding the range and working with the seasoned cowboys, especially some of the Mexican *vaqueros*, but there were a few that got into more trouble than good. One day, while in Tombstone, Ben was with some of those boys picking up supplies and they decided to take a break at the Oriental Saloon. One of the boys refused to check his guns and got into a scuffle with Wyatt Earp. The cowpoke was no match for the famous lawman, who grabbed the gun from his waistband and hit the fellow over the head with it before he could blink. They all spent a night in jail for the event, which nearly got them fired, but the rancher found the heart to give them another chance. It was a futile gesture, since within a year the silver ran out and Tombstone dried up.

Ben couldn't stomach going back east, so he kept heading west, and that's how he ended up on the ranch of L. J. Gorum. He'd worked there almost a year before he ever met the man. A big storm had come through and a lot of cattle were lost. Ben, talented with a rope and at handling spooked beeves, singlehandedly had them rounded up and returned to the ranch within two days. Impressed by this feat, Gorum had to meet the cowboy and offer him a promotion. Ben gladly accepted, but it wasn't long before he realized he was helping Gorum with unscrupulous activity. It became too much for Ben's conscience, so he asked to go back to being a cowboy. Gorum took offense at his request and made life difficult for him for several years. For over a decade he was given the toughest jobs on the ranch. They knew he'd want to leave, but the foremen made sure Ben knew about all the cowboys that tried to leave Gorum and ended up dead somewhere down the trail. Ben got the next worst thing, which was jail. Because of his refusal, Gorum had him framed, carrying a wagonload of stolen dynamite.

There were a lot of these details that he didn't want to tell his new companions, so he skimmed over most of it, except for the part about being arrested by Wyatt Earp. He knew they all would get a kick out of that story.

"Was he as tough as the stories tell?" Francis said.

"Wyatt Earp? I suppose you could say he was tough. His brother Virgil was friendlier, and seemed to have more interest in others. Many a day after that I would cross paths with the Earps and say howdy, but Wyatt would act like he heard nothing and just keep on walking."

Indigo stopped the burro and point westward. *"Allá en las montañas."*

The mountain range was in a much clearer view. Unlike the sun-baked playa, the mountains were a darker brown and sharp ridged from hundreds of years of erosion by the wind and occasional rains. There, in the mountains, where Indigo pointed, was his past, and somewhere beneath them, in the playa, Ben thought, could be everyone's future.

BY THE TIME YUDEXY HAD HOSTETTER'S BED READY IN the back of the wagon, José had showed up with the load of lumber, lanterns, and oil. Since the railroad didn't go through Cibola, it took two days to have the materials delivered from Yuma. The original plan was for José to return with Yudexy to the farm, but they surprised him with the news of the rising waters and that Felicia and Hostetter were also returning with them.

José helped Felicia carry Hostetter to the wagon. They had planned to use a makeshift stretcher, but Hostetter convinced them he could walk with their aid.

When they reached the barn near the wagon, the engineer noticed José's wagonload of materials. "What is that for?"

"It's for rebuilding the storage shed," Felicia said. "The one that was destroyed in the explosion."

"That's a waste of time," Hostetter said. "The Cashman farm is in the lower level of the valley. It will catch the heart of the flood."

Yudexy shared a glance of concern with José. After they got Hostetter into the back of the wagon, she helped cover him up. "But that is where we are going. What will we do when we get there?"

Hostetter coughed and took a deep breath. "The only thing we can do—help them evacuate."

It was a solemn moment for all of them as they headed out with the wagons, stopping only to give Hostetter the chance to speak to his foremen. The Colorado River had already risen above the dam levels, and water flowed into the amateur canals built by the settlers. Many of them celebrated out of ignorance, and Hostetter gave his foremen the uneasy task of informing them that the dams could break any minute. It was indeed a critical time for all, but all that they could do now was save themselves.

As word got around, many people scrambled to gather their belongings and head for higher ground. Others denied any belief that the flood would occur and sat stubbornly waiting or continuing to dig their own irrigation and plow their fields. Regardless, those that did give in decided to take their chances farther west and cross on the ferry.

Lucky for Hostetter's crew they were among the first to get on a very crowded ferry. There were as many as twenty-five people on the platform—men, women, and children—and at least five horses, besides the two mules and two horses hitched to the wagons. As they looked behind them, families with horses and wagons and all of their belongings milled and bottlenecked at the entrance. The four bits a head would likely make the ferry owners have a very good business day, but it was also likely to be the last ferrying business they would have for a while, if, that is, the ferry was to survive the rush at all.

The platform they called a ferry was more or less a large raft—a series of thick pine timbers tied together with ropes and metal spikes, with wooden rails on the sides and nothing but a single rope on each end. Another thick rope, nearly two inches in diameter, stretched from one side of the river to the other to help guide it across. The rope was threaded through a series of iron pulleys for easier navigation. If not for the rope, the wild rapids would easily have carried the ferry away. Hostetter did not ease their minds any when he commented that if the rope broke, it would be the fastest trip to Yuma anyone had ever taken.

Two men operated the tow rope with clenched teeth, while two other men stood on each side of the ferry with large oars that disappeared once placed in the muddy Colorado. The rapids were violent, and it was very challenging for José to keep the horses calm. He'd set the parking brake of the wagons, but that didn't keep them from sliding back and forth and sideways on the wet wooden surface. A large wave sent one front corner of the ferry up a good four feet higher than the rest, causing one man to fall into the river and the wagonload of lumber to slide back into the end rope. The man quickly disappeared into the rolling, muddy current, and his wife screamed and cried for his life. The people next to her held her and tried to convince her there was nothing anyone could do, but she remained hysterical. The back wheels of the wagon were inches from going off into the river, and should the rope break, the entire cargo, mules and all, would be gone. José called for Yudexy to hold the horses on Hostetter's wagon so he could try to save the other one. She obliged him by holding them each by the bridle while José climbed to the seat of the other wagon.

José snapped the reins frantically and tried to get the mules to drag the wagon forward without releasing the brake. The mules brayed from all the stress of the wandering ferry, which was preventing them from accomplishing any movement. If he didn't get them to move forward, the rope would eventually snap, therefore his only hope was to release the brake to free up the wagon for the mules.

Felicia sat next to her grandfather in the back of the other wagon, holding on tight to the side boards and peering out in fear of all that had just occurred.

Hostetter grabbed Felicia's arm. "What is happening?"

"The wagon with the supplies . . . it has slid back against the back rope. José is trying to save it."

"Tell him to cut the mules free," Hostetter said.

Felicia looked down at him with confusion. "But the wagon could fall and be lost."

"Better just the wagon than the wagon along with José and the mules. Tell him to cut it loose and save himself and the mules."

Felicia nodded slowly and did as her grandpa said. José balked at first, then understood the sacrifice. He climbed down quickly and produced a knife from a sheath on his belt. He cut all the harnesses on the doubletree and watched it drop to the floor of the ferry. The wagon continued to slide backward, putting more tension on the rope, and it eventually broke. The wagon wheels dropped off the edge, and the bottom of the wagon box lodged against the platform. All it took was one more big wave to tip the ferry up and send the wagon sliding, and all of its contents rolled into the current.

The next ten minutes seemed like ten hours as the ferry finally docked on the west side of the Colorado. Once everyone was off, the ferry workers were quick to repair the tail rope and head back for another load.

"They're crazy," Hostetter said. "Greed will cost them their lives, and the lives of others."

Though they were disappointed about the loss of the wagon and materials, they were thankful that they had survived. Now it was a matter of getting to the Cashman farm to warn them there of the coming flood and give them a chance to avoid further disaster. For Hostetter there were no more dam or canal projects. There was only his life and the life of his granddaughter and, God willing, the future of Imperial Valley.

Chapter Eleven

THE night before, upon arrival, they had made camp in the foothills of the mountains, near a shallow canyon where they could seek protection from the heat and desert wind. Early in the morning, on foot, they followed Indigo higher up into the southernmost ridge of the mountain range. Vegetation was sparser in this part of the desert than most places, and it was no better in the mountains. Ben found it hard to believe that anyone had ever lived here, but Indigo explained to him that they were known as the Sand People. The neighboring tribes lived the summer months along the tributaries, where they would irrigate crops, but Indigo's tribe lived in the canyons and foraged off of berries and plant roots, killed rattlesnakes and lizards, and sometimes jackrabbits when they could be found. Jackrabbit hides were a popular commodity among the tribes and could easily be traded for other things, especially corn. *Maíz*, they called it, was not taken for granted. It was rationed among the People, and only on special days was it ground into flour for bread or tortillas.

The shallow canyons, Indigo said, offered protection and shade, and the mountains were great lookout points. Up high they could see for miles across the playa and watch for warring tribes or any other threats to the People.

They reached a certain point on the trail where it leveled off, and Indigo stopped and gazed to the southeast. He removed his sombrero and untied his ponytail and let his long, stringy gray and white hair fall loose on his shoulders. The wind picked up his hair and whipped it back and forth in front of his furrowed, swarthy face. He raised his hands into the air and continued to let the wind embrace him and allow him to absorb the spirit of the past.

Raul got on his knees in front of his grandfather and looked out over the hazy, crusty flats. Indigo started a chant, and not in Spanish or English, but in the native tongue of the People. Ben and Francis found a place to sit and watch, and did so for about five minutes before Indigo stopped chanting and lowered his arms.

The old Indian turned and came to them, and both men stood.

"This is the place and the gods welcome us," Indigo said.

"What place?" Ben said.

"We came up from the canyon out of our shelters and stood here, after the storm." Indigo looked and pointed out into the playa. "There is where we saw the ship."

Ben and Francis both stepped forward and gazed to the southeast. Ben scanned the desert basin and wondered how on earth it could be true. Not a green plant in sight yet both Indian legend and science said that it was all once an inland sea. It was hard to fathom, but when he looked at the toothy smile on Francis's face, Ben was glad to know that he had both legend and science there with him.

RATHER THAN CROSSING THE DUNES, HOSTETTER'S crew chose a longer route through the mountain pass that guaranteed them a proven path and better terrain for the horses. They stopped along the pass at night to camp, and by morning Hostetter felt good enough to sit up in the wagon and eat with the rest of them. José had prepared biscuits in a Dutch oven, and Felicia brought her grandfather two on a tin plate, broken in half and smothered with honey, along with a tin cup half full of coffee.

"Do you think you can chew these?" Felicia said.

A lot of the redness around his cuts and bruises had gone away and the old man looked better, but he still complained of soreness on his lips. When he opened his mouth, the dry cuts separated and stung, but the bleeding was minimal. Regardless, he chewed slowly and was able to get the biscuits down without much pain or labor.

After they were done eating, Yudexy and José cleaned the camp and prepared for their departure. José checked the connections on the harnesses, then he walked around and inspected the wagon. The river ride had given the wagon quite a beating, and the rough mountain trails often gave the hubs and axels quite a test. All seemed okay, though, and when he was done, he rested his elbows on the wagon box to inform Hostetter that they were ready.

Yudexy put the last load of camping gear inside the wagon. "Speak for yourself, José," she said and followed with a smile. José laughed and went to offer her help, but she declined.

"Don't worry about it," Hostetter said. "We still have plenty of time to make it to the farm before nightfall."

Yudexy seemed confused. "But what about the flood?"

Hostetter swallowed a sip of his coffee and licked his sore lips. "Don't get me wrong, we don't want to dally," he said. "The only rush of water will be a few hundred feet from the dam breaks. It will eventually slow to a steady flow and follow the low passes, the gullies, and creep its way into the valley."

"I'm not sure what you're saying," Yudexy said. "How long will it take to reach the farm?"

"Once the dams break, five days. Even at that time it will be a slow fill and nothing but a muddy mess. In a week it will look like a rice paddy. In a month like a lake, and a lake that keeps getting bigger. It will be nothing that this part of the country has seen for hundreds, maybe thousands of years."

Even though there was no need for haste, the report was quite sobering. It didn't seem to affect Felicia, who rode contentedly in the back of the wagon, caring for her grandfather. Yudexy, however, rode next to José in the wagon seat with a look of great concern. She feared for not only the Cashmans, but also the lives of her family and the future of her people.

THEY FIXED INDIGO A PLACE TO SIT, AND HE STAYED AT the spot on the mountain, lit his pipe, and continued to reflect on distant memories. Raul stayed with his grandfather, retied the old man's ponytail and helped him re-don his hat.

Ben and Francis gathered the necessary items they needed from camp, and while Francis was sorting through his gear, Ben couldn't help but notice that he set aside a sawed-off shotgun.

Ben grunted. "That's quite a weapon for a college boy."

"Oh," Francis said, acknowledging the gun. "Never knew what I might run into out here in the desert."

"Do you have any shells for that?"

Francis reached over and picked up the gun, pressed the lever, and opened the barrels. "Duly loaded." He closed the gun, then reached into another saddlebag and retrieved a wooden box, slid open the lid, and exposed a nearly full box of red shells with brass primer heads.

"Bring that along, will ya?" Ben said. "And the shells."

Francis grinned and closed the lid on the box. "Plan on shooting some desert ducks?"

"No, but I have a feeling it will come in handy."

They returned to the mountainside on their horses, with the bag of corn, the wooden bowl, the compass, and a tall flag, the pole made from a rib of a saguaro cactus, with a red neckerchief tied on the end. Ben stood next to Indigo on the lookout point, held the compass out in front of him, and pointed it due north. Simultaneously he and Francis looked over the face of the compass and followed the plane of fifty-five degrees. In his mind Ben drew an imaginary dotted line and followed it all the way across the playa to the farthest mountain. He and Francis looked at each other and smiled.

Francis grabbed the flag and jumped on his horse. He rode down the slope, carrying the long flag at his side, and once he reached the playa, he kicked the sorrel to a gallop, dust flying up under the horse's hooves. He stopped about a hundred feet out from the foothills. He stabbed the flagpole into the crusty sand, then turned and looked back up at Ben. The red neckerchief whipped back and forth from the south-westward wind.

Ben looked over the face of the compass at his imaginary line and waved his hand to the left. He kept waving and Francis kept moving until Ben held his hand up to stop. Francis stuck the flag into the sand with a robust jab.

Raul shaded his eyes with his hand and peered out into the playa at Francis sitting on his horse next to the flag.

Ben knelt next to Indigo. "Does that look about right?"

Indigo removed the lit pipe from his mouth, leaned forward a bit, and squinted his eyes even more than they already were. He looked back up at Ben. "I don't see so good anymore."

Ben bit his lip, then waved at Francis to come back. Francis left the flag and kicked his horse to a lope.

The plane was right, Ben was sure, but the exact spot to

dig would be quite a bit more challenging to determine. They could just start digging, he thought, but then again Francis was right, they had to be right over the ship or they could be digging holes aimlessly.

When Francis returned, he dismounted and joined Ben in peering out at the distant flag.

Ben took a deep breath and let it out slowly. "Now what?"

"We have to get very close," Francis said. "Spanish galleons had a range of sizes. The largest of some of the treasure fleets were over a hundred feet long. Many were around seventy-five feet. A breadth of thirty-two feet at the most. That's a pretty big rectangle, but out there it's just a few grains of sand."

Ben looked at him quizzically. "How does a geologist know so much about old Spanish ships?"

Francis raised his eyebrows and lifted his chin, mocking his pride. "I took an elective course in Spanish naval history."

Ben shook his head. "I'll be damned." He pointed a thumb at Indigo. "Just wish you had a degree in optometry, too."

"Why do you say that?"

"I asked Indigo what he thought of the flag position and he said his old eyes can't see that far anymore."

Francis looked over at the old man, sitting quietly, catching the desert breeze. He walked over to him, squatted down in front of him, and peered into his glassy gray eyes. Francis nodded, then reached behind his ears and removed his eyeglasses. "Here, Indigo. Try these." He put his round wire spectacles on Indigo and then stepped to his side.

Ben squatted down beside them.

"Look out there now, old boy," Francis said. "Can you see the flag?"

"*Sí*," Indigo said.

Ben and Francis looked at each other in amazement.

"Farther," Indigo said.

Ben was wide-eyed. "How much farther?"

All Indigo could do was point and repeat his word. "Farther."

Francis looked at Ben and nodded toward Raul. "Maybe it's time you try your corn test?"

Ben nodded in agreement.

They all sat on the ground in front of Indigo with the wooden bowl and the corn. Ben handed Francis an ear of the corn. "Here, shell some of this into the bowl, and I'll shell the rest."

Francis began to do as he said, and Ben took the cotton sack, moved the pestle to the side, and shelled the remainder of the corn onto the sack. After Francis had cleaned off the cob, he looked to Ben for direction.

"Now what do I do?" Francis said.

"Practice," Ben said. He handed Francis the pestle, then looked up at Indigo. "Your mother would grind corn. How did she do it?"

Indigo held out his fist and moved it in a rotating motion. Francis held the pestle in his fist and pressed it into the bowl, smashing the corn.

"Faster," Indigo said.

Francis did as the old man said, moving quicker and mashing harder.

"No," Indigo said. "Faster."

Francis pinched his lips and ground harder, and Indigo responded with a nod. "*Sí*," Indigo said. "That is the way."

Francis dropped the pestle and rubbed his sore wrist. "Your mother must have been some woman."

Indigo only smiled and reached into his pocket for a match. He struck it on a rock and relit his pipe.

"Don't get too comfortable," Ben said. Ben grabbed the bowl and dumped out the contents, then grabbed two handfuls of corn and emptied them into the bowl. "Go grab your shotgun. When you get back, prepare to mash some corn."

"Are you planning to shoot the corn off the cob?"

"You'll see," Ben said. He turned to Raul. "You want to help us?"

Raul smiled exuberantly. "*Sí!*"

Ben stood behind him and pointed over his shoulder. "See that flag down there?"

"*Sí*. I see it!"

"Are you a fast runner?"

"*Sí*, very fast."

"Okay, when I say go, I want you to run as fast as you can toward that flag. Don't stop running until you hear the shotgun go off. When you hear it, stop right where you are and stay there. Okay?"

"Okay!" Raul removed his sombrero and tossed it on the ground next to his grandfather.

Francis handed Ben the shotgun, then knelt down in front of the bowl of corn, wove his fingers together, and cracked his knuckles.

He grabbed the pestle and nodded at Ben.

Ben looked down at the barefooted boy, crouched in a stance ready to run. "Okay, Raul. Go!"

The boy took off running down the slope, jumped over the areas of erosion, and when he reached the flat, he took off in a sprint. Francis worked vigorously with the pestle, and the yellow and brown kernels were quickly becoming a thick white powder. Ben kept watching Francis and occasionally glanced at Raul. In less than two minutes Raul was a good ten yards past the flag.

Francis made one final grind and dropped the pestle. "Done!" he yelled.

Ben held the shotgun up in the air and fired. The loud blast echoed throughout the valley, and Raul slid to a stop and created a cloud of dust around him.

As the dust cleared and the smoke from the shotgun whiffed away, Indigo leaned forward and peered through the spectacles at the position of his grandson. "*Sí*," he said. "That is the place."

Ben took a deep breath, then smiled at Francis. The scholar swiftly mounted his horse and headed down to the valley. He loped across the flat, reached out and pulled up the flag, then stopped the horse when he reached Raul. He dismounted and rubbed the boy's head, then stabbed the flag into the ground. He hugged Raul, then helped him up on the horse and rode back to the mountain.

In less than an hour the crew had moved the entire camp to a spot fifty feet from the flag. Ben calculated that if the flag was anywhere close to the mainmast, which was in the center of the ship, then fifty feet away was a safe distance to place their tent. After everything was set up, they built a campfire and cooked some beans and bacon out of Francis's provisions, then brewed some coffee and thought about the dig. Ben took his coffee and walked out to the flag, where he stood and looked down at the ground, trying to imagine what lay beneath. The excitement within him made him realize that this was the first time in his life that he felt a real purpose for his existence. All of his years had been spent learning and paying a hard price just to breathe the air. It was possible now, he thought, that his time had come. Time to forgive all those who had caused him pain. Time to truly live.

Chapter Twelve

❧

GORUM and Calhoun rode into Cibola to encounter a state of panic and confusion. Men worked frantically on the dams, bracing the cross timbers with pine logs twice as long as the men and a foot in diameter. They pitched the logs at a forty-five-degree angle and secured them on the ground with two-foot metal spikes. Water continuously flowed over the dam and into the homemade canals, and toward the small fields and gardens. Those who hadn't abandoned their claims worked feverishly turning the soil, hoeing and planting. One group of men celebrated with bottles of wine and mocked those who left.

Those who attempted to leave, nearly a thousand men, women, and children, with their wagons, horses, goats, pigs, and dairy cows in tow, bogged down the progress of the ferry by trying to defy the limit of twenty-five people at a time. Growing more and more impatient, the ferry owner made a rule that no animals were allowed that couldn't be carried. Those who abided by the rule carried their goats and small pigs, and those animals too large were quickly sold for next to nothing to those who stayed, or otherwise the animals were left to fend for themselves. Those who had to cross pushed and shoved, and fistfights developed over who was next in line. One man pulled a gun and shot his aggressor in the stomach. Those who wanted no part of the rush or the violence, but knew they had to leave, headed for higher ground on the east side or went south to Yuma.

Gorum located one of the foremen shouting orders on a dam. He was a slender, middle-aged man, with a sandy brown beard and wearing a gray vest over a white shirt.

"Hey you," Gorum said.

The foreman, who immediately recognized the tycoon, went quickly to attention. "Yes, sir?"

"What's going on here?"

"Chaos, sir," the foreman said. "Those dams won't hold much longer. It seems a mess now, but when those dams break, the mess will become hell."

Gorum gazed around at the scene. "Where's Hostetter?"

"He ordered the evacuation, then left with his granddaughter. I guess he was ill. He was laid up in the wagon."

Gorum and Calhoun exchanged glances, then turned back to the foreman.

"Which way did he go?" Gorum said.

The foreman pointed across the river. "They crossed on the ferry yesterday."

Gorum glanced at the ferry landing, and the rising disorder around it. "Did they say where they were going?"

The foreman wiped at his bearded chin. "No, sir, they didn't."

Gorum took another gaze around, then looked back at the ferry. "Foreman, I need to cross that river and quick. Is there another ferry anywhere near?"

"No, sir. Not until you get to Blythe. And word has it they have it just as bad up there."

Gorum nodded. "Well, Edgar, looks like we're going to have to shoot our way onto this one."

Calhoun grinned and drew his revolver. "It will be my pleasure."

Calhoun spurred his horse and took the lead, and Gorum followed him into the mayhem. The crowd wasn't too cooperative until Calhoun fired his gun twice into the air, which brought near silence, and when he started pointing the gun at a few people, they began to make way. Once they reached the landing, both men dismounted and forced their way through the remaining crowd. Calhoun held the reins of his horse with his left hand and his gun with his right. He pointed it into the air and shot again.

The ferry owner held up a hand in a stopping motion. "What the hell is this?" He was a tall, stout-looking man with a red beard, and he wore a brown vest over a white band-collar shirt. He tipped back his straw hat when he addressed the men.

Calhoun walked close to him, pointed his revolver under the man's chin, and cocked the hammer. "We're taking your ferry, that's what it is."

"Whatever you say, sir," the ferryman said nervously.

"Yeah, no shit," Calhoun said, pulling his revolver down. He and Gorum led their horses onto the crowded ferry. Calhoun turned back to the ferryman. "Now latch that rope and let's get moving."

"But sir, we could fit another ten, maybe twelve people—"

Calhoun clenched his teeth, grabbed the man by the shirt placket, and pulled him onto the ferry. "I said let's get moving!"

The ferryman quickly latched the end rope but not without protest from his waiting customers.

Calhoun shouted out to them. "Ah . . . go write a letter to the president." He followed with a heckling laugh.

The ferryman released the dock rope while the men with the long oars pushed the ferry off the bank. As the men pulled the thick rope through the pulleys the platform was already swaying with the rough current. Gorum and Calhoun held the side rails with one hand and the reins of their uneasy horses with the other.

"Damn," Calhoun said. "This ride certainly isn't for the meek and mild." Being a professional gunman, he avoided circumstances where at least one hand wasn't free, so he tied his horse's reins to the side rail and did the same for his boss.

Gorum studied the faces of the other passengers. He took a good gander at a well-dressed man wearing brown riding pants, knee-high black boots, a white shirt, and a gray felt hat. A leather satchel rested on the platform at the man's feet. He sported a black mustache waxed on the ends and held the reins of a white Percheron draft horse fitted with an English saddle. The man smoked a cigar until the need for balance forced him to spit it into the river. He noticed Gorum's glance and nodded with a smile.

Gorum responded with a similar nod. "Where are you headed?"

"Los Angeles," the man said. "Samuel Bradford is the name. Made my bones as a contractor for telegraph lines. Was looking to buy land here and start a produce operation." The entire platform made a steep, rocky swing, and the passengers struggled to hold on. The man laughed. "But suddenly it has the appearance of a poor investment."

"You're a wise man, Bradford," Gorum said. He acknowledged the horse. "Fine-looking animal."

"Thank you, sir. First-rate bloodline. Paid a good price for him." Bradford acknowledged Gorum's horse. "I see that you, too, got past the ferryman's rule. I slipped a twenty-dollar bill into his hand. He never blinked an eye and let me on through. Curious, how much did it cost you?"

Gorum raised his eyebrows and made a sideways glance toward Calhoun. "I'm not sure. My friend here paid the bill."

"Oh, I see," Bradford said.

Gorum shifted his attention to a young man struggling to keep his balance while holding a goat. Along with his threadbare clothes, he wore a tattered derby and a hint of the first growth of a beard on his chin. The young woman next to him, wearing a soiled bonnet and long dress, held an infant child and had the appearance of being pregnant with another.

Gorum kept his balance by holding the rail and stepped closer to the young man. "How much did you pay for that goat?"

The young man seemed timid and caught off guard. He glanced quickly at his wife, then back at Gorum. "Sir?"

"The goat," Gorum said. "How much did you pay for it?"

"Nothing, sir. It was born to us. Had to leave its mother behind."

"What about a horse? Did you have one?"

"Yes, sir. And a wagon, too. But we couldn't afford to bring them."

"I see," Gorum said. "Where are you headed?"

"Not sure, sir. Heard there was a farm a day's ride into the valley. Thought we might find work there."

Gorum took another glance at the young man's wife, pondered a moment, and then nodded toward the goat. "Put it down."

"Beg your pardon?" the young man said.

"I said put it down."

"But the ferryman said—"

"I don't give a damn what he said. Put it down."

The young man struggled with the swaying ferry and nervously set the goat on the platform. The animal bleated repeatedly and wandered aimlessly on its lead rope. Gorum took the rope from the young man, who then looked at his wife with dismay.

Gorum led the goat and staggered with the swaying ferry

over to the Percheron, swiftly jerked the reins out of Bradford's hand and gave him the rope in return.

Bradford returned a fiery glare and refused the rope. "What the hell do you think you're doing?" He lunged to grab the reins back from Gorum but quickly met the end of Calhoun's six-gun in his stomach. Calhoun cocked the hammer.

"I'd take that goat if I were you," Calhoun said.

Bradford reluctantly did as Calhoun said and watched Gorum lure the Percheron over to the young man and hand him the reins.

"It might be a good idea to tie these to the rail," Gorum said.

The astonished young man quickly did as Gorum said. The tycoon reached in his vest pocket and pulled out a small white card and handed it to the young man. "When you get off this ferry, sit your fine wife here up on this horse and take her north to Blythe. It's not much farther and a whole lot safer ride. When you get there, show any farm owner that card and tell him I said to give you a job."

The young man smiled at his wife, then shook Gorum's hand vigorously. "Thank you, sir! God bless you!"

Gorum nodded toward the young woman. "You might want to relieve your wife there of the weight of that infant. I'd say she's carrying enough already."

He glanced at his wife awkwardly. "Oh—of course." He reached for the child, and his wife willingly let go.

Gorum pointed a thumb over his shoulder. "And you can thank that gentleman there for paying the ferry toll for the horse. He was in a very generous, giving mood today."

The young man and woman peered over at the man and nodded their thanks. He sneered back at all of them with a look of both fear and contempt.

Gorum touched the tip of his hat. "Good day to you both."

The young man hugged his child and revealed a stained, toothy smile. "Good day to you, sir!"

Gorum staggered back to Calhoun. The gunman leaned close to him and gazed over at the young couple. "So why did you help them?"

"Reminds me of me when I came out west," Gorum said. "Pregnant wife. Barely two pennies to rub together. Hungry. Was just outside of New Orleans when I acquired a nice stallion that got us all the way to Texas, where I made my first fortune."

"A rich man give you a horse?" Calhoun said.

"No, I got it in a poker game."

"You won a horse playing poker?"

"No I lost. But the bastard took my pocket watch that had belonged to my grandpa. I met him in the alley behind the saloon. He was about to mount the horse when I stuck my skinning knife in his kidney. Got my watch back and took the horse because he wasn't going to be needing it."

Calhoun shook his head in amazement. "I'll be damned."

"Yeah," Gorum said. "Doubt the lad there would feel that desperate or have the sand to take control like that. Man has to be rock-hard if he wants to win in this life."

Calhoun nodded. "You're right, sir."

Gorum leaned closer to Calhoun and spoke quietly into his ear. "All the same, make sure Fancy Britches doesn't get off the ferry. He looks just like the bastard that took my watch."

Calhoun glanced over at Bradford, who had let loose of the goat and let it roam the platform. "You got it."

When they reached the dock, Gorum assisted the young pregnant woman off the platform and onto the horse. Her husband handed her the baby, then thanked Gorum again and took the reins.

Calhoun followed them off the ferry then turned to deal with Bradford. Bradford picked up his satchel and stuck a hand inside. He clenched his teeth and pulled out a nickel derringer. His arm was barely half-raised by the time Calhoun had drawn his gun and fanned the hammer. Three shots to the chest sent Bradford backward onto the platform. All grew silent, and the ferrymen and former passengers all looked on in shock.

Gorum grinned at the young couple. "I guess he was trying to renege, eh?"

The young couple gazed in horror.

"Don't you worry none," Gorum said. "Now, get on your way. You still have time to get to Blythe before sundown."

Gorum watched the young man drop the business card, then swiftly lead the horse away.

"Ungrateful bastard," Gorum said, then turned back toward the ferry. He walked down to the ferryman and nodded toward Bradford's body. The white shirt was soaked with blood.

"You saw that it was self-defense, right?" Gorum said.

The ferryman looked dismally at Bradford's corpse. "Yes."

"Good," Gorum said. He gathered both of their horses and led them up the bank. "Now that that speck of business is cleared up, we need to resolve something else."

"Resolve what, sir?" the ferryman said.

"I need you all to step off that ferry."

The ferryman glanced back at his men, then back at Gorum. "Why?"

Calhoun pointed his gun at the ferryman and cocked the hammer. "Just do as he says."

The ferryman looked down at the gun fearfully, then nodded back to his men. They all walked slowly off the ferry and Calhoun followed them onto the sandy bank.

"Thank you, gentlemen," Gorum said. "You boys have heard of Edgar Calhoun, right? Yes. The one and only, and you have the pleasure of looking down the barrel of his gun.

Now, you might be thinking that he's already spent three of those bullets, and there are four of you. But just so you know, his rig carries two guns, and he's very fast."

Gorum grinned, stepped out of the way, and glanced at Calhoun. "Show them how fast you are, Edgar."

Calhoun spun to his left and fanned the hammer three times, shattering the thick rope that guided the ferry across the river. Before the men could absorb what had happened, Calhoun twirled, reholstered the empty weapon, and had the other one drawn, cocked, and pointed back at the men.

Gorum stepped back toward his smirking gunman and put a hand on his shoulder. "Gentlemen, the ferrying business in Cibola is now over."

They all watched in shock as the wild current pulled the loose ferry into the river.

Gorum walked toward the head ferryman and drew a more serious stare. "You may think you can start over, but you need to remove that idea from your mind. I don't want any more people in this valley. You hear?"

The ferryman nodded slowly.

Gorum smirked. "I knew you'd see things my way."

The tycoon backed away, and he and his gunman mounted their horses. As they spurred and loped away, the ferrymen all ran to the river's edge. The head ferryman cursed, took his hat off, and slammed it on the wet, sandy ground. The others stood in disbelief, and one actually fell to his knees. The farther the ferry drifted, the faster it traveled, and carried with it their way of life, as well as the bloody body of Samuel Bradford. But their anger and sorrow were short-lived when they heard the cracking of wood and looked upriver to see a dam collapse and hear the thunderous roll of water that followed. People screamed, while those who could flee grabbed their children and ran with all their might toward higher ground. The pressure of roiling water was more than the other dams could bear, and one after the other they collapsed, allowing the Colorado River to rupture like a bloated vein and set forth to make its mark on the valley.

BERNARD CASHMAN DIDN'T GRIPE TOO LONG ABOUT THE loss of his wagon. When Hostetter sat him and Verona down and gave them the hard facts about what was coming, it left them in a calm bewilderment. But he knew beforehand that he was the only one who could convince them of the truth. He knew it would not be easy for a man and a woman to look out at all they owned, all the progress, the time and money invested, the livelihood of so many, and fathom that none of it could be saved. Nothing but their lives and the belongings they could carry in their arms or load in wagons.

Verona wasn't the type to give anyone an answer on something so important without giving it careful thought. They couldn't compare it to a warm afternoon in Kansas when the sky grows dark and a funnel cloud appears and you only have seconds to find cover. This foretold disaster had not yet showed its ugly face. She took a walk with Bernard, and they went to their fields, looked over the many rows of foot-high cornstalks, beans, cabbage, lettuce, carrots, potatoes, strawberry patches, and cotton fields, and peered out to the canal that took two years, their life savings, and the blood and lives of others to build. It was hard to believe it had all been in vain.

They walked back by all the bunkhouses and by the faces of their workers who peered out the doors and windows and watched them walk by. It was more than sobering, and almost surreal.

Verona sat with her husband on a wooden bench on the porch in front of the adobe. They talked for two hours while the farm sat dormant and waiting, and then they called to everyone to meet them in the courtyard.

They all came. Curious men, women, and children stood

in a half circle in front of Verona as if it were Judgment Day. They knew that Verona would be the one to do the talking, not so much because she knew what was right, but she just knew how to say it right.

José and Yudexy helped Hostetter out to the porch, and he sat on a bench close enough to hear. Redman, now fully dressed, was up and about, and he and Felicia stood not far behind the proprietors as they began to speak.

"I'm sure this is all quite a shock to you as it is to us," Verona said. "The news that Mr. Hostetter brought us has to be taken seriously. I trust his expertise, and I know he wouldn't tell us such a thing if he didn't believe it was really going to happen. In all likelihood our farm will be under water in a month. But, it's not here yet—and I believe in miracles. Now, I can't make any of you stay, but I am going to ask you to wait this out with us. When Hostetter left Cibola, the dams hadn't broken yet. According to his calculations, when the dams do break, the water could be here in four to five days. That considered, there are mountains fifteen miles from here that are safe from flooding, and we own those mountains. I would like to ask you to make a shelter there and take your possessions to where they will be safe. Then I would like to ask for your help in making a safe place for our animals. Once we are done, you will all be paid for your time, then we will wait this out and see what happens. Think about it and report back here in an hour with your decision." She offered a tender smile that attempted to cover her sadness. "I thank you all."

In less than a minute Verona had said all she needed to say and left them all in a somber silence. She and her husband walked hand in hand back toward their adobe. They walked up to Hostetter, and Verona reached out and offered her hand. When Hostetter gave her his hand, she squeezed it tight.

"I know this wasn't easy news to deliver," she said. "But I want to thank you for having the courage to make the trip in your condition. I've wondered what it would be like to have a crystal ball—if you're right, you may be the closest thing." Hostetter nodded and she squeezed his hand tight, then the two proprietors walked inside their adobe to pack their belongings and, if nothing else, pray for that miracle.

Chapter Thirteen

NEAR the tent and a hundred feet from the digging area Francis used his finger to draw a map of a ship in the sand. An intrigued Raul sat on the ground next to him and watched. Ben stood with his hands on his hips looking over their shoulders.

Francis first drew the outline, then added the keel along the bottom. He drew a line across the top representing the top deck, then three lines below that line, to represent the four decks below. On the top deck and at the stern he drew a narrow, rectangular area representing the captain's quarters. He drew a long line at the bow representing the bowsprit, then three lines upward, spaced evenly along the ship, representing the masts. When he had finished, he held his finger on the center line.

"This is the mainmast," Francis said. "It's the tallest mast, so one would presume that if the top of a mast at one time presented itself, it would be the taller one. Now, there is a possibility that the mainmast broke during the collapse, which means that the storm could have revealed one of the other masts, so it's hard to say."

"So what you're saying," Ben said, "is if that flag is near the center mast, then we have thirty to fifty feet on either side of it to hit the ship."

"It's not that simple," Francis said. "It also depends on what direction the ship was pointing. The breadth of the ship will be somewhere around thirty feet, which means fifteen feet on either side of the mast."

Ben glanced out at the flag. "But if it's the front or rear mast, then we have a good chance of missing it entirely."

"I'd say the chances are fifty-fifty, hit or miss."

Ben wiped around his mouth with his thumb and forefinger and took in a healthy breath. "And I suppose it's unlikely that the ship will be sitting straight up and down."

"Exactly," Francis said. "And that's where it gets even more complicated. But we'll have a guide if we find the mast." He ran his finger down the height of his sketch. "We just follow the angle of the mast."

Ben pondered a moment, then nodded back down at Francis's diagram. "What else you got there?"

Francis pointed toward the body of the ship. "This section on top and at the stern is the captain's quarters. There might be a chest there with some things of value." The scholar moved his finger to the next deck. "The next two decks are the gunnery areas, where we'd find mostly cannons, cannonballs, powder kegs." He moved his finger to the bottom of the diagram. "The lower deck is likely nothing but ballast, large rocks and gravel to help stabilize the ship. But there could be stores and valuables. It's worth checking." He moved his finger up to the deck above the bottom. "But here are the storage areas where, if it exists, we'd find the real treasure."

"Like what?" Ben said.

"If this was a ship from the treasure fleet, chests full of silver coins, some gold. Chests of pearls, emeralds, gold and silver jewelry. But the best of it all, gold and silver ingots—bullion."

Ben's mouth fell slightly agape as he nodded, then scratched his chin. "How much money are we talking about?"

"You mean, how much would it all be worth?"

Ben nodded. "Yeah."

Francis shrugged. "It's immeasurable. Or a better word, unfathomable. You'd have more money than all the railroads. The richest man in America, no doubt, and quite possibly the world."

Ben was speechless, and a wave of fear swept through him. A man that had never had much more than a hundred dollars at any given time, he was not sure what he would do with more money than he could count. He remembered back to a time when he wanted to save up a thousand dollars to buy a small homestead outside of Yuma, and even that had been a hard number for him to contemplate. This was wealth beyond comprehension, and for the better of him he decided to remove it from his mind.

"Well," Ben said, "let's not start counting the money yet. We have to find it first."

Ben started to walk away, but Francis stood and grabbed his arm. "There's one other thing."

Ben turned and looked back over his shoulder. "What is it?"

"You said that you were told you'd be digging down maybe forty or fifty feet?"

"That's right," Ben said.

Francis shook his head. "That mainmast—it's as long as the ship. We're talking sixty, maybe even eighty feet. And we have to find the tip of the mast first."

Ben stood and pondered these new facts. "Well then, I guess we better start digging." He looked down at Raul, who now stood in front of him. "Raul, better fetch me my shovel."

The boy smiled widely. "*Sí*, Señor Ruby!"

* * *

FRANCIS STOOD WITH HIS SHOVEL READY AS BEN stepped off a six-foot-diameter circle around the flag. With the heel of his boot, he made four marks in the ground to indicate a three-foot radius, removing the hard layer of crust and revealing softer sand. Ben started on one side and Francis on the other, and they both dug into the crust to make a complete circle. Once the circle was drawn, they dug across from each other in steady, easy strides. Ben remembered what Hostetter had told him about the alkali in the soil, and Francis agreed that the man was right. Both men covered their mouths and noses with their neckerchiefs and went back to digging. In an hour they had dug down three feet, and the sand began to have dampness to it.

Ben stopped for a moment and wiped the sweat from his brow. He stood down inside the hole and reached up to Raul, who held his canteen. The boy handed it to Ben, and he took a small sip and swished it around in his mouth, then swallowed. After another small sip he handed the canteen to Francis. The student accepted, and Ben shaded his eyes and peered up into the sky. It was a dull blue, and the sun was high above them, creating a blinding white and yellow glow.

Francis handed the canteen back to Ben, but he refused, and then handed it back to Raul.

"Better not overdo it," Francis said as he commenced back to digging. "The sun out here can steal your energy."

Ben pinched his lips as he stabbed the shovel blade into the sand, then pushed down with his foot and tossed another shovelful out of the hole. "Small sips of water and keep your hat on. Keep digging and before long we'll be in the shade."

Francis laughed. "You're so right."

GORUM AND CALHOUN HAD HEARD THE CRASH OF THE dams and rode quickly to higher ground and found a lookout. River water rushed through the broken dams, and a steady flow filled the low washes and headed for the gullies. The east side and the town of Cibola faced total destruction, and the screams of women trying to save their lives and the lives of their children echoed in the valley. The worst of the flooding, however, was on the west side, below where the tycoon and his gunman got their near bird's-eye view.

Calhoun grunted. "There goes the irrigation project."

Gorum continued to watch the destruction develop and the paths of the water. "It's more than that," Gorum said. "If we don't hurry out of here we'll be on an island. Let's go."

The two men spurred their horses and galloped across the mountainside and down into the pass. Calhoun looked behind him and could see the water coming in a rushing, steady flow. He spurred his horse harder, and Gorum kept up, the two of them eventually beating the pace of the current. They would be safe, for now, but they could not stop for anything. Gorum was no engineer, but he knew enough to know that the valley was in dire straits.

THE FARMHANDS HAD FILLED EVERY WAGON THE Cashmans owned, five in all, with whatever belongings they could haul, and then they'd made a convoy for the mountains. Each of the farmhands had built a shelter, and the Cashmans put up a tent and built a ramada. After a full day of loading and unloading, and eight trips back and forth, the Cashman farm had the telltale appearance of abandonment.

To stay ahead of the danger Verona sent José into the mountain pass and instructed him to find higher ground and keep a lookout for the water. At first sign, he was to hightail it back and make sure everyone, wagons and all, were safe on the mountain.

It was late in the afternoon when José came galloping into the courtyard, where the wagons were lined up and the farmhands were putting finishing touches on another load.

Three of the wagons were loaded down with furniture from the adobe. Verona came out of the house to greet him, as did Hostetter, who now walked with a cane to help with his balance. Felicia and Yudexy helped load crates of dishes and kitchen supplies onto a wagon, and Redman and one of the farmhands brought a heavy trunk filled with clothes outside the adobe.

José quickly dismounted and tied his horse to the hitching rail.

"There are two men coming," he said. "It's Calhoun and Señor Gorum. They are riding fast."

Verona stepped out into the sunlight. "What about the dams?"

"They have broken, señora. Gorum, well, he was riding fast to outrun the coming water."

A deep level of concern formed on the faces around him.

Hostetter took two steps forward, guiding himself with his cane. "How far back did you see the water?"

José looked away in thought, then looked at Hostetter directly in the eyes. "Eight, maybe ten miles from Cibola."

Hostetter looked directly at Verona. "I'd say we still have two days before the water hits. But Gorum will be here by nightfall."

Verona let out a long breath. "So much for miracles, eh?"

"I can differ with you a bit," Hostetter said.

"Oh, how's that?" Verona said.

"The fact that I'm even standing here alive is testament enough for me."

Verona nodded and offered a slight smile. "You may be right. Regardless, when Gorum gets here, I want him to be spared a greeting."

AFTER THE FARMHANDS LEFT FOR THE MOUNTAIN WITH the wagons, Hostetter met with Felicia and Redman inside the adobe. Yudexy was following Verona's instructions and pulling photographs and paintings off the walls and arranging them in large crates.

The two men sat at the table that was the only piece of furniture left in the house. Felicia brought the coffeepot from the stove and poured them each a cup.

"This is the last of it," Felicia said. "Mrs. Cashman said we have to pack it up."

"Thank you, dear," Hostetter said. He took a sip of the coffee, then looked across the table at Redman. "We need to go warn Ruby."

Redman nodded. "I will take you."

Felicia put her arm around her grandfather. "I should go with you."

"No," Hostetter said, patting her hand. "You will be safer here with the Cashmans. Plus, I have an idea."

"What sort of idea?" Redman asked.

Hostetter turned in his chair toward Verona, who pointed at items on the wall for Yudexy to remove.

"Mrs. Cashman," Hostetter said.

Verona wiped her hands on her apron and walked closer to the table. She looked down at Hostetter. "Yes?"

"Whatever become of that dynamite?"

"It was unloaded on the mountain somewhere I believe," she said. "You'll have to ask Bernard. He put himself in charge of that little detail."

"I may need your help in getting it loaded back up," Hostetter said.

"Why?"

"I have an idea to lure Gorum away from here. When he comes, the sooner he leaves the better."

Verona nodded. "Okay. Let's make a final load, then head up to the mountain. I'll do anything to keep that son of a bitch off my farm."

Chapter Fourteen

GETTING Bernard Cashman to let go of the dynamite was not as difficult as they had expected. Verona did all the talking, which meant Bernard had very little to say about anything.

When one of the wagons was available, three of the farm-hands loaded the crates of dynamite, covered them with a gray tarp, and tied it down with short ropes. Two draft horses were already hitched to the wagon, which Hostetter complimented, based on his experience with working teams.

Felicia kissed her grandfather good-bye, then walked to the other side of the wagon and up to Redman. She smiled at him tenderly, and he responded by removing his hat and reaching for her hand.

"You be safe out there," she said.

"I will," he said, looking deep into her eyes.

Without hesitation, Felicia reached up and kissed him softly on the lips. They both closed their eyes and left their lips together, and all Redman could do was put his arms around her and try to pull her closer to him. He didn't want to let go, but he knew he had to. He opened his eyes and ran a hand over the top of her head, feeling the silky texture of her hair.

"I'll see you soon," he said.

"You better," she said, barely allowing him to get loose of her.

Redman climbed into the seat of the wagon, and two of the farmhands helped Hostetter onto the seat as well. Once he was situated, Yudexy walked up to the side of the wagon and handed him a folded blue neckerchief.

"Please give that to Ben," Yudexy said.

Hostetter looked down at Ben's name embroidered on one corner.

Hostetter nodded. "I'll be sure he gets it."

Yudexy backed away from the wagon, and the two men glanced back at the shelters and the tent, and the Cashmans and all the farmhands that had gathered to bid them farewell.

Hostetter nodded at Verona. "When they come, don't be afraid to tell them what I said."

"Don't you worry," Verona said. "I hope we see you again."

Hostetter offered a hint of a smile. "You will."

Felicia blew a kiss at Redman as he snapped the reins, and they all watched them ride away, down to the mountain pass and toward the sun.

"God be with them," Verona said.

Yudexy wiped a tear from her cheek. "God be with them all."

THE SUN HAD LEFT A HINT OF PINK CLOUDS THAT partially covered the fading blue sky when Gorum and Calhoun rode into the Cashman farm. The smell of water was in the air, just like life around the river, and the fields were plush and green. But there was no movement of workers, of farm animals, of poultry, just a freak calmness and an occasional tumbleweed drifting across the courtyard.

They both approached the hitching rail, dismounted, and let their lathery horses drink from the trough. Both men took a gander around the courtyard.

"Place looks deserted," Calhoun said.

Gorum walked up onto the porch and Calhoun followed. Their spurs jingled as they walked across the planks and up to a window. Gorum peered inside, then went over to the door, opened it, and walked into the dimly lit room. It took several minutes for his eyes to adjust.

Calhoun stepped up beside him. "Hell, there's no one here."

Gorum looked down at the wooden floor and took note of the dusty footprints. "But they were here, not too very long ago. See all those wagon tracks? They've received word of the dam break, which means Hostetter was here. They can't be far."

"How will we ever find them?" Calhoun said.

"We won't tonight," Gorum said. "They won't be moving, either, so we'll camp here and head out at first light."

"What about the river?"

"We're way ahead of that." Gorum walked over to the stove and opened the cast iron door. "Build us a fire here and make us some coffee. We'll relax tonight, and tomorrow we'll bring them hell and high water."

DARKNESS HAD SET IN ON THE PLAYA, BUT BEN REFUSED to stop working. He had Raul bring a lantern, and the boy hoisted it above the hole while Ben kept digging. Francis had agreed to work in shifts, and they each took periodic breaks to eat or sleep, but someone was always digging.

During his break Ben sat on the floor next to Indigo, who lay snoring peacefully, and grabbed some beef jerky from his saddlebag. He stuck the jerky strip in his mouth and chewed on it while he lay back on his bedroll and massaged the muscles in each arm. All of the digging was making him stiff and his thighs cramped. He rubbed his legs, too, for a couple minutes, then he bit off a piece of the jerky and lay there and chewed. It seemed like a million things roamed through his mind. Everything from the digging of the hole, the details about the ship, the treasure that might lie beneath, the words of Jeb Hostetter, the threats of L. J. Gorum, and his days in prison with Abel Winthrop. But it was his last thought that consumed him and made his body feel almost numb. He thought of the moment he first saw Yudexy; the light in her dark eyes and the glisten in her hair. It was the perfect thought as his eyelids grew heavy and he swallowed the last bite of his meal, allowing his mind and body to completely relax.

WHEN HE WOKE, IT WAS TO THE SOUND OF FRANCIS calling his name. It startled him to a sitting position on his bedroll. It was still night, and the only light was a faint glow from the half moon that cast an iridescent blue onto the playa. He heard his name again, and instantly Francis opened the tent flap and stuck the lantern inside.

Indigo rose to his elbows to inquire about the commotion.

Ben got up to his knees and Francis crouched inside. The student held the lantern out in front of him and his other hand in front of the lantern.

"Look!" Francis said.

Ben squinted at the tarnished, ball-shaped object, about the size of a chicken egg, that rested in Francis's soiled hand.

"What is it?" Ben said.

"It's an ornament off of a lanthorn—a lantern," Francis said. "The kind that hung on the rails around the stern of an old ship. I saw a complete specimen once in a museum. I'd recognize it anywhere!"

Ben wiped at his sleepy face and tried to get a better look at Francis's find. Francis handed him the ornament, which felt heavy and likely formed out of brass.

"Where did you find it?" Ben said.

"I dug it up in the hole," Francis said. "I hit it with the tip of my shovel and thought it was a rock until I got a better look at it."

"But it feels so heavy. If the ship is below it, how could something like this keep from sinking?"

"It makes perfect sense to me," Francis said. "It used to be attached to a lanthorn, which likely broke off from the ship when it collapsed. Or maybe it was knocked off the ship by a rum-drunk crewman. Who knows? The point is that the lanthorn would float."

Ben rose to his feet and grinned. "I'll be damned."

"Yes! And there's something else!" Francis said. "Smell it."

Ben brought the object up to his nose and sniffed. There was definitely an odor.

"Sea life," Francis said. "I've dug in this area and found shells and other signs of sea life, but this is the first time I've ever smelled it. It's preserved under the ground. I've dug almost ten feet now. I can smell it in every scoop I make!"

Ben laughed out loud and slapped Francis lightly on the shoulder. "All right then, let's get back to digging!"

"You got it!" Francis said.

Ben started to walk out to the digging site, but he did a quick about-face and turned to Francis. "Wait a minute. I've had my rest. It's your turn now."

Francis shook his head. "Are you kidding? I'm wound like a Swiss watch. I couldn't sleep now if it meant saving the world."

Ben smiled and put his arm around the student. "All right then, let's go save the world a different way!"

THEY REACHED A POINT OF DEPTH IN THEIR SIX-FOOT-wide hole where soil removal was more of a challenge. Ben had estimated a depth of twelve to thirteen feet deep, and he could no longer scoop dirt and toss it out of the hole with any efficiency.

They had already tied a rope to a stake several feet from the hole, which they used to climb out, and Francis came up with the idea to tie a second rope to a stake and tie a bucket on the end of each rope. With two buckets tied to ropes and lowered down into the hole, the routine now was for one man to dig inside the hole and fill the buckets, while one man pulled the first full bucket up and emptied it, then lowered the empty bucket back down and pulled up the next. It wasn't as fast a process, but with the level of commitment they had, along with an ounce of patience, it got the job done.

Another challenge was light, because the deeper they got, the darker it became. Even as the sun rose and shed light into the hole, it wasn't enough for them to see the bottom. Ben alleviated the problem by driving a stake into the tunnel wall at arm's length above his head and hanging the lantern on the stake. It worked so well that he did the same on the opposite side and doubled the luminance.

The two men agreed to change positions, and Francis secured the rope and helped Ben out of the hole. When Ben got to ground level, he squinted as he looked out and saw that the sun began to peek over the eastern mountains. As he crawled out he couldn't help but notice Raul not far from the hole, curled up on his side sleeping.

Ben laughed. "Looks like you lost your helper."

"He deserved a break," Francis said.

Ben got to his feet and took a good look at Francis, who seemed a bit droopy as he removed his hat and yawned.

"Raul is not the only one who deserves a break," Ben said.

Francis stretched his arms above his head. "I suppose I could use a cup of coffee."

"No, you could use some sleep."

Just as Francis was about to speak, they both turned their

heads at a clanging rattle to the north of the tent, out on the flat. Ben stepped farther out and looked closely into the hazy dawn until he saw faint movement and heard the rattle again.

"Looks like we got company," Ben said.

"Should I get the shotgun?" Francis said.

"No, let's just stay calm and watch them come in. It appears to be a wagon. In my experience trouble usually comes on horseback."

Francis continued to gaze out into the playa while Ben walked over and woke Raul. He helped the boy to his feet.

"Better go inside the tent with your grandpa," Ben said.

Raul rubbed his eyes with his fists and did as Ben told him. After the boy ducked inside, Ben got a closer look at the coming wagon, and the closer it got the more sure he was that these were peaceful visitors.

He walked out from behind the tent and Francis followed him. As they came into clear view, the man on the right waved and Ben immediately recognized the hats: the gray Stetson of Jeb Hostetter and the brown plainsman of Casey Redman.

Ben waved back, as did Francis, and within two minutes Redman brought the wagon to a halt near the tent.

"Whoa!" he said, pulling back hard on the reins. The horses took one step back before they completely stopped.

Ben reached up to shake Jeb's hand. "It's good to see you're all right, Jeb." Ben nodded at Redman. "Casey, looks like you've healed up."

Redman nodded and looked soberly at Jeb.

"What's wrong?" Ben said.

"Help me down," Jeb said.

Ben and Francis both helped Jeb down, and when he reached the ground, he looked behind them, and Indigo and Raul came out of the tent.

Jeb looked at Ben. "The dams have broken."

Ben studied the concern in Jeb's eyes. "How long do we have?"

"Out here . . . three or four days. Five if you're lucky."

Ben tried to absorb the sobering news. "What about the Cashmans?"

"They have evacuated the farm and moved to higher ground. They're safe. From the water anyway."

"Why do you say that?"

"Gorum. He's likely already there. That's why we're here." Jeb walked toward the back of the wagon, untied one of the ropes, and lifted the tarp.

Ben recognized the crates of dynamite immediately.

Jeb dropped the tarp. "There's nothing at the farm for him now. I thought maybe we could lure him out here with this."

Ben nodded. "Good idea." Ben looked at Redman. "Did you bring any guns?"

Redman reached behind the wagon seat and produced a model '92 Winchester. "Compliments of Verona Cashman." The kid patted the rig on his waist. "And I've still got my six killer."

"Very good then," Ben said. "All we need to do is be on the lookout. Can you handle that?"

Redman smirked. "You bet I can."

Ben looked again at Jeb, but did a sideways nod toward Redman. "Did you fill him in on what we're doing out here?"

Jeb shook his head. "No, not really. I just told him you were on an archaeological dig."

Ben smiled. "Well, you're not wrong."

The men laughed, and Ben invited them all to the tent for coffee and some breakfast. Since their supply of firewood had all but diminished, and fresh supplies were pretty much nonexistent where they were, Francis got the idea of busting up one of the dynamite crates for wood to create a fire and brew some coffee. It worked well, and because of the tiny bit of gunpowder residue on the wood pieces, he had no trouble lighting the fire.

*   *   *

THEY ENJOYED A SHORT BREAK AND MUCH NEEDED REST
before getting back to work. Francis, who hadn't slept in
over thirty-six hours, still had the energy to continue on.
Ben took the time to give Redman a tour of the site and
explain to him what he hoped to find under the desert floor.
He didn't bother with the details of all the treasure, mostly
because Ben himself had yet to grasp the idea of anything
actually being there and didn't want to get his hopes up.

It was also nice to have an engineer appear on the scene
to whom Ben could explain the digging and dirt-removal
situation. Hostetter walked with his cane over to the hole
and peered down inside. He didn't contemplate long before
he looked around the camp, then toward the wagon, and
came up with a solution. A solution, he said, that might be
to more than one problem.

Chapter Fifteen

GORUM walked out of the adobe and into the courtyard, where Calhoun had already saddled their horses and had them ready to ride. He took a deep breath of the morning air, then put on his black leather gloves. He untied his horse from the hitching rail and walked it about ten feet into the courtyard.

"Where do you think they went?" Calhoun said.

Gorum looked up over the adobe and to the far north horizon, where a mountain could be seen in the haze. "Where else would people go in times like these? They moved to higher ground."

At that very moment Gorum heard the sound of water trickling. He listened more carefully, then ascertained that the sound was coming from below him, and he looked to his feet to see water flowing around his boots.

Calhoun noticed it, too, and immediately jumped up in his saddle. "We better get out of here."

Gorum looked east, toward the entrance to the farm, and

saw the steady flowing and widening stream working its
way into the courtyard. He looked around again at all the
fields, the buildings, and the adobe. "Such a pity."

He mounted his horse, and he and Calhoun rode out of
the newly formed mud and back into the dust. When they
reached the edge of the courtyard, they spurred their horses
to a gallop, and Gorum believed without a shadow of a doubt
that destiny had now run the Cashmans from the valley. *His*
destiny.

JOSÉ SAT MOUNTED ON HIS HORSE, HOLDING HIS WIN-
chester upward, with the butt of the rifle resting on his thigh.
He had spotted them leaving the farm and heading toward the
mountain and gone back to warn the Cashmans. Now he stood
on the slope below the shelters watching Gorum and Calhoun
trek up the rocky grade.

Gorum nodded at José as he rode by, but José returned
only his serious, unwavering stare.

Bernard and Verona stood outside their tent watching the
tycoon and his gunman approach. Two other farmhands
came close to them and stood with rifles ready. Other men,
women, and children stood in or near their shelters watching. One of the children held the white puppy, which commenced barking the moment it saw the riders.

Gorum and Calhoun stopped no more than twenty feet
from the Cashmans. Gorum looked around the encampment,
sporting his trademark smirk, and removed his gloves.

"Quite a setup you have here," he said.

Calhoun followed with a gravelly snicker.

Gorum pointed at Calhoun with his thumb. "I guess
you've already met my foreman here."

Bernard shifted on his feet. "Foreman? Hired gun is more
like it."

"Well, call him what you want. You, sir, don't have much

room to talk. He said that you killed one of my men. A valuable man to my business."

"We have a business to run, too, and he was a threat to it."

Gorum laughed mockingly. "What business?"

Calhoun followed with similar laughter.

Verona stepped forward angrily. "What do you want, Gorum?"

"You know, I was just thinking," Gorum said. "What a shame it was that not so very long ago I offered you a generous price for your 'business.' Too bad you refused. Now it's not worth two bits in a puddle of puke."

Bernard clenched his teeth. "I'd rather be dead and broke than sell you my land, in any condition."

Gorum snorted. "You may just get your wish, then. You're halfway there already."

"Then what's the purpose of this?" Verona said. "If you're so damn happy that you won, then go on, try and humiliate us and rub it in. Have your fun, then get the hell out of here."

Gorum raised his eyebrows. "You're so right. I shouldn't boast too much about my advantage. But I have other interests."

"Being what?" Verona said.

"Oh, I think you know exactly 'what,'" Gorum said. "Three of my former employees. Deserters. One a man named Ben Ruby. They are here."

"Were here," Verona said.

"Were?"

"They purchased some dynamite from us, then headed out into the desert."

"Dynamite? What for?"

"How the hell am I supposed to know? They didn't state their business—no more than you would."

Gorum laughed under his breath. "Very well then." He took another, long look around at the men with guns and the women and children near their shelters watching him. Then he looked contemptuously back at the Cashmans. "Before you feel too happy about things, I want you to know that I won't walk into a trap like Paulson Duff. If we ride out of here and find that you were lying to us, you'll all be out of business in a different way."

"Your threats don't scare me." Verona nodded to the men behind her with their weapons. Both of them ran the levers on their rifles and pointed them at Gorum. Verona stared hard at the tycoon. "Now, get off my mountain."

Gorum nodded toward Bernard. "That's some wife you got there, Cashman."

After a mocking stare, the tycoon put his gloves back on, then touched the tip of his hat and turned and rode away.

WHEN THEY REACHED THE PLAYA, CALHOUN KEPT watching the ground and eventually he saw where a wagon had entered the flat. The two men stopped riding and followed the tracks as far as they could see.

"I'm not sure I trust this," Calhoun said.

Gorum studied the wagon trail. "I don't want to over-complicate this. It just seems too logical to me. Abel Winthrop knew the Cashmans. He would have known they had explosives. Ruby went to see Hostetter about something, then came here to buy the dynamite. Whatever they're looking for, somehow Redman found out about it and Ruby made him a deal."

"What do you think it is?"

"An old mine maybe. I can't be sure. But what I can be sure of is that if Hostetter is involved, it must be real, and it must be big. He's not the type to wander off on a fantasy."

"So what do we do?"

"We follow that wagon trail." Gorum looked behind him into the valley and at the farmland that now glistened with

the pooling water. "And we better not waste any time or
we'll be trying to track them in the mud."

HOSTETTER SAT BEN AND THE REST OF THE MEN DOWN
to explain his ideas to improve their excavation. After Francis had convinced Hostetter that the ship would be much
deeper than the forty to fifty feet, the engineer knew there
would need to be a better plan.

Borrowing Francis's technique, Hostetter used his finger
to draw an image of the tunnel down and how it would
appear. "It's nearly impossible to dig a five- or six-foot-
diameter shaft a hundred feet down and make it safe. It's
bound to collapse at one time or another. Plus, we can't
forget that the Colorado River has decided to join us."
Hostetter poked a hole in the ground with his finger, then
grabbed a canteen of water, removed the cap, and poured
just enough water to simulate a flood. "See how the water
flows and fills the hole? Imagine that's your tunnel down to
the ship. Water will always fill the lowest points first."

Ben tipped back his hat and ran the fingers of both hands
into his hair. "Then what do we do now?"

With his forefinger, Hostetter drew a series of rectangles
in the sand, one on top of the other—with each rectangle
longer than the one below, like an upside-down pyramid
made of blocks. "We dig a series of holes that get smaller as
we go down, in tiers. The top hole, at ground level, can be
twenty feet across and nearly as deep. The next level, fifteen
feet. The next, ten. Then at five we are a lot closer to the ship
and the tunnel won't be so prone to collapse."

"Wait a minute," Francis said. "Where is the manpower
to dig holes that big? We have a flood coming. We don't have
the time!"

"There's a solution to both those concerns," Hostetter
said. "As for the coming water, we build a levee around the

top edges of the hole. We use the sand and soil that we've dug up, pile it at least two feet high and pack it hard with our shovels. I figure the water will rise no more than a foot a day, so that will buy us two days." Hostetter then grinned, reached behind him, and grabbed a stick of dynamite. "As for the digging—we will rely on the science of Alfred Nobel."

"Whoa, wait a minute," Ben said. "If there's a ship down there, won't the blasts disturb it?"

"Not with the amount we'll be using. There will be some ground vibration that will no doubt be felt by the ship, but most of it will be absorbed by the ground around it."

Ben looked at Francis. "Well, what do you think?"

Francis shrugged. "It sounds a bit crazy, but what the hell?"

"All right then," Ben said, putting a hand on Hostetter's shoulder. "Let's get to blasting."

HOSTETTER HAD WORKED ENOUGH WITH EXPLOSIVES during his years in the mine to know just about how much was needed to remove a certain area of rock or soil. Ben and Francis watched while he prepared the charges and educated them on how to use them safely. He placed fuses two feet long into three sticks of dynamite, then tied them together with short ropes. He twisted the fuses together all the way to the end, making one thick fuse. After setting that charge aside, he prepared three more sticks with short fuses that would be used separately.

"The idea now," Hostetter said, "is to concentrate more on soil removal and less on digging. Our dynamite is going to do the digging for us. All we have to do is remove the loose soil from the hole."

For the sake of safety, Raul helped Redman move the tent another hundred feet away. All of the men gathered around the tent while Ben walked out with the first charge. He stood above and looked down inside the twelve-foot hole that had taken almost two days to dig. He looked back toward the tent to make sure all were accounted for, then struck a match on his belt and lit the fuse. He dropped the three-stick bundle into the hole and sprinted back toward the tent. He could only get halfway there before the explosion rocked the ground. He stopped running and covered his head, and a shower of sand and soil fell all around him. He turned slowly and looked at the new crater that had formed, which amazingly was as big as Hostetter had predicted. Nearly twenty-five feet in diameter and nearly as deep at the center of the bowl.

They all joined him at the edge of their creation and gazed in awe.

Hostetter patted Ben on the shoulder. "Now we make the second tier."

THE SUN WAS HIGH ABOVE THEM, AND A SCORCHING heat forced Gorum and Calhoun to make frequent stops to wipe their brows and drink from their canteens. The wagon tracks were easy to follow, and they seemed to go on and on toward the southwest, without any clear destination.

Gorum put the cap back on his canteen, then peered out across the flat. He squinted at something that he couldn't make out. He pointed. "There's something there."

Calhoun tried to locate his discovery. "What do you see?"

"Let me see your binoculars."

The gunman reached into his saddlebag and grabbed the binoculars. Gorum took them and looked out down the trail they followed, and after focusing he eventually found what he had seen.

"What is it?" Calhoun said.

"It looks like a wagon." He handed the binoculars back to Calhoun. "Let's get a little closer, but not too close."

Calhoun looked through the glasses. "You think it's a trap?"

"I don't know yet. But we won't get close enough to find out."

The two men followed the tracks a bit farther, taking frequent stops and glances through the binoculars. At one stop Gorum was satisfied that he could see what they were after clear enough to make a decision.

"Strange," Gorum said.

"What?" Calhoun said.

"It's a wagon all right. Wooden crates in the back all labeled DYNAMITE."

"Why is that strange? We knew that's what they had."

Gorum lowered the optics. "No, what's strange is that all the wheels and axels are missing, and some of the crates are stacked on the corners underneath holding it up."

"What do you make of it?"

Gorum gazed around him and looked for other signs but saw nothing. "I think they left it there for us to find. And I think that they are looking at us right now."

Suddenly they heard an explosion that came from due south. Gorum brought the glasses up and looked at the small cloud of dust in the aftermath. A smile grew on his face. "Ah, we've just located the enemy."

"What about the wagon?" Calhoun said.

"We're not going near that wagon. That's exactly what they want us to do."

"Then what are we going to do?"

"We are going to circle around it and head toward that explosion. But they'll be watching for us now. So we'll get as close as we can, then wait. Until dark. Sneak up on them like a couple of Apaches."

REDMAN LAY ON HIS STOMACH AND PEERED THROUGH the telescope at Gorum and Calhoun as they circled far around the wagon. Hostetter was right; Gorum was leery of the wagon and took no interest in it. But it made them circle wide and bought some time. How much time, and when they would present themselves, was still an unknown.

The kid collapsed the telescope, then crouched as low as he could and ran back to camp. He would try to find them again later, when he figured they'd be close. Otherwise he would just remain on the lookout.

IT ALL WORKED JUST LIKE HOSTETTER HAD PREDICTED, and Ben had never imagined they would have gotten so far so soon. Three tiers had been carved out of the ground, with fairly level platforms at the bottom of each tier, around the hole. The most ingenious invention, Ben thought, was how Hostetter had designed a hoist by using the axels from the wagon. Just outside the top tier on the playa, he cut foot-deep grooves in the soil where the wagon wheels set, to keep them from rolling. The axel, however, spun, and using steel support rods from the wagon box, he created a makeshift crank that wound the rope. Using wood from the crates, he built two tripods, where he fastened pulleys that helped keep the ropes off the ground. He positioned them at the edge of the hole, where they allowed the buckets to drop freely and not drag on the sides of the tunnel. Each of the buckets was attached to a hundred feet of rope, which allowed it to go all the way to the bottom tier.

In order to double the amount of soil removal, the system was duplicated with the other set of wheels and their axel; however, they lacked the labor to operate it. Francis worked on top hoisting the buckets while Ben filled them. Raul stood at the bottom and had the job of attaching the buckets to a metal hook on the rope. Ben could fill twice as many buckets as Francis could hoist, but until Redman returned from his lookout, they had to be happy with the rate it was going. Considering the amount of time that was saved using the dynamite, Ben felt no cause to complain.

When the sun was at its apex, there was sufficient light

inside the holes to work; however, as the sun fell farther to the west, the need for lanterns arose. Two stakes were driven in the walls at the bottom tier and lanterns were hung on the stakes.

Regardless of the success, the work was tedious and tiring. Francis and Ben rotated the tasks to relieve the monotony, but only periodic breaks to rest and massage their cramping arms allowed them to keep going at any kind of productive rate. It was also a lot hotter on top than it was in the hole, so much that when they changed shifts it was almost as refreshing to get down in the hole as it was to have a cool drink of water.

When it was time to change shifts, the man in the hole put a foot in a bucket and held on tight to the rope, and the man on top fixed the rope to a horse and it hoisted the other man up. When this system was explained to Francis, he rubbed his sore arms and asked why they didn't use the horses to pull up the buckets of dirt. Hostetter was quick to explain that there wasn't enough drinking water to work the horses that hard; humans consumed a lot less than horses.

At suppertime Raul was hoisted out first, then Ben. They ate some beans and bacon that Hostetter had cooked and then rested for a moment to let it digest. They were about to start up again when Redman came jogging back into camp. He came up to them panting, his face red and sweaty. Hostetter gave him a canteen, and the kid took a couple sips between breaths.

"See anything?" Ben said.

Redman nodded. "They're out there—Gorum and Calhoun. They circled around the wagon. They're still three or four miles out."

"Just two of them?" Francis said.

"That's right," Redman said.

"That's a good thing for us," Ben said.

"But I don't know what will get here first," Redman said.

Ben wrinkled his brow. "What do you mean?"

Redman pointed toward the west. "There's a storm coming."

The sky was a pale blue above them, but as it went west the shades of blue grew darker, and the western horizon was an eerie charcoal gray.

Ben stood to take a good look at the sky. "If they see it, too, they won't be coming here now. They'll be looking for shelter."

"That's right," Hostetter said. "But what if the only shelter is our camp?"

"We just have to be on our toes," Ben said.

"We will be," Redman said.

BEN WALKED UP TO THE EDGE OF THE HOLE AND PEERED over the two-foot levee. It was amazing how deep they had gone, he thought. The lanterns on the sides gave it a cavernous appeal. The depth, he figured, was seventy to seventy-five feet. All sand and silt, some rock sediment, along with an occasional clamshell or mollusk, and the scent of sea life.

He figured the storm was a good two hours away, and he decided to keep working until it came time to take shelter. Francis and Raul went to the bottom and Redman and Ben doubled up on the hoists.

They worked steadily until Ben's arms felt so stiff and fatigued from cranking the handle that he could barely move them. He had two buckets of dirt halfway up when his arms locked and cramped and he could no longer hold on to the handle. He yelled for help, but no one was near enough to keep the buckets from falling. All they could do was yell for Raul and Francis to take cover. Ben staggered to the side of the opening and was almost afraid to look down. Luckily the buckets didn't make it past the ledge on the second tier. Ben collapsed to a sitting position, then lay back on the ground.

When Redman had his buckets to the top, he quickly ran to Ben's side.

"Everything all right?" Redman asked, looking down into the hole.

"Luckily, yes."

Redman looked to the west. "Storm is getting closer. We probably should think about getting in."

Ben rose up to his elbows and peered toward the charcoal sky. "What are we doing here, Casey?"

"What do you mean, Ben?"

Ben sat clear up, put his elbows on his knees, and buried his face in his hands. "This is just crazy. I'm crazy."

"No, you're not," Redman said, squatting down beside him. "You're just following a dream."

Ben uncovered his face. "Yeah—a pipe dream." He looked up at Redman, a once freckle-faced kid who now, for some reason, had more of the appearance of a man. Ben couldn't place what it was that caused it. Maybe it was just a change in the young man's level of comfort that gave him a gleam of confidence. Hard to say, Ben thought, but whatever it was he had a hard time thinking of Redman as a kid anymore.

Ben held out a hand and Redman helped him up. They both looked down in the hole, and Raul and Francis both looked up with concern.

"Let's get the horse and get them out of there," Ben said.

Chapter Sixteen

━━━◦━━━

WHEN they saw the storm coming, they knew that they had only two choices, which were to turn back and try to outride the storm or to get close to Ruby's camp and take cover until it passed. To Gorum, however, turning back was rarely an option, and this time was no exception.

To keep their horses out of sight, Gorum stayed a good mile behind and held the animals while Calhoun crept slowly into camp. The gunman crawled on his hands and knees for a quarter mile, then lay on his stomach and retrieved the binoculars. As the wind picked up, he saw the men at the camp start to stir. He caught a glimpse of the wagon wheels but still couldn't figure out what they were up to. A sudden gust caused whirls of sand that stung his face like biting ants. He closed his eyes and put his head down between his arms, and when the wind calmed again, he looked back up.

Through the binoculars he could place Redman. The kid tied their horses to the wagon wheels, then scurried to the tent while trying to keep the wind from taking his hat. Once he was in the tent, Calhoun kept gazing around, gusts of wind picking up and occasional clouds of desert dust hindering his view.

He lowered the binoculars and glanced up to the sky. The blue was slowly being conquered by the gray, and dark clouds on the horizon were only minutes away. Though he thought it might be a good time to retreat back to their horses, the gunman decided to get on his hands and knees again and crawl closer. All the men at the camp had taken cover, and once the sand clouds made better cover he stood and ran in a crouching position. When he got close to the horses and burros tied to the wagon wheels, he fell back to his stomach. The horses whickered and shifted from his presence, but he presumed the howling wind kept the men in the tent from hearing him.

He gazed around and noticed the piles of sand, most of them waist high. He scurried to them, and that's when he saw the large hole. He dropped again to his hands and knees and crawled to the edge of the hole and peered over. Several feet down he could see the first tier and the unlit lanterns hanging on the inside walls, but after that it was too dark.

Satisfied he'd seen enough, Calhoun glanced again toward the tent and realized his visibility in the blowing sand was diminishing quickly. He jumped to his feet and ran back behind the horses and toward where he'd left Gorum. The gusts grew stronger, and the stinging sand forced him to shade his eyes with his hand and squint as he ran. The wind knocked his hat off, but it was caught by the chin cord. He ran a quarter mile before he saw Gorum walking toward him with the horses.

When he met back up with Gorum, he immediately gave his report. "There's something big going on there."

Both men shaded their eyes and tried to speak above the howl of the wind.

"What did you see?" Gorum said.

"There's a huge hole in the ground. It was so deep that I couldn't see the bottom."

"Interesting. Did you see a place where we could hole up until this passes?"

"Other than the tent, no. It's a good two hundred feet from where they're digging. The wagon wheels are next to the digging site. They've tied their horses there and we could do the same."

Gorum nodded. "All right. Let's get that far, then after that I'm sure we'll think of something."

BEN RECALLED HAVING THOUGHT THAT FRANCIS'S TENT would easily sleep eight people, but once bedrolls were laid out for five men and a boy, there barely seemed enough room to breathe. To make room, Indigo moved toward the back center and had taken quite a liking to Francis's foldout table and chair. He sat on the chair in usual form, smoking his pipe and listening intently to the goings-on around him. Raul found comfort at the same end of the tent and at the head of his grandfather's bedroll. The other four men spread out evenly across the floor, with Hostetter and Redman on each side and Ben and Francis in the middle. The lantern hung on a hook in the center and cast just enough light for the men to see their food and each other's faces.

Francis walked around the inside of the tent securing the seams to lessen the influx of sand from the storm. He spent a great deal of time at the center flap, making it overlap enough that very little sand seeped through. But there was nothing that could hide the howl of the wind and the ticking of the sand as it beat on the sides of the canvas.

It was all enough to remind Ben of the melancholy he was feeling. His body ached from all the digging and cranking, and something in his mind made him look at all of the men and their presence there in a new way. What was it all about? Since when did grown men go off into the middle of a desert and search for a five-hundred-ton Spanish galleon? Just because some withered-out prison inmate, incarcerated for thirty years, says so? He glanced at Indigo and watched the old man gum his pipe stem, and remembered that he was the reason they were on this very spot, digging large holes in the desert floor. Elderly, senile, Ben suddenly thought. Too many years in the sun had baked his brain to where his entire life was spent reflecting on the past and living on a cloud. Then there was Hostetter, a third old man, who predicted the demise of Cibola and went along with Ben's quest for the sake of indebtedness to an old friend. A week later, after having his skull beat on by one of the biggest brutes in the Southwest, he was here, too, coming up with fancy ways to make big holes in the desert, which he'd likely decided was an improvement over sitting in an infirmary playing checkers with other failing minds.

It was a sick feeling for Ben, not just to belittle them, but to think that he had talked them all into it. His passion and persistence for foolishness had gotten them all here. Two old men and a young boy aching to go on an adventure. Plus a beady-eyed college boy who was already in the desert digging holes in the sand, so it didn't take much to lure him along. And Casey Redman, the size of a man but still really a kid, who just wanted to fit in with the right crowd and had found a safer haven with Ben.

No, Ben couldn't blame them. He was the real fool, who'd already spent half of his parole allowance on supplies for a chance at nothing. How could he criticize those who left the Yuma prison and blew all their money in the saloons or the opium dens? There was the *real* pipe dream. And, above all things, they were trying to outrun a flood. God himself was trying to cover up this valley, and he thought he could outwit God?

He was certain now that the eight years in prison had done something to his mind as well. Luckily now reality had truly set in, yet he didn't quite know how to tell them.

They all seemed content being inside out of the wind and talking about their day. The sound of the wind and sand hitting the tent did nothing to weaken their spirit. No fear that all the work they had done was now being covered back up by God and Mother Nature. He knew it now: there was no ship out there in the sand. No fortune bigger than all the king's purses. No truth to the legend. No matter how many times he'd felt hated by his stepfather—the humiliation, the woodshed beatings—the bastard was right: life is not a fairy tale.

What once was just a tired body was now nothing but a bundle of nerves, and there was no way he could rest, let alone sleep. He lay there on his bedroll listening to the others talk and laugh while the wind continued to howl as if it were feeding their energy.

Since Francis had been the last one out of the hole, he and Hostetter jawed about their discoveries. The student showed the engineer some of the clamshells and he studied them under the magnifying glass.

"Incredible," Hostetter said. He held the magnifying glass out in front of him. "You mind if I bring this out to the dig? With my old eyes, it might come in handy."

"Help yourself," Francis said.

Hostetter put the magnifying glass in the pocket of his trousers. "We have made good progress."

"I'd say we're at about seventy-five feet," Francis said. "If Indigo is right, we have to be close."

Indigo removed the pipe from his lips and blew out a long puff of smoke. "It is right," he said. "I will never forget such a place. The gods will not let me forget."

Ben wove his fingers into his hair and let out a long exhale. This bit of motion got the attention of the others, which brought silence to the tent, save the sound of the gusting wind.

"Are you all right, Ben?" Hostetter said.

"I'm just tired," he said.

"Then get some sleep. Might as well take advantage of the idle time."

Ben lay back on his bed. Yes, he would try to get some sleep, he thought. But in the morning he would end the project. The foolishness stopped now.

BY THE TIME THEY GOT THEIR HORSES TIED TO THE wagon wheels, the visibility had decreased to the point that they could barely see ten feet in any direction. The south-westward wind was whirling, gusty, and strong but not overly powerful. It was just enough to drift the sand and annoy the eyes. Both men had tied their neckerchiefs over their noses and mouths to keep the sand and dust out of their airways. They donned dusters that were tied in with their bedrolls, which would keep them warm during the cool desert night.

To make shelter Gorum showed his gunman an old trick where he dug a hole in the sand and covered himself with his horse's saddle. Fortunately for them, the piles of sand and silt left by Ben and his system of excavation, along with the nearby shovels, made for easy digging. The two men each took a shovel and hollowed out a place on the sand piles, then they laid out their bedrolls and crawled down in the pits. They pulled their saddles over them, and the curvature of the skirt worked like a protective dome over their heads. The technique would not suit the claustrophobic, and though they were consumed by the smell of horse sweat and leather, with a pocket of air over them, it beat having to have a blanket over their heads, with the wind and sand beating against them. Now all they had to do was wait out the storm, and when it passed, the lord over Imperial Valley would be ready and waiting for Ben Ruby's secret to be revealed.

Chapter Seventeen

B EN woke to complete calmness save the snoring of
Hostetter and the slight movement of Francis as he went
about trying to open the flap of the tent. Ben rose to his
elbows, yawned, and looked around him. The air smelled
of bad breath and flatulence. Raul, too, was awake and when
they made eye contact, the sleepy-eyed boy offered a broad
grin. Indigo was still in his bedroll, but he made short moans
and slow movements. Redman, like Hostetter, snored a good
song and gave off no signs of waking anytime soon.

The sleep had done Ben well, but as if he had an emo-
tional hangover, his head ached with resentment for starting
this so-called project. Once they were all up, he would tell
them, and the only digging they would be doing today would
be getting themselves out of the tent.

Raul took interest in Francis's work and walked around
the sleeping men to observe and offer a helping hand. The
opening of the flap revealed a drift nearly as high as the tent,
with a hint of the morning sun peeking over. Francis reached

out and pushed sand from the top, expanding the opening, then looked down to Raul for help.

"You're a better fit for this," Francis said. "How about you crawling through and fetching our shovels?"

Raul readily agreed, and like a lizard he bellied onto the drift and worked his way over the top. A quick avalanche of sand fell into the tent, and Francis tried to kick it back out with his foot.

Ben rose to his knees and stretched his arms. The muscles in every part of his body were sore, but his arms felt the crux of the tenderness.

"Good morning," Francis said. "Looks like we have some other digging to do first."

Ben took a deep breath and was about to inform Francis of his request for a meeting, but he was suddenly interrupted by a call from Raul.

"Señor Ruby! Señor Ruby! Come quick! Come Quick!"

Francis and Ben jumped to their feet, and the excitement in the boy's voice along with the commotion stirred all the men awake and out of their bedrolls. Francis was the first to dive into the opening and push through the sand like a frantic gopher. Ben appreciated Francis's work, as it made it much easier for him to crawl through.

The scene around them reminded Ben of the aftermath of a nighttime blizzard, only with golden remains rather than white. Most of the flat remained clear, but the wagon wheels and newly built levees had become traps for drifting sand.

Still unsure of the purpose of Raul's alarm, they found him standing near the edge of their hole, his back to them and looking down inside. They ran to him, and when they reached the edge and saw Raul's discovery, their bodies locked from motion.

"I don't believe it," Francis said.

During the night the southwestern winds had eroded the easternmost side of their hole, and there, no more than three feet down, was the damp and weathered tip of a ship's mast, topped with a tarnished ball, and another six feet down and five feet out of the sand were the beginnings of the rope sail lifts and netted shrouds. All of it pointed back into the ground at a slight angle toward their hole.

Ben could not have been more stunned. After all his doubt, his entire loss of faith, the evidence of truth stood below him. The myth had been dispelled. The realm of fantasy was gone forever.

Francis ran around the edge of the hole, grabbed the hoist rope, then jumped in the hole and slid down. He rubbed his hand on the preserved, weathered wood of the stump then looked up at Ben and smiled. "Can you believe it?"

Ben exhaled a long breath. "I'm trying to."

Francis spun around the stump pole, studying it and wiping off the sand, then worked his way as far down as he could. "Do you see the angle Ben? It's fifteen, maybe twenty degrees! We're going to hit it, Ben! We're almost there!"

"Do you know which mast it is? Can you tell?"

Francis looked it over, wide-eyed. "This ball on top is likely brass, but I see nothing here that indicates the type of flag that was attached to it."

"Flag?"

"Yes, on the mainmast was the pendant, like a long narrow flag that I'm sure was the flag of Spain. But on the foremast or mizzenmast was merely a much shorter, narrow flag used as a wind vane." The student followed the length of the stump down, then pointed at the sail lifts and slid down to them. He rubbed them vigorously, removing the silty soil. "But these lifts and shrouds indicate a topsail, which most likely indicates either the mainmast or the foremast." He looked up at Ben. "There's only way to find out!"

"Yeah," Ben said. "Then let's get down there and start digging!"

By this time Redman had joined Ben by the side of the hole, and Hostetter was working his way out of the tent. Ben shared a smile with the kid, and they gave each other friendly pats on the back.

"You did it," Redman said.

"*We* did it, kid. We all did it."

Hostetter yelled from the sand drift outside the tent as he struggled to wade through the drift. "Would somebody give me a hand? I want to see what this damn fuss is all about!"

Ben laughed. "Better go help the man. We're going to need him."

"Will do," Redman said.

Redman started to run but came to an abrupt, sliding halt when Gorum and Calhoun stood up from behind their horses and cocked their pistols. They still wore their dusters, and their dirty neckerchiefs hung under their necks. Gorum walked on past Redman, his spurs jingling, his face and hat dusty from the night in the storm.

Calhoun kept his gun on Redman, walked slowly to him, and pulled the Colt out of the kid's holster. Not once losing eye contact with Redman, Calhoun opened the flap of his duster and stuck the gun under his belt. The gunman pointed with his chin toward Ben. "Go over there—nice and easy."

Gorum walked closer to the hole, and as he walked he acknowledged Ben with a crooked smirk as mocking as his squinting eyes. "Quite a task you have here, Ben," he said, then peeked over the edge of the hole. When he cocked his head toward Francis and saw him hanging on the tip of the mast, his smirk vanished and his eyes widened. "Well, well, what do we have here?" They tycoon gazed in astonishment and with a hint of lust. "Get out," he said to Francis.

The student quickly did as he said, climbing up the rope and stopping fearfully when he reached the top.

Gorum looked back up at Ben. "So this is your ten thousand in gold? Some estimate, I'd say. And it looks like you've already done a lot of digging."

The tycoon walked slowly around the edge of the hole, and while keeping his gun pointed at Ben, he reached down and picked up a shovel. He walked farther around the hole, and when he was close enough, he tossed the shovel to Ben. Ben caught it with both hands.

Gorum pointed at the shovel with his gun. "Keep digging."

Then men exchanged hard stares, which were suddenly interrupted when Hostetter walked back into the scene.

"What the hell is going on here?" Hostetter said.

Gorum grinned. "Howdy, Jeb. Wondered why you left your town under water. Now I understand."

"There was nothing more I could do there."

"So are you retired then?"

"Let's cut through all the bullshit, L.J. What do you want from us?"

Gorum lost his smug grin. "You know exactly what I want. For starters I want everyone out of that tent and I want to see shovels swinging. Got it?" Gorum walked over to the pulley stand and tugged on the rope. "I am anxious to see how this contraption works."

Ben tossed the shovel down into the hole. "There's no one else in that tent but Indigo Juarez, and he's no threat to you. So leave him be."

Gorum grunted. "That old Mexican? What's he doing clear out here?"

"He's not Mexican," Ben said. "He's Cahuilla. And this is his desert."

"Whichever," Gorum said. "You know it's all the same to me." Gorum's spurs jingled in unison with his slow steps. "But I beg to differ with you about this being his desert. You see, California sold claims to this land many years ago. Your friend Bernard Cashman staked a lot of it north of here, but this here valley belongs to me." He stopped walking three feet from Ben, cocked his head, and delivered a wry smile. "I don't remember being asked for permission to dig here. But I can be a very forgiving man when the right circumstances arise. Now, like I said—get digging."

Ben studied the situation with Gorum and Calhoun both standing, guns pointing, and knew that they were taking on a lot if they thought they could control them all. But that was how Gorum worked. His level of confidence, along with hubris, always exceeded his capability and left room for failure. The fear that he imposed, however, usually won out, because no one ever had the guts to seize the moments of opportunity. Ben had never really had the guts, or the will, either, but after eight years of his life had been taken away, and with the hard truth resting now beneath his feet, there was too much at stake not to try. For L. J. Gorum to be the richest, most powerful man in Imperial Valley was one thing, but to extend that influence to the world would mean pain and suffering for a lot of people. Though it was still yet to be determined the value of the treasure in that ship, if there was any treasure at all, such wealth could not fall into Gorum's hands. One thing was certain now: a ship did exist. Digging was what Ben had to do even if it was at gunpoint.

Gorum forced everyone into the hole except Redman, who stayed on top to operate the hoist. Calhoun was instructed to stay up there also and watch Redman, plus keep an eye on the tent to make sure Indigo stayed put.

Francis swung on the other hoist rope and lit the lanterns, then joined them at the bottom. Both Francis and Ben dug while Hostetter and Raul filled the buckets and attached them to the hoist hooks.

Gorum sat on a pile of dirt at the bottom of the third tier, gun in his hand and resting on his thigh, while he ate a red apple he'd fetched from his saddlebag. After the last bite, he tossed the apple core and it landed at Hostetter's feet. The engineer looked up at Gorum with disgust.

Gorum lifted the gun from his thigh and made a circular motion with the barrel. "Keep moving."

The hole they now dug was six feet in diameter, and they'd dug for over an hour without a break. The sun was high over the hole, and though it was cool deep inside, Ben feared for Redman working at the hoist.

Ben stopped digging and wiped his brow with his shirt-sleeve. After lowering his arm, he looked at Gorum. "Can we make sure the kid has water?"

"Let me worry about the kid," Gorum said. "Keep digging."

Ben knew there was no swaying the man's greed, and he went back to digging. He and Francis both stabbed at the soil with their shovels, breaking up the silt and sediment, then lifted up the loose soil with the shovel blades and tossed it out onto the tier for Hostetter and Raul to scoop up with the buckets. After another fifteen minutes of breaking the soil, Ben made a hard jab into the hole and hit something hard. He and Francis both stopped and looked at each other wide-eyed. Ben did it again, and the same clunking sound echoed throughout the hole. They both dropped the shovels and fell to their knees and dug frantically with their hands. Raul and Hostetter took notice and leaned curiously over the hole to see what they had found.

Gorum stood up from the dirt pile, pointed his gun, and looked over Raul's shoulder.

With their hands flat, Ben and Francis brushed the soil away from the hard surface and immediately recognized it as a wooden platform.

"Is it the top deck?" Ben said.

Francis studied it carefully, then smiled. "It has to be."

The two men used their shovels to break away more of the soil and toss it out of the hole, and when a good four-foot area was clear, Ben looked up at Hostetter.

"I need a lantern," Ben said.

Hostetter used the hoist hook and handed one down to him. Ben held it over the cleared area and could see the texture of the wooden deck. He and Francis smiled at each other until Gorum took the moment away.

"What do you got there?" Gorum said.

"It's the deck of the ship. I'm going to need an axe to chop through. We have one at the camp."

Gorum thought for a moment, then pointed his gun toward Francis. "You, go get it."

Francis crawled out of the hole, and as he reached for the hoist rope, Gorum pressed the end of his gun barrel against the student's jaw. "And don't try nothing stupid, right, college boy?"

After they hoisted Francis out of the hole, Gorum instructed Calhoun to have Redman come down so he could keep an eye on him, then to follow Francis to the tent. For safe measure Gorum grabbed on to Raul and held his gun to the boy's head, then reminded Francis that if he tried anything foolish, the boy's blood would be on his hands.

CALHOUN HELD THE FLAP OF THE TENT OPEN AND KEPT a sharp eye on Francis as he rummaged through his belongings for the axe. Indigo sat calmly on the chair smoking his pipe and winked at Calhoun while he watched. Calhoun grunted and wrinkled his nose at the old man.

Francis moved around on his knees and found the bag where he kept his tools. When he opened it, the first thing he saw was the shotgun. A wave of fear swept through him that made his stomach tingle and his face feel hot. Though he wanted badly to turn with the gun and shoot Calhoun dead, he knew that Gorum would hear the gun blast and kill the boy. It was a risk he couldn't take. He pushed the gun aside and found the hatchet. He stood on his knees and took a good look at Calhoun.

"Get it and get out," Calhoun said.

Francis also noticed Ben's pickaxe leaning up against the tent wall. He grabbed it, too, then stood and looked down at Indigo.

The old man removed his pipe. "The gods are with you, my son."

Francis took a deep, stuttering breath and then walked to the opening. Calhoun held the flap, then after Francis was through, he let it fall back down. The student had never felt so nervous and scared. The situation made him think about where he would be if he hadn't crossed paths with Ben Ruby. Somewhere, he figured, much farther south, maybe in Mexico, studying rock surfaces and soil samples, or maybe even at a cantina sipping tequila with a young, beautiful *señorita* on his lap. Though that scene in his mind seemed safer and a lot more comfortable, he didn't tarry long with the thought. Never in a thousand lifetimes would a man have the chance to experience what lay beneath these sands. It was more than just fame of discovery or potential wealth. Like Ben had told him, it could mean a better future for an entire civilization.

Chapter Eighteen

FRANCIS held the lantern while Ben used the pickaxe to break a hole through the deck. The aged hardwood of the deck had been preserved by the salty sand, and breaking through was no easy task. The smell of the splintered wood now mixed with the damp scent of the soil and the fragrance of a once abundant sea life. Before long, as the hole in the deck widened, a musty odor rose into the air that seemed to drown every other scent. Once Ben had a sizable opening, Francis handed him the hatchet, which he used to chop off the large splinters and smooth out the jagged edges.

The mystery of what lay inside the hole sent a wave of nervous anticipation through Ben, to the point that he wasn't sure how to handle it now that Gorum was calling the shots. What would they do if they found treasure? Should they try to take Gorum now? He had to think, and quick.

Once satisfied that he could fit through the opening, he looked up at Gorum. "It's ready."

Gorum looked down at the hole with his mouth slightly

agape and his eyes as wide as silver dollars. "You wait there."

Gorum called up to Calhoun and told him to send Redman down and for him to follow.

"What about the Indian?" Calhoun said.

"Don't worry about that old raisin," Gorum said. "Just get your ass down here."

The two men did as he said and stopped on the bottom of the second tier. Gorum had Hostetter and the boy move up, and then he looked down to Francis.

"You," Gorum said. "Up here, too."

Ben glanced at Francis with concern, then looked back at Gorum. "I can't do it without him."

"Him?" Gorum said, pointing at the student with his gun.

"He knows the ship layout. He's the only one that knows how to find the money."

Gorum appeared perplexed by what he didn't know, and therefore he resorted to the only thing he understood. He grabbed Raul by the arm and lifted him up. He held the boy's arm up for the others to grab. "Take him, now!"

Redman lifted the boy, and Raul crawled up to the edge of the second tier. Gorum looked at Calhoun with what now seemed a permanent glare. "I'm going in that hole with them. If anything happens, kill the boy."

Calhoun grabbed Raul by the arm and pulled the boy to him. He cocked his gun and pushed the barrel into Raul's cheekbone. The boy's face was ridden with fear.

Gorum reached a hand toward Hostetter. "Now, give me those lanterns."

Hostetter handed down two lanterns, then Gorum handed them to Ben and Francis. The tycoon nodded toward Ben. "All right, let's go. Nice and easy."

Ben took his lantern and lowered it through the hole. The immediate area lit up, and though there were many areas of sand and silt, Ben could see the floor. His stomach churned, and he felt a twinge of excitement mixed with frustration and fear. He lowered the lantern down farther, then bent over and stuck his head into the hole. Though looking upside down, he could see a good twenty feet in any direction. Support beams still intact had kept the deck from collapsing, although areas of pressure from the weight of the soil on top had caused cracks and separation where sand and silt had seeped through. He moved the lantern around and saw many opened doors and what appeared to be the butts of cannons partially covered by an avalanche of sand.

Satisfied it was safe, Ben leaned back up and had Francis hold his lantern, then took a deep breath and went feet-first into the hole. Once on the floor, he looked up and acknowledged it was a fairly low clearance, only as tall as his six-foot frame. He held on to the edges of the hole and bounced slightly to test the sturdiness of the floor below him. Though unlevel, it appeared solid. Satisfied, he reached up for his lantern. After Francis handed it to him, Ben stepped aside from the hole.

"All right," Ben said. "Your turn."

Francis lowered himself into the hole, and because he was a bit shorter Ben held him by the waist until his feet met the floor. Francis reached up for his lantern, and Gorum handed it to him, then the tycoon lowered himself down. Once all were inside, Ben and Francis held their lanterns as high as their heads and scanned the area. Gorum continued to gaze in awe.

"My God," Francis said. "It's nearly as I had imagined." The student balanced himself on the tilted floor and took three steps to his right, then knelt down and held the lantern above his head. He reached toward the floor near a pile of sand and brushed with his fingers in swiping strokes, which ultimately revealed a round, black object.

Ben held his lantern closer to Francis, and Gorum looked between them.

Francis looked up and grinned. "It's a cannonball." He stood with his lantern held out in front of him and pivoted the room. "This is the upper gun deck."

He continued to pivot around, looking as far as he could

see from the lanterns. "See there? Kegs of blasting powder. Absolutely fascinating."

Gorum pushed his way between them. "All right, that's enough history. Let's keep moving."

The excitement had been almost enough for Ben to forget Gorum was there, but the tycoon helped him realize that he couldn't forget. As much as he'd have liked to get caught up in the moment, Gorum was too serious a matter for them to let down their guard. "So where are we?" Ben said.

Francis shined the lantern to his right. "We've definitely hit near center."

"How can you tell?" Ben said.

"There," Francis pointed. "The base of the mainmast."

They all looked at what appeared to be a rectangular wooden structure that extended from floor to ceiling.

"You mean that box?" Ben said.

"Yes," Francis said. "It's a housing that goes clear to the keel and secures the base of the mast. I can tell by looking in each direction." He pointed to his left. "See there? Another one, which is either the mizzenmast or the foremast." Then he pointed to his right. "And there, the other one."

"How will we know which is which?"

"We split up and search for the officer's quarters."

"Bullshit," Gorum said. "We're going together."

Francis turned to the tycoon. "You're forgetting that we don't have much time. If we don't gather our wits, this entire discovery will be under water and we'll have gained nothing."

Gorum contemplated Francis's statement, then laughed and punched him in the stomach. Francis gasped and clutched his abdomen, then buckled to the floor.

Gorum leaned over and grabbed him by the back of the collar and pushed the gun barrel down on his jaw. "And you're forgetting, college boy, who's in charge here. Now, you better head us in the direction of that loot or I'll leave your brain-splattered remains behind and go find it myself."

It was all Ben could do to keep from pouncing on Gorum, and he felt confident enough to do it, but Gorum still had the advantage with Calhoun. It still wasn't the time, so they had to keep working under his thumb.

Gorum picked Francis up by the collar, and the student struggled to regain his composure.

Clutching his stomach with one hand, Francis held the lantern up with the other and gazed at each end of the ship. He looked back to the southwest and stared down as far as the light could travel. "If the ship was anchored, then it was likely pointed north or northeast. Being that the captain's cabin and officer's quarters are at the stern, I say we head that way."

Francis pointed to the south and Gorum nudged him with his gun. "Then get moving."

Francis led the way, and he and Ben held out their lanterns while Gorum followed close behind. Though the atmosphere felt damp and cavernous, there was no echo. Nothing but deadening sounds, which Ben presumed were muffled by the soil that surrounded the ship.

As they kept walking, Ben tried to imagine what had gone on here while the ship was sinking. He looked at the many cannons that lined the walls, the portholes and the sand that flowed through them onto the deck floor. If the story that Indigo told was true, the battle would have been hand-to-hand and not with cannons. But he saw no human remains to fulfill the legend. At least not yet.

They walked another twenty feet and came to a series of steps, one set going up, the other going down. The steps going up were almost entirely covered by sediment that had drifted in from above the deck. The steps going down, however, save the dust, were nearly clear to the lower level.

Francis held the lantern over the stairway and peered down. "Looks like another gun deck. This was definitely a war vessel."

Ben wondered how much they should reveal to Gorum

about the locations of the treasures. He wasn't sure how much the tycoon knew about Spanish naval history. Probably no more than Ben originally had, drawn mostly from wild children's tales of pirates and shipwrecks. He thought about luring him to the captain's quarters, where there might only be a small chest filled with various valuables. Still a fortune, it might appease him to the point of leaving the rest behind to find later. In most circumstances that would likely work just fine, if they lured him back out and overpowered him. But they didn't have time for that. They had to find the treasure now and get it out and take their chances with Gorum later.

Ben stepped down with Francis, and they shined their lanterns in each direction. Like Francis had explained, it was another gun deck, similar to the one above only with larger cannons and portholes. There was another stairway going down, but Francis turned south again and eventually led them to another set of stairs. Though one stairway went down like the others, perpendicular to the ship, the one going up was parallel, and it led to a door.

Ben held his lantern closer. "Where does that go?"

Francis added his lantern to the area. "That is the officer's quarters. The captain's cabin will be above it." He smiled. "We're at the stern."

Gorum shoved his gun into Ben's back. "All right, quit fooling around. Where's the loot?"

Ben nodded downward toward the stairway going down. "It's in the stores."

Francis seemed alarmed that Ben had revealed that information, but after Ben nodded to him, the student didn't tarry long with the thought, and he led them all down the stairway.

When they reached the bottom, Francis looked in both directions, then walked back to the south. Much different from the other levels, this one was nothing but stores and supplies—barrels, crates, bundles of goods, all covered in thick layers of dust. Francis walked over to one of the barrels and brushed his hand across the top, revealing a large wooden plug. He gripped the plug firmly and removed it, then held the lantern over the hole. A sweet perfume penetrated the air, and Francis leaned over and sniffed inside the barrel. He looked up and grinned. "It's rum."

He put the plug back in the barrel, then continued to walk north, pointing at various items as he walked. "Those bales are likely tobacco. The crates could be all sorts of things. Blankets, clothing, cooking utensils, or even fine goods from the Orient. Of course it's hard to tell without opening them."

"Let's not waste our time with that shit," Gorum said.

"The chests of money and valuables will be in either one of two places. Maybe both." Francis pointed southward. "Down there."

They kept walking, shining their lanterns over objects to their right and to their left as they walked. After about ten feet they came to an abrupt halt and Francis took two quick steps backward, nearly dropping his lantern. Ben held his lantern higher, and there before them were the dusty skeletal remains of a man still in his clothing: buckled shoes on his feet, torn leggings, a long, velvet tunic with brass buttons, and near his side the widest brim on a hat Ben had ever seen, with a flat crown and a two-foot plume all matted and dusty. The most interesting thing, he thought, was the man's rusty sword, which was still clutched in his hand and draped over a wooden chest.

Ben squatted down closer and noticed that the man's skull revealed a long gash. "Looks like this man was clubbed with something. Indians probably ganged up on him."

"Yeah," Francis said, holding his lantern higher. "And it looks like he was trying to protect something. Something that the Cahuilla cared nothing about."

Gorum pushed his way between the men. "Move out of the way!"

The tycoon knelt down and with one fell swoop brushed the Spaniard's remains onto the floor and then wiped the dust off the latch. He tugged hard on the rusty lock and it wouldn't budge. "Dammit!" Gorum grimaced, then leaned back and put his gun point-blank against the lock and fired. The loud blast quickly deadened throughout the deck and the lock split into two pieces. Gorum knocked it away, and like an impatient kid at Christmastime he opened the lid.

Ben and Francis both held their lanterns over the chest, and Gorum dug his hands into a tray of jewels. "Sweet Jesus," he said, while he lifted up a string of pearls with his gun barrel and a gold-shrouded emerald with his free hand. He dropped the jewels and pushed them aside and discovered they were all in trays. He lifted the trays out of the chest, and the sight below created a big lump in Ben's throat. Cloth bags, the size of flour sacks, and all tied with ropes. Gorum lifted one and it jingled. The tycoon's breath stuttered as he untied one of the ropes and poured out scores of silver coins.

"God Almighty," Gorum said, looking all around him and then back at the sacks of coins. He counted them with his forefinger. "There has to be more here. This is downright obscene! Hell, I'll do more than own the valley now. There's enough loot here to buy the presidency!" The tycoon swished his hands back and forth into the pile of spilled coins and laughed giddily.

Anger boiled up inside Ben as he listened to Gorum revel in the results of the hard work of others. The tycoon was used to that, he supposed. All the mines, the ranch, the irrigation projects, might legally be owned by Gorum, but none of the sweat and blood that built it all was his own.

Just as Ben was trying to rid his head of all the negative thoughts, he felt a slight vibration under his feet. Gorum raised up quickly and pointed his gun toward the men.

"What was that?" he asked.

"I'm not sure," Ben said, gazing around. "I felt it, too."

Before another word was said, the ship began to tremble. The men took wide stances to brace themselves, and sand began to fall from the cracks above them.

Francis grabbed Ben's arm. "It's an earthquake! We have to get out of here!"

The men ran toward the stairs with Francis in the lead and Gorum at the tail. They dodged up the stairway, trying to keep their balance in the shaking ship while sand fell down on them like rain. They ran down the second level toward the north end of the ship and to another stairway and had barely made it to the top level when the floor cracked and separated and Gorum's right leg fell through the opening all the way to his hip. He yelled as he fell, his gun thrown from his hand as he tried to brace himself. Ben and Francis stopped and looked back. Gorum braced himself with both arms as the ship still shook and steady streams of sand fell down on him as if he were in the bottom of an hourglass.

Ben yelled over the sound of the rumbling. "I've got to help him."

Just as Ben turned back, the shaking and groaning of the earth ceased. He knelt down in front of Gorum and inspected the area around his trapped leg. His trouser leg was torn and there was blood.

"Get me out of here, Ruby," Gorum said, grimacing and breathing heavily. "Half of everything is yours. You have my word. Just get me out of here."

Ben studied Gorum's face a moment, then looked over at his gun lying on a pile of sand.

Gorum looked at the gun, too, then back up at Ben. "You kill me and I can't promise you what Calhoun will do. But you help me out of here and I assure you I'll call him off."

Ben picked up the gun and slid it underneath his belt, then turned to Francis. "Help me lift him up."

Ben grabbed one of Gorum's arms and Francis grabbed the other. They tried to lift, but Gorum's leg was wedged tightly among the broken floorboards.

The tycoon cried in agony as they pulled upward. "Stop! Stop!"

Both men let Gorum's arms down and Ben inspected the area again.

"We're going to have to cut him out," Ben said. He looked north and could see the daylight through the opening of their hole. "Go get the hatchet."

Francis looked fearfully down at the opening. "What do I tell Calhoun?"

"Tell him I'm hurt," Gorum said. "Because of the earthquake he will believe you. Tell him and I'll call him off the boy."

Ben nodded his agreement to Francis, and the student turned and walked toward the opening.

CONVINCING CALHOUN THAT GORUM NEEDED HELP WAS not as difficult as Ben had thought it would be. Judging from the look in the gunman's eyes, the earthquake had been an eye-opening experience. Though equally cautious, for the moment everyone was cooperative.

Cutting Gorum out of the hole in the floor was no easy task, and neither was getting him through the opening and up the rope to the desert flat. Redman climbed the rope first, then hoisted everyone out. The tycoon's thigh was cut badly by the splinters of the broken floor, and blood dripped all the way down to his boot. They laid him out on the ground, and Francis inspected the wound while Calhoun stood over him and Ben helped the others out of the pit. Eventually they all crowded around Gorum, and Ben knelt down beside him.

"I need some water," Francis said. "And there's a first aid kit in the tent. I'll go get it."

Calhoun quickly cocked his pistol and pointed it toward Francis. "No." The gunman reached out his other hand to Ben. "Gorum's gun—give it to me."

Gorum rose up to his elbows and looked at his gunman in deliberation, then looked at Ben but said nothing.

Ben looked sternly at Gorum. "Remember what you said?"

Gorum sat up and reached a hand to Ben. "Shut up and give me the gun."

Ben sucked in a deep breath and retrieved the gun. After he handed it to Gorum, the tycoon pointed the gun back at him. "Everyone back away. Get out in front where I can see you." Then he looked at Francis. "Except you. You stay right here."

All of them followed Gorum's orders and stood in front of him while he contemplated the next move. He looked up at Calhoun. "Go to the tent and get that first-aid kit. I'll hold them here until you get back."

Calhoun nodded and backed away, then turned and jogged toward the tent.

Gorum looked up at Ben and sneered. "Someday you'll learn, Ruby, that there's only one way to stay on top in this world. I've seen men try other ways and they end up regretting their defeat. My motto is to be true only unto thyself, because no one else will be."

Ben wondered why he felt no contempt for Gorum, because truthfully all he felt was pity. "You should read some of those books in your office, Gorum."

"Don't patronize me, Ruby."

"Especially one," Hostetter said. All eyes looked toward him, but the engineer looked only at Gorum with a confident air. "The poet, Shelley. 'Rulers, who neither see, nor feel, nor know, but leech, like to their fainting country cling, till they drop, blind in blood, without a blow.'"

The two men stared at each other until a sudden gun blast startled them to attention.

With the exception of Gorum, they all rose to their feet. Indigo stood outside the tent with the smoking shotgun and Calhoun dead on the ground in front of him. Gorum found the strength to stand, hopped on one leg, and looked on with disbelief.

Raul quickly ran to his grandfather, and Gorum pointed his gun toward the running youngster. Ben turned swiftly to Gorum and kicked the gun from his hand. Gorum lost his balance and fell against Hostetter, and both men dropped to the ground. Redman picked up the gun, and when he turned toward them, Gorum had rolled back with Hostetter in front of him and a knife to the engineer's throat.

"Easy does it," Ben said.

The tycoon pulled Hostetter's head back by the hair. "All right, on your feet."

The two men stood slowly, and Gorum hopped on his good leg to gain his balance. He nodded toward Ben. "Get my horse."

"Come on now," Ben said. "We can work this out."

Gorum pressed the knife harder. "No!"

Hostetter's face was red with fear and his voice gurgled. "Do as he says."

Ben hesitated only for a moment, then walked to the wagon wheels and untied the horse. Though bridled, the animal was still unsaddled. Ben led the horse to Gorum, and Gorum nudged Hostetter.

"Take the reins," Gorum said. "Everyone back away. We're going to get up on that horse. Any sudden moves and ol' Jeb gets a knife in the heart. Get it?"

Hostetter slowly took the reins and Gorum nodded toward Redman. "Drop the gun."

Redman looked at Ben.

Ben nodded. "Do it."

The kid put the gun on the ground and kicked it away.

Gorum stood back and forced Hostetter to get on the horse. After he had mounted, Gorum stood with both hands up, one reaching toward Hostetter and the other firmly gripping the knife. "Now you help me up, and if you try anything stupid I swing this knife into your back."

Hostetter looked at the knife, then reached a hand out. Gorum pulled himself onto the horse and positioned himself behind Hostetter, quickly putting his arm around him and pointing the knife upward to his chin. The tycoon put his other arm around Hostetter's stomach and wasted no time spurring the horse to a full gallop.

As they rode north into the playa, Redman ran for the gun. Before he could pull it up to aim, Ben grabbed his forearm.

"Don't. It's too risky," Ben said. "Come on, let's get our horses and go after them. The way Gorum is bleeding, I have a feeling he won't last too long."

Francis came forward. "I'll go with you."

"No," Ben said. "Go make sure Indigo and the boy are all right. Help get the tent torn down and packed up and move them back to the mountain where it's safe."

Francis nodded. "What about the ship?"

Ben looked over at their hole in the ground and took a deep breath. "God willing, we'll be back."

GORUM KEPT SPURRING THE HORSE, AND HOSTETTER held tight to the horse's mane. They rode about a mile before the tycoon's strength started to fade. The horse slowed to a lope and Gorum dug his chin into Hostetter's back.

"You're losing a lot of blood, L.J.," Hostetter said. "Let's turn back."

Gorum pulled his arm tighter around Hostetter's stomach and his fist firmer against his chest, reminding him he still had the knife. "Keep riding."

They had ridden another quarter of a mile when Hostetter noticed the abandoned wagon in the middle of the playa. He steered the horse toward it, and by the time they neared the wagon, Gorum's chin had drooped below Hostetter's shoulder and he could no longer hold the knife firmly.

Hostetter pulled back on the horse's mane and brought it to a halt. He reached down and took the knife from Gorum's hand.

"What are you doing?" The tycoon slurred his words.

Hostetter dismounted and Gorum fell forward. Hostetter pulled him off the horse, and it was all he could do to hold him under the arms and drag him to the shade of the wagon.

"You lay right here," Hostetter said. "I'm going to get you the help you need."

The engineer stood, then looked to his right and saw a pool of water creeping toward him and over the cracks on the desert floor. When he looked up he could see the pool widening to the north all across the playa. He quickly grabbed the reins of the horse and pulled the animal to the back of the wagon. He looked over the crates in the wagon box, and there it was, dangling down over the edge just like they'd left it.

He mounted the horse, then reached into the pocket of the trousers and retrieved the magnifying glass. The sun to his back, he positioned the magnifying glass until it captured the perfect angle, and then he turned the lens until it made a bright spot on the ground. He guided the spot until it reached the end of the two-foot fuse, held it steady, and in seconds, like magic, the fuse ignited and sparks flared from the tip.

BEN AND REDMAN HAD RIDDEN THEIR HORSES A HARD mile when they saw Hostetter on the horse alone, galloping toward them in front of a trail of dust. A sudden explosion far behind him forced them to pull back on the reins and bring their horses to a rearing halt. Other powerful explosions immediately followed, and balls of clouds and orange flames mushroomed above the playa.

Ben and Redman looked on in puzzlement as Hostetter rode up to them. Then it suddenly hit Ben. "The dynamite."

Hostetter stopped next to them and leaned forward out of breath. Ben was speechless. He knew the man was clever, but this beat all he'd ever seen.

Hostetter patted the horse's neck, then looked up at Ben and grinned. "Well, Gorum got his dynamite back. Payment in full."

Ben shook his head. "I don't believe it."

Hostetter looked back at the black and gray smoke that rose into the dull blue sky. "Isn't that evidence enough?"

"Yes, I'd say it is," Ben said. "Now our worries are over."

Hostetter's face quickly sobered. "No, there's still one left. The flood. It's reached the flat."

Ben's mouth fell slightly agape and he looked sharply to the north. "Then we have to get moving."

Chapter Nineteen

ᵀᵀ

HOSTETTER worked steadily as he helped pack the folded tent and all the gear onto Francis's modern travois. The only gear he didn't pack was all the lanterns and the three shovels that Redman, Francis, and Ben used to repair and build up the levee, which had partially collapsed during the earthquake.

Though there was no wagon now, there were four extra horses to look after. Besides Gorum's and Calhoun's, there were the two draft horses. Hostetter took Gorum's, a sorrel with a white blaze, and Indigo and Raul each rode a burro. Packed down with the gear, they all mounted, ready to ride.

The three men came to see them off, and Hostetter offered a military-style salute. "Be safe down there."

"We will," Ben said, returning the salute. "See you soon."

BEN KNEW THE FLOODWATERS WERE ONLY HOURS AWAY. Though Hostetter originally had said the levee would hold them for a couple of days, he reduced that to one day, considering the rate at which the water had already reached the flat.

A new spiritual feeling swept through Ben, which caused him to retrieve the tin box and find the medicine bag. He took a leather chord and made a necklace of the bag, pulled it over his head and tucked it underneath his shirt. Before closing the box, he took special notice of Yudexy's blue handkerchief, folded neatly and monogrammed with his name. He pulled it out and removed his old, dirty neckerchief and dropped it to the ground, then tied Yudexy's around his neck. He couldn't imagine anything more spiritual to take along with him.

They all crawled down the rope and into the hole. The earthquake had caused only moderate damage to the ship, but an avalanche of sand and silt had formed below the hole. Francis warned them to watch every step carefully. They went first to the storage level, to the chest where they had found the jewelry and silver. It was all the three of them could do to drag the chest down the deck and up the stairs and at the same time watch their footing and carry a lantern. After reaching the next deck, they decided to have Francis lead the way with the lantern and warn them of loose planks, and Ben and Redman carried the chest. They made periodic stops to catch their breath and rebuild their strength, then got the chest as far as the top opening.

They decided there was no way to get the heavy chest through the hole, so they had Redman crawl up into the lower tier and hand them buckets. They filled the buckets full of jewelry and handed them back to Redman, who set them on the bottom of the next tier. They removed the bags of silver individually, then handed them one by one up to Redman. Once everything was through, Redman climbed the rope to the top to hoist everything out. When he reached the top he called down to Ben.

"Get up here, quick!"

"What is it?" Ben said.

"The floodwaters!"

Ben grabbed the rope and pulled with his arms as he walked the side of the pit up to the top. Redman sat on the levee and reached for Ben's hand and pulled him next to him. The water made slow ripples and pooled around the wagon wheels. The three horses were a bit spooked by it, and they shifted and whickered.

"Hostetter was right," Ben said. "It is coming fast."

"What are we going to do?" Redman said.

"Take your boots and socks off and roll up your trousers. That way your feet won't get too bogged down. There are six bags of silver. That's two for each horse. I'll put a bag in a bucket and you hoist it up. After that you can hoist up the buckets of jewelry and fill our saddlebags."

"What do we do with the stuff in the saddlebags?"

Ben grinned and put a hand on Redman's shoulder. "Don't worry about it, kid. We can buy more of that crap later."

Redman laughed, then did as Ben said and took off his boots.

Ben climbed back down in the pit to the bottom tier and helped Francis attach the buckets loaded down with the bags of silver. Redman pulled them up two at a time, and after loading the last two buckets of jewelry, Ben and Francis stood at the bottom of the pit and watched them go up.

"You think there's more in there?" Ben said.

"It's hard to tell," Francis said. "War vessels were a part of the treasure fleets, too. They were well equipped with guns to protect their cargos. The chest we found likely belonged to the man that we found draped over it. There were often passengers on the ships besides the officers and crew. Businessmen. They would carry money and other valuables to purchase goods in other countries, or that may have been payment from some Oriental noble for his worldly commodities."

Ben nodded. "What we already found—how much do you think it's worth?"

"You're already rich, if that's what you're asking. There's at least fifty thousand in silver alone. That jewelry, another hundred thousand, maybe more."

Ben grinned shyly. "That is a lot of money."

"It will set you for the rest of your life, Ben."

"You, too, Francis. And Redman up there. Hostetter. Indigo. The boy. Truthfully, this is Yuma's gold. We will all share it."

"You're a generous man, Ben Ruby."

"What are you going to do with your share?"

Francis shook his head. "Haven't given it much thought, really. But the first thing that comes to my mind is education."

"You want to get more education?"

"No, I want to give it. This is proof that Indian legends are worth listening to. It's enough that I imagine I could convince the university to start a center for Indian studies."

Ben grinned and nodded. "That's perfect."

There were a few seconds of silence while Ben looked up out of the hole and toward the bright desert sky.

"The water will be over our levee in just a few hours," he said. "How about we have one more look around the ship?"

Francis took a deep breath and raised his eyebrows. "Our horses are already loaded down with more than they can carry, and not to forget wading in water. What would we do with it if we found it?"

Ben shrugged. "Pray for another miracle."

REGARDLESS OF THE DANGERS, WHEN BEN INFORMED Redman they were going back into the ship he responded with a broad smile and rushed to find his boots. He skipped putting on his socks, pulled the boots on over his pant cuffs, and slid down the rope before Ben even had the lanterns ready.

Ben also handed Redman a shovel. "Here, we might need this."

All three men carried lanterns, and they walked down the first stairway to the third level and gazed among the stores of barrels and crates. Though the crates were likely filled with some sort of antique valuable, Francis did not have to explain why their limited time would be better spent searching for wooden chests. The men walked one in front of the other, Francis in the lead, Redman at the tail, scanning the area with their lanterns. The student stopped when he found another human skeleton, this one without clothing save a dusty breechcloth around its groin.

Francis knelt down in front of the remains and held up his lantern. Ben and Redman held up their lanterns and looked over his shoulder.

"Wonder what that fella was up to," Redman said.

"I think we have one of Indigo's ancestors here," Francis said.

It was a sobering sight to Ben, thinking about the legend of the great battle, and though the Cahuilla had claimed victory, there were still casualties. However, a deeper, more personal thought swept through him as he thought of Indigo and that the human whose remains lay before him was a member of Indigo's family.

Francis stood back up and the men continued walking down the third deck, searching the area, only to find nothing but the typical stores.

Francis stopped walking and took a deep breath. "Maybe we should split up. That way we can cover more area in less time."

"No, we should stay together," Ben said. "There may be a fortune in treasure in here, but it can also be a trap."

"All right," Francis said. "Then we need to check the most logical places first."

"Tell us where to go first, partner," Ben said.

The student led them to the far south end of the boat, near the officer's quarters, and to where a stairway led up to the captain's cabin. Damage from the earthquake, and maybe others from the past, had created openings in the upper deck that had allowed sand to flow through and create barriers to the entrance. Redman used the shovel to clear the sand away from the door. Once it was fairly clear, Ben tried to open the door, but it wouldn't budge.

"The hell with this," Ben said, taking the shovel from Redman. "Stand back."

Redman and Francis stayed clear of Ben as he used forceful punches with the shovel to break through the door. The blade of the shovel ripped into the wood like a dull axe, breaking more than cutting. The harder Ben hit the door, the more damage he did, and the quicker the shovel broke through. He held it like a battering ram, clenched his teeth, and made persistent jabs until the long boards of the door broke in two and hinged forward at the crosspiece.

Ben knocked them away, then stepped back, letting Francis peek through with the lantern.

"A lot of sand in there," Francis said. He backed away and let Ben look into the room.

Ben held the lantern to the side of his face. There was indeed a lot of sand on the floor, but as he looked up he could see the walls and the appearance of furniture. Not wanting to waste another second, Ben set the lantern down on the other side of the hole in the door and crawled through. His hands felt nothing but damp, gritty sand, but it offered a soft landing for his elbows and knees as he crawled on into the room. He stood and raised the lantern to peer around as Francis and Redman followed him inside.

The three lanterns woke the roomy quarters after nearly three hundred years of complete darkness. Though Redman held his up high, Ben and Francis both secured their lanterns in the sand piles. Far from luxurious, the captain's cabin had still offered the nicest accommodations on the ship. Even the aftermath of battle and hundreds of years of creeping sand and dust couldn't hide the omnipotence bestowed on the occupant of the room. The bed had a mattress, covered in linens, which was a far cry more than the wooden bunks afforded the crew. A wooden desk that appeared permanently attached to the wall bore the filthy remnants of a quill and an inkwell that lay on its side.

"Well, I don't see the captain anywhere," Ben said.

Francis gazed around the room. "If there was a battle going on, he would have been out on the deck with his men."

Ben knelt down and peered under the desk. Thinking he saw something there, he dug into the sand and pushed it away in large clumps, finding what looked like a box. Though much smaller than the other chest they had found, it was still a good foot in length, and half that in height and breadth. He brushed off the sand enough to get a better look, and when he noticed the wood grain and tarnished brass on the corners, he tried to pull the box toward him. Whatever was inside had significant weight and it required a hardy effort to pull the box into the opening.

"What do you have there?" Francis asked, looking over his shoulder.

Ben tried to open the rusty latch, but it wouldn't budge. He turned to Redman. "I need your gun."

Redman handed Ben his gun. Ben rose to his feet, then took a step back and aimed the gun at the latch. The deafening shot of the .45 sent splinters flying, and the lid to the chest flew open. Gun smoke clouded the room, and Ben waved it away as he knelt over the open chest. It was filled with small leather bags the size of tobacco sacks, and all were tied closed with leather strings. Ben picked one of them up. It was heavy and it jingled.

Excitement brewed inside of him as he pulled the leather string and watched several gold coins fall out over the other bags. "Dear God, it's gold!"

He vigorously opened the other bags and they all had the same contents, which he poured into a pile inside the chest.

Francis put both of his hands on Ben's shoulders and shook him excitedly. "There it is, Ben! You found it! You found the gold!"

Ben scooped up a pile of the coins with both hands, then let them fall and clank together into a pile. "There is a lot of money here."

"It was the captain's purse," Francis said. "But now it's yours! All yours!"

Ben turned and nodded at both men. "It's ours, boys. We all earned it."

They all laughed and embraced, then Ben grabbed the others by the arms and looked at them earnestly. "Let's get this out of here, then let's keep looking around. There may be more."

Francis got a look of concern on his face. "Don't be greedy, Ben. With what's on our horses now and that gold, we have more than enough to last a lifetime. Let's get out of here while we can."

"I understand your concern, but it's not greed, Francis. I feel like the first half of my life was nothing but a blue funk. I want to do more than just provide for me. If there's a bigger fortune in this ship, I could do more for Indigo's people. In a way, they seized it three hundred years ago. I'm just retrieving it for them. And now Gorum is gone. The valley will be flooded. Much will need to be done to give people of the valley new hope. If there is more here, it can give them that hope."

The student shook his head. "That's all very noble. But what if it costs you your life? Or ours?"

"I'm not Gorum. I'm not telling you to do anything. And I don't want you to feel pressured to do it. If you're done, then go. Take a third of this gold and head out while it's safe. But I'm staying here and looking for more. In just a few hours there will be no more chances to look. So I'm looking now."

Francis bit his lip and nodded. "There's just no arguing

with you, Ben Ruby. All right. But I still think you're forgetting about one thing."

"What?"

"Our horses are packed down now the way it is. If we find anything else, how are we going to get it out of here?"

Ben shrugged. "I have no idea. But we've come this far on blind faith. Let's find it first, then—I'm sure we'll think of something."

FRANCIS WENT ON TO LOOK AROUND THE SHIP WHILE Redman helped Ben carry the small chest back to the opening. The chest had a brass handle on each end that eased the lifting and allowed each man to hold a handle with one hand and carry a lantern in the other. Ben led the way down the slanted floor, but as they approached the stairway on the second deck, he stopped abruptly when he heard a strange sound. He looked all around him and heard it again, then raised the lantern upward and looked toward the tip of the stairs. A steady stream of water started to flow down toward them. He quickly looked back toward Redman. "The water is over our levee! We have to hurry!"

The two men moved up the stairs as fast as they could, and if it wasn't hard enough to walk on a slanted, earthquake-damaged floor, shuffling through the pooling water on the first deck was more of an undertaking than Ben had expected. Trying to move faster, he got ahead of Redman, causing the kid to stumble and eventually fall. The chest made a loud splash into the flowing stream, splattering both men with water and mud. Worried that Redman had fallen through the floor, Ben went quickly to his aid.

"You all right?" Ben said.

Redman breathed hard as he got back to his feet. "Yeah, I'm fine."

Ben studied the flowing water and peered down to the opening, where he could see it come in at a steady flow, bringing muddy sand with it. He put a hand on Redman's shoulder. "Take a second and catch your breath."

Redman shook his head. "No, I'm fine. We have to keep going."

They each grabbed a handle on the chest and got moving again, reaching the entry hole and pushing the chest through the rushing water and onto the deck above. Ben was the first to crawl up through the hole, the water drenching him as he pushed himself through. He climbed up the slippery, muddy grade to the next tier and gazed upward to ground level. The floodwaters had broken through the levee in two places. He contemplated climbing the rope and trying to fix them, but he knew the current would be forceful and they would be wasting precious time.

He and Redman struggled on the muddy edges of the pit to get the box on the ledge of the lowest tier. Once there, the breathless men rolled to their backs.

Ben turned to Redman. "So how does it feel to be rich?"

Redman shrugged. "It feels good. But I will say this; it feels better to be away from Gorum."

Ben nodded. "I guess we both got out of prison."

Redman broke a short laugh. "Yeah, I guess you're right."

"So what are you going to do with your money?"

Redman thought for a few seconds. "Keep doing what I've been doing."

"Digging in the sand?"

"You might say that. I want to help you."

Ben grinned, then reached his muddy hand toward Redman, and the two men gave each other a firm handshake.

"It will be a pleasure working with you," Ben said.

Redman gazed upward at the flowing water. "But how are we going to get all this out of here?"

"I don't know," Ben said. "We can't worry about that anymore. We have to go get Francis."

Redman laughed. "I guess this is one time where it would pay good to swim like a fish!"

Ben had been able to laugh while trying to keep his balance, when suddenly he looked at Redman with wide eyes and grabbed him by the shoulders. "That's it!"

"What?"

"I don't have time to explain. Let's get Francis and get out of here!"

Chapter Twenty

꩜

REDMAN followed Ben back down into the hole and found their lanterns. One of them had tipped over and been forced by the flowing water to the stairway, causing the glass globe to shatter. The two men stayed close together, and guided by a single lantern they treaded the slippery deck until they reached the next stairway. The water now flowed steadily down the stairs of the top deck and across the floor of the second. When they reached the third deck, Ben cried out for Francis.

A response came from another level below. "Down here!"

They went down to the bottom deck and looked in each direction. Ben saw the light of Francis's lantern at the south end. They walked quickly down the slanted slope, and as they drew near, Francis lifted his lantern to see them.

Francis looked closely at them and squinted. "What's that mud on your face?"

Still somewhat out of breath, Ben looked at him solemnly. "The floodwater is over our levee. It's in the ship."

Francis looked as though he'd seen a ghost. "We have to hurry then," he said. "I think there may be more."

Ben stopped him from turning. "No, you were right. We have enough. Come on, let's get out of here while we can."

Francis held up a finger. "Let me show you something first."

They followed the student to stairs at the very end of the deck. He walked behind the stairs and pointed toward the floor.

Ben held the light over the area and saw nothing but empty space. "There's nothing there."

"No," Francis said. "Look closer." He bent down and pointed at an area where he'd brushed away the dust. "See the drag marks? Something very heavy was dragged across the floor to carve these grooves. As you can see, something the same width as a chest." He pivoted and pointed behind him. "And here, the same thing. And there. And there. At least four chests were moved from this point."

Ben was confused at the student's logic. "But that could have been a crate, or something else."

"Maybe," Francis said. "But I thought of something else." He raised his lantern and walked back north down the sloping deck, and Ben and Redman followed him. Francis kept looking down at the floor, and eventually he stopped and looked all around him.

"There," Francis said. "They dragged them here."

Ben held the lantern above the marks on the floor and saw where they turned into large piles of rocks.

"Ballasts," Francis said.

Both Ben and Francis held their lanterns over the rocks. Redman stuck his head over their shoulders. "Ballasts?"

Ben nodded. "I remember now. You said these rocks were added to the bottoms of the ship for stability."

"Right," Francis said. "The crews on treasure fleets were trained to protect their treasures first and foremost. If they thought the treasure was ever in danger, they hid it.

Sometimes they even removed the treasure from the ships and buried it until there was a safe time for retrieval. A time of battle was one of those moments when the captain ordered his men to protect the treasure."

Ben nodded at Francis, then grinned. "I know what you're thinking."

Ben and Francis quickly set the lanterns on the floor and crawled up on the pile of rocks. They frantically picked up rocks bigger than their hands, some bigger than their heads, and tossed them aside. The adrenaline kept Ben from noticing how the sharp edges of the rocks cut through the top layers of skin on his fingers and palms, and he tossed them as fast as he could lift them.

In a matter of seconds Francis was the first to speak. "Oh, Mary—dear mother of God."

Ben and Redman turned quickly.

"What is it?" Ben said.

Francis seemed to be speechless as he kept tossing rocks aside, then with the palm of his hand wiped the dust off the top of a large wooden chest.

Ben and Redman helped with the rest of the rocks, and they quickly revealed more of the chest, and as they wiped away the dust, they could see that it was decorated with curved steel plating. It was as large as the chest they'd found full of silver and jewelry. They cleared a way to the latch and found a rusty lock dangling on the clasp.

Redman quickly pulled his revolver, but Francis put a hand on the kid's wrist above the gun.

"Wait!" Francis said. "Let's keep digging."

Redman put his gun back in the holster while Francis jumped to the side and started removing more rocks and revealed yet another chest. The men laughed like children as they kept clearing rocks, suddenly revealing a third chest equal in size to the others. They jumped enthusiastically across the walkway to the other rock pile, where they uncovered a fourth, then a fifth, and ultimately a sixth chest.

They worked feverishly clearing around the top of each chest to allow the lids to open, and discovered they all were guarded with locks.

Redman pulled his gun again and popped out the cylinder. There were five bullets and one empty chamber. He took another bullet from his belt and put it in the empty chamber, then snapped the cylinder shut. "Stand back," he said.

Ben and Francis crawled down from the rock piles and stood clear while Redman walked in a half circle, stopping at each chest and shooting the lock. After the sixth lock, the kid spun the gun in a circle around his trigger finger, then smoothly shoved it back into the holster. He looked at the men and smiled.

Ben took a deep breath. "I'm almost afraid to look."

They climbed up the rocks to the chest closest to them. Redman held up a lantern as Ben removed the broken lock.

Ben glanced at Francis. "You ready?"

Francis nodded. "Do it."

Ben lifted the lid and Redman looked over his shoulder holding the lantern higher. The glare of the contents was almost blinding. Never in his life could Ben have imagined such a sight. His mouth fell agape as he reached forward and ran his hand over the porous metallic surfaces.

"I don't believe it," Francis said. "It's gold bullion."

Ben had only seen pictures of bullion, both in silver and gold, and they referenced perfectly shaped, smooth, tapered bars. These, however, though clearly the real thing, were a much cruder shape, some almost oval, and none truly identical. He picked one up and held it in his hand. Heavy like lead, but shiny like gold.

Francis and Redman each grabbed one, too. Francis caressed his with both hands, like petting a kitten. Redman bounced his hand up and down demonstrating the impressive weight.

Ben put his bar back into the chest, then scooted fervently

to the next chest, tore off the broken lock, and flipped up the lid. Exactly the same. Redman set down the lantern and joined Francis in opening the other chests. In seconds they had the lids on all six chests standing tall. They stepped down into the walkway, and Redman and Francis held up their lanterns, revealing six identical chests, sitting randomly in a bed of jagged rocks. The reflection off the gold bars was spellbinding, and all the three men could do was gaze in awe.

"Do you realize what we are looking at?" Francis said.

"I know what it is," Ben said. "But the thought of anything outside of that overwhelms me."

At that moment Francis looked down at his feet and saw the water pooling around them. "Yeah and here comes the misery of it all."

Redman held his lantern up and got a better look at the flow of water. "What do we do?"

"There's nothing we can do," Francis said. "Maybe put a bar in each pocket, but that's about it."

"There's got to be a way," Ben said.

"No, Ben, there's not. We can't just wheel this stuff out of here as if it were a gold mine."

Ben put his hands on his hips and walked farther up the walkway. He grabbed a lantern and shined it toward the stairway. He turned back toward them. "I've got an idea."

Francis shook his head. "No, Ben, there's no way. It would take hours for us to unload these chests and get it all to the top. Then, suppose we do get it up to the top deck. How do we get it out of the hole? There's no time."

"We can move it all," Ben said.

Francis could only stare in confusion. "You mean carry them? There's at least a ton of bullion here!"

Ben grinned. "Help move the rocks away from the chests." He pointed to the south. "Pile them back there and keep the aisle free."

Ben turned to Redman. "Leave Francis your lantern, we'll use mine. Now, come with me!"

Francis looked speechless as Redman handed him his lantern, then walked swiftly with Ben up the walkway, through the rushing water, and climbed the stairs. They returned in less than five minutes, each carrying a wooden crate. They set the crates down, then knelt to help Francis move the remaining rocks.

Francis raised his eyebrows. "You think you're going to carry all of that bullion up in crates?"

"I don't think," Ben said. "I know. It will be a tedious process, yes, but it will work if we're patient."

"Tedious? Patient? Ben, don't you see this water running in here? We don't have time for tedious and patient! There's another thing that you don't understand. It's not just the water inside the ship that we have to worry about. The flood-water on the playa will be soaking into the soil. The weight of the soil on top of the ship will increase tenfold. There will be subsidence. If we don't get out of here soon, the entire ship could collapse down on top of us. We could all be trapped. We could all drown."

Ben looked at the student, an austere feeling inside him. "I understand your fears. But I don't want to look back on all this and wonder. I'm not speaking for you, but I'd rather die here than have to live with that regret."

Francis took a deep breath, then looked down at the running water in thought.

"Just listen a moment," Ben said. "Here's how it will work. I will go find two more crates and bring them here. We transfer just one layer of the bullion from the chest to the crate. They are easy enough to hold and strong enough to withstand the weight of one layer. It will still be heavy, yes, but we can carry it. You carry the crate to the steps and set it on the next deck. The kid will be on the third deck and he will pick up your crate and take it to the top of the stairs on the second deck. I will be there and take the crate to the top of the stairs on the first deck. I will take the bullion out of the crate and stack it near the opening, then bring the empty crate back to the stairway. Redman will bring the crate back to you, only to find the next crate filled with another layer of bullion."

Francis nodded. "All right. But there's still a safety factor here. We are in a ship filling full of water. Anything can happen at any given moment. Are you prepared for that?"

"There's no way to prepare for that, Francis. We just have to take the risk."

"I'm a man of science, Ben. I don't know how to calculate risk."

"You can't put odds on this," Ben said. "There's no way to measure it. This whole expedition has been one giant leap of faith. And so far it's paid off more than we could ever have imagined."

Francis pondered Ben's logic. "We may not have time for all of it, but we could get a majority of it up there. But then comes the next challenge. We have no wagon. We have nothing to put this in to get it out of the valley. The valley will be flooded. It will be all we can do to get ourselves and our horses out."

"Will you trust me on that one?"

Francis exhaled slowly. "It may all be balderdash, but I can't find the nerve to doubt you."

Ben grinned, then looked at Redman. "Kid, are you in?"

Redman smiled. "I'm in."

They both looked at Francis, and the student rolled his eyes.

"I have to be in," Francis said, "or you'll never forgive me. Or maybe I'll never forgive myself."

BEN FOUND TWO MORE CRATES ON THE THIRD DECK. LIKE the others they were filled with cargo items, some glass china originally packed and protected by straw, tinware, silverware, felt hats, boots, and even some silk from the Orient. Ben found it funny that if they had not found the treasure the cargo goods alone would have been salvageable and could have been shipped to the East Coast and sold to seventeenth-century antique shops.

By the time they had all the rocks moved away from the front of the chests and piled out of their way, the water had reached the farthest, lowest point of the ship, near the ballasts, and started to rise. Their system of shuttling the crates worked as planned, which also meant it was slow-going. It was mostly a lot of trekking up and down the tilted decks, watching their footing on the wet surfaces, which was nerve-racking to say the least.

WHEN FRANCIS HAD ONE CHEST EMPTIED, THE WATER was up to his ankles; with the second chest it came to the middle of his shin, and with the third, to his knees. He had found a place to hang the lantern, but he worried, too, that it would soon be out of fuel. With three more chests of bullion to go, the student was reaching under water for the gold. The water was cool, and he'd grown used to it, but the worst part was the cloudiness of the water caused by the silt. Mixed with very dim light from the lantern, the reddish, muddy water made it impossible to see anything past the surface, and he had to feel for the bars to retrieve them.

He did the math, and at the rate the water was raising, he knew the strategy had to change or he'd soon be dunking his head under water to work. He gave the report to Redman, who relayed the information to Ben, and within five minutes Ben came down with all the empty crates. He and Redman walked down the stairs onto bottom deck and high stepped through the water with the crates.

"Could you use some help?" Ben said to Francis.

Francis responded fearfully as he watched the water flow

like a river down the steps. "Much longer and I'll need some gills."

"Don't worry," Ben said. "We're going to get you out of here."

THOUGH IT WAS NOW A SYSTEM THAT REQUIRED THREE times the effort, the three men filled their crates with as much as they could carry and took them to the top of the stairs and dumped them. With three chests left and each man working on emptying one, along with a lantern almost out of fuel, they managed to get all the chests emptied by the time the water was waist-high.

As Redman was nearing the stairs with his final load, his wet crate collapsed and the gold bars plunged into the water. He cursed and flung the broken pieces of the crate away from him and looked angrily into the rippling current.

Ben looked back at him. "Let them go. That's the last of it."

Redman wouldn't hear of it. He'd worked for a man that sucked the valley dry of its soul. Just like the water that flooded the valley, Ben would bring it new life. Every bar of gold they found could build a city. They couldn't leave any of it behind.

"No!" The kid ducked under the water in pure darkness, feeling around his feet for the bars. When he came up, he had a bar in each hand. Ben and Francis dumped their crates and moved quickly to help him. Redman handed the bars to them, then went down for more. Though he had no idea how many bars he'd lost in the water, he felt confident he'd retrieved them all. He breathed heavily as he walked up the steps and fatigue forced him to his hands and knees.

Ben knelt beside Redman and put an arm around him. "You all right?"

Redman nodded, his red hair dripping wet and hanging over his face. "I just need to catch my breath."

"You rest here a minute. I'm going to go find you another crate."

"All right."

Ben slapped him on the arm and grinned. "Hey, we're almost out of here. And you're a rich man!"

Redman smiled through his heavy breaths. "Well, let's make it quick. I don't want to be a dead rich man."

Chapter Twenty-One

❦

WET, dirty, and exhausted, the men crated the gold bars to the first deck, dumped them in piles, then returned for more. The water had now risen to waist level on the second deck. Unlike when the water first came in, the ship now creaked from the weight of it, both inside and out.

After they had gotten all the bullion moved to the upper deck, the final task of transporting it to the opening was now in full swing. The reddish, cloudy water rushed through the opening into the ship, bringing with it a steady flow of mud, but Francis and Redman crawled fearlessly through into the lower tier. Francis used the hoist rope to climb up to the next tier. Water flowed over the complete circumference of the top opening, and the pit they had made was now badly eroded, slick, and muddy.

Francis looked down at Redman, who sat in the hole near the opening, pushed his wet hair back with his hands, and wiped away the water from his face. The two made eye contact and nodded at each other.

Ben pushed through the rushing water and set all but two of the empty crates through the hole. Redman took the crates one by one and handed them up to Francis. The student set them all along the tier, side by side, and waited for Ben to hand them the bullion.

THOUGH THE REDUNDANCY OF THEIR WORK HAD MORE than set in, along with sore, cramping muscles all through his wet body, the adrenaline fueled by achievement kept Ben moving. From near the lantern that rested on the floor atop the stairway, he grabbed bars one at a time from the pile, filled the crate with a single layer, then waded through the mud to the opening. Not only was it heavy and hard to push through to Redman, but the muddy water rushing into his face forced him to hold his breath. Once one transfer had been accomplished, he went back and filled another crate, and the timing was nearly perfect, for when he returned, Redman lowered the empty back to him.

Though the tedium was not over, Ben was confident now that it all would work.

It was a good feeling to be this far, and to have the two young men out of the ship and in safer elements. He was proud of them, their hard work and unique contribution to making it happen. It made him smile to think back and remember that big, freckle-faced kid in the Yuma alley. And to think back to when he rode out of the dunes and crossed paths with a newly educated, aspiring geologist. No, such things don't happen by mere chance.

It was a hard hour of toting crates back and forth, holding his breath under the water, but when he realized there was only one crate left, there was an immediate feeling of triumph.

He picked up the last crate and walked toward the opening. Though he was used to his head being wet and being doused by incoming water, he suddenly noticed that water now dripped inside the ship. He looked up at the ceiling, to where the cracks of the top deck had once seeped sand and now dripped water. Before he could observe much more, a loud creak resonated across the deck, then a rumble. He turned quickly and looked toward the lantern burning near the stairway, and before he could take another breath, the deck collapsed, and along with the splintering wood, the thick, silty mud crashed down over the lantern and filled the stairway.

With death at his tail and the rest of his life waiting at the opening, Ben turned in a rush, the deck rumbling beneath his feet and above his head. Common sense told him to drop the crate and run for the opening, but neither time nor logic would allow him to let go. As he ran, the cold water and thick mud dripped on his back, the floor broke under his feet, and as the opening drew closer and closer he felt himself lunge, then fall to the splitting floor, the crate of bullion flying from his hands.

The weight of the mud and sediment was paralyzing. Ben lay on his stomach, covered from the waist down, and there was nothing he could do to pull himself out. He looked up to the only light and was relieved to see that the opening was still there. Muddy water still flowed through at an increasing rate, and he knew, too, that the cavities of the ship were no longer void of water but filled with mud and sediment, and that he had only a few short minutes before the entire ship was forever a grave.

He looked at the crate that lay on its side, gold bars in a disorderly pile, all four feet from his reach. He tried to crawl toward them with his elbows, but there was not enough strength in his tired arms to pull himself out. There was too much weight on his legs and buttocks. Fear and melancholy bit at his nerves, but he kept breathing long, deep breaths searching for strength.

The sound of creaking wood fueled his anxiety, but when he looked up and saw Redman running toward him the fear quickly subsided.

Redman reached down and grabbed his hand. "Ben, are you all right?"

"Yeah," Ben said. "Get Francis. Get the shovels. You've got to dig me out."

Redman ran back to the opening, and Ben reached under his neck and untied his neckerchief. Though muddy and wet, he could still see his monogrammed name. He kissed it, then held it tightly in his fist.

In less than a minute Redman was back with Francis, each with a shovel, both holding them like boat oars and digging frantically at the mud and sediment.

Though already cold and wet, Ben felt a new wetness around his waist. He looked underneath him and noticed the water rising.

"You have to hurry," Ben said.

Redman grimaced as he made stronger thrusts with the shovel and suddenly felt the blade hit something solid. He scraped the mud and sand away and exposed a long timber that lay crossways over Ben's legs.

Redman dropped the shovel and moved to the front of Ben. "Grab an arm," he said to Francis.

They each grabbed an arm and pulled, but the weight of the timber and the remaining mud was still too much to free him. The water was now up past his chest, and Ben could feel it splash against his chin.

Redman scooted back to his shovel and pushed the blade under the timber. He looked back at Francis. "I'm going to pry this up and you pull!"

Redman clenched his teeth, and using the shovel as a lever he pushed downward and could see the timber raise two inches. "Pull!"

Francis sat on the floor and reached forward, grabbed both of Ben's hands, and pulled with all his might. Ben could feel the roughness of the wood floor move underneath him.

Redman yelled as he kept the pressure on the shovel. "Keep going! We've almost got him!"

The water had risen to where it was all Ben could do to raise up on his elbows and keep his head above it. Francis scooted farther back, then reached forward again, and with a firm grip on both of Ben's hands, he drew back. Ben closed his eyes and held his breath and let his face fall down into the water. He could feel his body move, and Francis pulled him forward a good foot. When Francis let go of his hands, Ben raised back up on his elbows and gasped for air.

Redman let loose of the shovel and the timber dropped quickly back into the mud. He scooted through the water to help Francis and they both took an arm and lifted Ben to his feet.

He could tell his legs weren't broken, but they were cramped and weak. He was grateful for the assistance of the other men, knowing that at the rate the water was rising he wouldn't have had the physical ability to make it out alone.

As they stood at the opening, the water had now risen to their chests. Francis and Redman both pushed Ben out of the hole. Though water rushed around him, it was good to feel the clean air.

Francis was the next to come out, and he climbed up the rope to the tier above Ben, then reached down and helped Ben up. Ben found the strength in his arms to pull up, and with Francis's help he made it.

As he reached the muddy and eroding platform, he watched the water rush down the sides of the pit and over the crates that were stacked full of gold bullion, and across from them the chest of gold coins from the captain's cabin. What a feat, he thought, remembering where the bars came from. All the work getting to the ship, the searching, the challenges of Gorum, the tedium—it all seemed like a blur now.

Suddenly Redman called their names and they looked down into the hole, where the kid stood in the rushing water pushing the final crate of bullion into the open air. Francis slid down quickly to help him, and once the crate was securely on the platform he grabbed Redman's arms and pulled him out of the hole.

Once they were all on that tier, they stopped to catch their breath and look down at the hole. The flow of the water slowed and bubbles of air came up from inside the ship.

"The ship is full now," Ben said. "We got to get out of here."

REDMAN STRUGGLED UP THE ROPE, HIS FEET CON-stantly slipping on the muddy slopes of the pit, with water flowing all around him. It took him nearly five minutes to reach the top, and when he looked down Ben and Francis stood in water up to their knees and the gold had disappeared out of site beneath them.

"Hang on!" Redman said. "I'm going to pull you up with the horse!"

The kid ran through the thigh-deep water, which was chest deep to the horses. He was happy to see all three of them still tied to the wagon wheels and the bags of silver still hanging in front of the saddles.

He high stepped up to Ben's black horse and rubbed its neck affectionately. "Thanks for hanging on. We'll get you out of here in a jiffy."

WITH WATER UP TO THEIR NECKS, BEN AND FRANCIS reached above them, each grabbing a rope.

Redman looked down over the edge. "You ready?"

Francis yelled. "Ready!"

Immediately they rose out of the water, clinging to the ropes as they slid over the sides of the pit, being doused with muddy water. With the aid of the horse they were out in no time, standing thigh-deep in the middle of a lapping sea. Ben looked all around him in awe, at the muddy, glistening

ripples that extended in all directions for as far as he could
see. He didn't have to stand there long to feel the sun on his
face, and he reached to the sky to absorb its warmth.

Francis peeked over the rushing water and down into the
hole. "Well at least we tried."

"We did more than that," Ben said. "We were victorious."

"How can you say that? All that work, which you well
know nearly cost you your life—a king's fortune was in our
hands and is now at the bottom of that hole, and in just a
few minutes it will be a hundred feet under a sea and ten
leagues from dry land."

Ben put a hand on Francis's shoulder. "I have a feeling
that before long you'll realize the fruits of your labor."

The student didn't seem convinced, and Ben knew there
was nothing more he could say now to help him understand.

STILL MOUNTED ON HIS HORSE, REDMAN COILED THE
ropes out of the water, and when he reached the ends, he felt
resistance and discovered that the hooks were still attached
to the buckets. He started to remove them, but Ben quickly
stopped him.

"Don't," Ben said.

Ben waded through the water and grabbed the end of
each rope and made sure both buckets were tied firmly.
"That should do it."

"Do what?" Redman said.

"Let's mount up," Ben said. "We have one more thing to
do before we get out of here."

Regardless of their confusion, Francis mounted his horse,
as did Ben. Working together, the three of them towed the
wagon wheels, still attached to the axels, up to the edge of
the slowly filling hole.

Ben dismounted into the water. "Come give me a hand."

Redman and Francis both wrinkled their brows, but they
dismounted and waded over to the wagon wheels. They

followed Ben's lead and pushed them into the hole. The wheels and axel tumbled and made a big splash in the rising pool, the ropes and buckets twirling behind. They followed suit with the other wheels, and as they watched the second one lodge in the muddy edge and ultimately sink, Ben put his arms around both of the other men. They took one final glance into the hole and acknowledged the floating buckets with a grin.

"Well, boys," Ben said, "that's the grand finale. It's time to go home."

The three men waded to their horses, mounted, and headed them west toward the mountain range where Hostetter, Raul, and Indigo waited for them. It was almost surreal, Ben thought, riding a horse through a sea. But it was only appropriate considering the legend of how it all began. The old Indian was right. The gods would answer in their time, but no one had known that it would take them three hundred years to do so.

Chapter Twenty-Two

꧁ ꧂

Los Angeles, California, 1905

B EN Ruby held on to the mahogany handrail as he walked down the wide Victorian staircase of the Bissell House. He felt a bit foolish in the neatly pressed white coat, vest, and trousers, the starched white shirt and shoes so shiny and white he could see his reflection. The only thing that wasn't white was his black bow tie. Not used to the feeling of a tie, he'd developed a habit of sticking his fingers behind his shirt collar and stretching it outward.

He stepped off the final tread, onto the landing, and walked toward the front desk.

A slender, balding gentleman worked behind the counter and greeted Ben with a polite smile. "Good morning, Mr. Ruby. Did you sleep well?"

"I did, thanks. Do you have any mail for me?"

The desk clerk turned to a section of wooden bins behind him. "In fact, I do."

He handed Ben the envelope, and Ben immediately read the return address:

Bernard Cashman
Imperial Valley, California

BEN REACHED INTO HIS INSIDE COAT POCKET AND
pulled out a pair of wire reading glasses. The clerk stopped
him as he turned to leave.

"Oh, Mr. Ruby," the clerk said.

"Yes?"

"Congratulations on your big day."

"Thank you." Ben reached in his vest pocket and pulled
out a twenty-dollar gold piece. He looked at it a second, then
tossed it to the clerk.

The man caught it with both hands. His eyes widened
after he opened his hands and saw the coin. "Thank you!"

Ben put on the glasses, then walked over to a leather chair
in the lobby, sat down, and opened the envelope. Just like
when he read the name on the envelope, her first words
brought an instant smile to his face.

10 March, 1905

Dear Ben,

Don't let the name on the envelope fool you. My husband wouldn't sit down and write a letter to anyone, even if it was a formal complaint. I do hope this finds you well in Los Angeles. We were all happy to get your letter announcing the engagement to Yudexy. I couldn't ever imagine a more perfect match for the two of you. Matters are fine here but busy as ever with the irrigation projects. You were right, Jeb Hostetter made the perfect engineer to design our new canals. The needed labor was not hard to find either and the place looks more like a city now than a farm. It is all hard to believe at times that things worked out the way they did. There

is a lot of gossip on the farm about how you found your
rainbow connection. I think if they even knew all the
facts the story still wouldn't come out right. The next
best part is that we have you as a partner and don't
have to worry about Gorum coming around harassing
us anymore. Though his ghost makes its presence felt
from time to time, all I have to do is sic Bernard on him
and he goes away. Give my best to Yudexy and Jeb
sends his love to Felicia. We all look forward to the day
when we see you all again.

> *Warmest Regards,*
> *Mrs. Bernard Cashman*

Ben felt immense warmth from the letter and was tempted to read it again before a strong voice called his name from the foyer. He stood from the chair to find Casey Redman walking toward him dressed in a nearly identical white suit, only with a silver ascot rather than a bow tie.

"Come on, Ben," Redman said. "We're going to be late."

A WHITE-BEARDED MAN WEARING A LIGHT GRAY SUIT and matching top hat drove the horse-driven carriage down a brick-covered parkway. The carriage approached a stand of palm trees surrounded by a garden of stones and yucca, mixed with a variety of red, blue, and yellow flowers. When the carriage stopped, the driver stepped down and opened the side door. Ben and Redman stepped out onto the red tiled walk. Ben tipped the driver a gold piece, then he and Redman walked side by side down the walk into the garden.

They'd let Yudexy and Felicia pick the place, and Ben couldn't have imagined anything more appropriate. The tile path led to a spacious wooden patio, surrounded by more palm trees, save the far side, which looked out at a sunset over the Pacific Ocean. The only other people on the patio, besides the priest, were the four-man mariachi. Along with their singing, the ensemble of musicians each played an instrument: an acoustic guitar, a trumpet, a violin, and an accordion. They played a bolero that Ben recognized as *Tres Regalos*, meaning "three gifts."

The two men stood on one side of the priest and listened to the sound of the Pacific waves as the mariachi began the procession.

The procession began with Felicia walking out of the garden and down the tiled path. She carried a bouquet of blue and white irises that blended perfectly with her long, pale blue dress. Though it was not their day, most of her smiles of affection were directed toward Redman. When she stood opposite him Ben had little doubt that the next wedding he attended would be theirs.

Since the day Ben had gone to prison, he'd never imagined this day would ever come, when a woman as beautiful as Yudexy would see past the headlines and see the good in him. He felt the connection before he found the treasure, and he held off telling her about it until he was sure of her love. It was on the day when he visited the Cashmans and delivered the news about Gorum's death, when he told her about his desire to free Indigo and their people from a life of poverty and hard labor. It was then that he confessed his true feelings for her.

"Just what did you do out on that mountain?" she had asked.

Ben had smiled and held her hand. "We just had some strong spiritual time."

"It's good then, because my papa likes you. And so does Raul."

"What about you? Do you like me?"

Yudexy had looked down shyly. "Yes, I do."

Ben had lifted her chin and looked deep into her eyes. "How much?"

"Very much, Ben Ruby."

Ben had dropped to one knee, and Yudexy put both of her hands over her mouth. He reached into his shirt pocket and pulled out the blue handkerchief she had given him. He unfolded the handkerchief in the palm of his hand, the edges draped over, and in the center of his palm was a golden band studded with a sparkling diamond.

Yudexy's eyes had welled with tears.

"Will you marry me?"

Yudexy had removed her hands from her mouth and given Ben her hand. "*Sí*. Ben. *Sí*, I will marry you!"

He had put the ring on her finger, then stood in front of her, studying the look of love and desire in her eyes, a look he was sure would be engraved in his mind forever. She had put her arms around his neck, and he held her tight around the waist. When their lips touched, Ben had immediately understood the meaning of life. He knew that recovering the world's richest treasures couldn't buy the feeling he had at that moment.

Ben never thought he would see the day when Yudexy was more beautiful than the day when he proposed to her, but when she walked from the garden in a long white dress, her long raven hair accented by a white floral headband, he thought he saw an angel. He knew the smile she offered was only for him, and their eyes never drifted from each other's as she came to him.

The sound of the ocean waves couldn't have set a better tone to the words of the priest and the vows they exchanged. And though it could never replace their first kiss, it was a perfect kiss, and Ben immediately understood the difference between a kiss of passion and a kiss of eternal love and commitment.

The mariachi played a recessional of *De Colores*, and the new bride and groom, along with their best man and bridesmaid, joined one another at the waiting carriage.

Felicia and Yudexy embraced and kissed each other on the cheek.

"Please let us know when you're back from San Francisco," Felicia said.

"It will be at least two weeks," Ben said. "After our honeymoon, we are helping Francis with the opening of his new school. Dexy is helping with the dedication."

"Did they ever come up with a name for the school?" Redman asked.

"Yes," Ben said. "That's why she's a part of it. It will be the Indigo Juarez Center for Indian Studies."

The young couple smiled and nodded.

"Perfect," Redman said.

Ben shook the kid's hand firmly. "I'll see you soon."

"Just have fun," Redman said. "I'll hold the fort down for you."

The driver held the door open while Ben helped Yudexy into the carriage. They waved at Redman and Felicia as they drove off and Ben noticed a tear running down Yudexy's cheek.

"Are you okay?" Ben said.

"Yes," Yudexy said. "I'm just very happy."

Ben smiled and wiped the tear with a soft swipe of his fingertips. "I'm very happy, too."

"I do wish Papa could have been here," she said.

Ben laughed and looked out toward the road. "I know you do, but I have a feeling that Indigo is happier right where he's at."

INDIGO REVELED IN THE STORIES OF HOW HIS ANCES-
tors once fished in the great sea. Having lived his whole life in the desert, such an experience had been left only to his imagination. Now that the sea had returned, it was his wish to celebrate the legend. It did not matter to him that it took a few years for the fish to hatch in the sea and populate, he did not mind only simulating the actions of the People.

He sat inside the skiff holding a cane pole, with a line of

string tied to the pole and tossed into the water. The old Indian opened the can of Stag tobacco and pinched out enough to stuff inside his new clay pipe. It was a nice gift from Ben, as was the new red cotton shirt with pockets on the chest, where he kept his matches, and the crisp blue dungarees. Ben thought also to get him a pair of moccasins, which were nothing like the ones Indigo remembered from the past, but they kept his feet warm, and at this point in his life nothing else really mattered.

Francis, too, had left him with a gift of his wire spectacles, mentioning that he would purchase a new pair when he returned to his home. The student encouraged Indigo, however, to see an eye doctor the first chance he got. Being that the closest eye doctor was in Yuma, they all knew that the old Indian would find Francis's hand-me-downs to be more than he would ever need.

Raul had been gone for almost a minute, and Indigo looked over the edge of the skiff at the bucket bobbing in the current. Like a frog Raul popped his head up out of the water, then put his arms over the edge of the skiff. He dropped the gold bars into the hull, then looked over at his grandfather.

"That is enough," Indigo said.

Raul swam to the end of the skiff and rolled his naked body up over the edge. Once inside, he lifted the tarp and placed the gold bars next to the others, then covered them back up. The boy untied the dock rope from the bucket, then grabbed the oar and proceeded to row them toward the northern shore.

Indigo rolled in his line, then looked across the broad expanses of the new sea, the sparkling waves, the gulls that soared not far from the surface, and west toward the mountain range and up at the brilliant, cloudless blue sky. It would make a good story, he thought. The gods were definitely smiling on him today.

Author's Afterword

Although the legends of buried Spanish ships in the Imperial Valley of Southern California are mere myths, there is strong scientific evidence to prove that the Gulf of California did in fact exist farther to the north, as well as geological theories explaining continental drift in that region.

The return of the sea in 1904–1905, however, is a historical fact. Due to the buildup of silt from building a dam on the Colorado River, the dam eventually breached and flooded the hottest, driest desert in America. The key result of that flood came to be known as the Salton Sea, the largest lake in California, covering 376 square miles. Though too salty for human consumption, and polluted by raw sewage, the large body of water still exists today and is surrounded by wildlife refuges and an oasis of farmland, irrigated by man-made canals connected to the Colorado River.

In 1911, while the Salton Sea was still in its infancy, acclaimed author Harold Bell Wright was so fascinated by the sea and the transformation of life that occurred that he penned a novel, *The Winning of Barbara Worth*, a drama that centers on the irrigation projects.

About The Author

Steven Law comes from a family of storytellers that inspired him with both folklore and the written word, all which derived from their pioneer days and on up to the novels of Mark Twain and Laura Ingalls Wilder. During college Steven felt inspired to write his first novel, which a constant busy schedule forced him to put on hold. After receiving a bachelor's degree in business administration, Steven spent several years in corporate America, and he also nearly completed a master's degree in business education. Increasingly disenchanted with his career and course work, he dropped out of graduate school to devote his life to writing. While struggling to make a name for himself, Steven has worked as a community newspaper reporter, a columnist, and a freelance Web publicist for writers and writing organizations. For more than twelve years he has worked with several acclaimed authors, such as *New York Times* best seller Stephen Harrigan; *New York Times* columnist Peter Applebome; award-winning novelist, singer, and songwriter Mike Blakely; Pulitzer Prize finalist Sam Gwynne, and the late Elmer Kelton. He also works as a Web publicist for Western Writers of America and the Alamo Society. Now a successful novelist, Steven lives in the Missouri Ozarks with his son, Tegan, a Siamese cat named Cowboy, and a Shih Tzu named Obi-Wan Kenobe. *Yuma Gold* is his fourth novel. Visit his Web site at www.stevenlaw.com.

Don't miss the best Westerns from Berkley

LYLE BRANDT
PETER BRANDVOLD
JACK BALLAS
J. LEE BUTTS
JORY SHERMAN
DUSTY RICHARDS

penguin.com

M10G0610

Penguin Group (USA) Online

What will you be reading tomorrow?

Patricia Cornwell, Nora Roberts, Catherine Coulter,
Ken Follett, John Sandford, Clive Cussler,
Tom Clancy, Laurell K. Hamilton, Charlaine Harris,
J. R. Ward, W.E.B. Griffin, William Gibson,
Robin Cook, Brian Jacques, Stephen King,
Dean Koontz, Eric Jerome Dickey, Terry McMillan,
Sue Monk Kidd, Amy Tan, Jayne Ann Krentz,
Daniel Silva, Kate Jacobs...

You'll find them all at
penguin.com

Read excerpts and newsletters,
find tour schedules and reading group guides,
and enter contests.

Subscribe to Penguin Group (USA) newsletters
and get an exclusive inside look
at exciting new titles and the authors you love
long before everyone else does.

PENGUIN GROUP (USA)
penguin.com

M224G0909